*To Rita Roberts for believing
and Aile Roberts for enduring.*

By the Banks of the Rheidol

GERAINT ROBERTS

Cover design: Y Lolfa
Cover painting: *The Vale of Rheidol Light Railway,*
Eric Bottomley (Guild of Railway Artists)

ISBN: 978 1 78461 559 8

Published and printed in Wales
on paper from well-maintained forests by
Y Lolfa Cyf., Talybont, Ceredigion SY24 5HE
e-mail ylolfa@ylolfa.com
website www.ylolfa.com
tel 01970 832 304
fax 832 782

Foreword

IN MY WRITING I have always looked to explore the hidden histories of places that are dear to me, using the reality as a background and weaving a tale of human interest in front of it.

The north of modern Ceredigion was late into the railway age and many projects were mooted. In many cases, had they been brought to bear twenty years earlier, they would have made a considerable difference. As it was, many arrived too late for the industries they were set up to serve.

So it was with the Plynlimon & Hafan Tramway and the Vale of Rheidol. Thankfully the Rheidol railway survived and today people can take the trains and dream of the past, whilst admiring the present.

Acknowledgements

I would like to thank the Leicester Writers for advice at the start of this project. Kay Green for assistance in fashioning the draft and the Lolfa team for making the dream happen. Deb Lea for being the alpha reader. Robert Gambrill and Llyr ap Iolo of the Vale of Rheidol railway, who have allowed me to check some of my ideas and quietly remove some of the wackier ones... The Vale of Rheidol railway suffered at its start but has a bright future, due to the work and dedication of the team, led from the front.

Geraint Roberts
July 2018

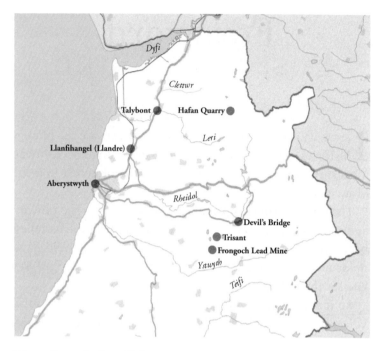

Map of north Ceredigion

NB A glossary of Welsh terms is provided on page 265

CHAPTER ONE

Lost and Found (1896)

HOW LONG HAD he been running? He couldn't think of where to go, except away from his loved ones and the land of his birth. After years of torment, he had finally stood up to his tormentors, and disaster had struck.

'Who the hell do you think you are anyway?' Parry had said. 'Jones Foreman says you've been seeing my girl in Aber again.'

He reached the old coach road along the top of the Rheidol Valley. It marked the end of his world and the beginning of the unknown.

'Should throw you down the bloody shaft, Dafydd Thomas,' Parry snarled, looking to his friends for support. 'Do Frongoch a big favour, there's no place here for the likes of you.'

Dafydd had spent his life in this land, working at the mine as his father and grandfather had before him. Now he had the choice of two roads – Aberystwyth or Devils Bridge and beyond. He'd been down to Aberystwyth a few times. At least he knew the place a bit, although it had been the cause of his current crisis. Taking a deep breath, he stumbled on towards the town.

'I told you enough times to stay away, but you're just too big for your boots. Taken my place on the Aber run, now you're trying for my girl,' Parry shouted, shoving Dafydd back with a prod. *'Who the hell do you think you are?'*

It had all gone too far. He had let it go on for too long. With no energy left, Dafydd loped on awkwardly. He knew the coach road by day. The view was rewarding, like being on the roof of the land, looking over the Rheidol Valley at the hills beyond. On this night, though, the hollows were dark and full of foreboding, the land bleak and silent. A few miles on, the road ran next to an old mine, a rocky outcrop cut away in a long-ago search for silver-lead, one of many ventures that had foundered without return. All that was left of this one was the shaft and a mound of spoil: 'an epitaph to someone's struggle', Dafydd's school teacher had once called it, lamenting the desecration of the valleys.

Sharp black and silver in the moonlight, the vertical opening was larger and more dangerous than Dafydd remembered. As dark as the space between the stars above, it drew him until he stood at the edge. It offered ultimate escape. Why not, what was there left?

'Right,' Parry said. *'It's time we put you in your bloody place once and for all.'*

It was the girl; those louts were happy enough just taunting him before she came along. It changed when he got chosen to help Jones Foreman with some business in Aberystwyth. There, he met Gwen, and his world got nastier.

A chill wind from the direction of the mine shaft stirred his hair. If he just jumped... If he didn't jump, they would catch him, he knew. Catch him and hang him for his moment of anger. They wouldn't understand.

He closed his eyes and sighed. It was a simple choice.

Carry on along the road into the unknown, or step forward and end his plight.

He felt light-headed, surprised by a sudden urge to giggle. Then the anger rose again, frightening him more than despair – and he stepped back.

'To hell with them,' he spat into the pit. He'd go to Aberystwyth, perhaps take a boat, perhaps to become a sailor. Weren't his family supposed to have been seamen once? Something about his tad-cu being the bastard son of a Spaniard? He'd never believed it, but now the idea gave him a future of a kind.

The shaft still pulsed its terrible offer, but he stepped back slowly until he was free of it and trotting along the road to safety. Funny that it was anger that saved him from the pit. Not too long ago his anger had set him on this road.

With his arms pinned by the other two, Dafydd was helpless as Parry lined up with his stick. 'Now then,' he snarled. 'Time you got taught a lesson, good and proper, you bastard.'

This, after an innocent tease by Jones Foreman.

'He's taken to your old girl at the harbour Parry,' Jones had chuckled. 'I think you'd better watch him, the hwrgi. *I'll be handing him my job next.'*

Parry had erupted at the mere thought of "his girl" in the arms of another. Dafydd hadn't even held her hand.

Dafydd had been taught well by his father. As Parry took his first swing, Dafydd lashed out a kick straight for the man's groin. Parry crumpled, mouthing soundless curses.

The other two were paralysed for the moment, and Dafydd took advantage, pushing back, knocking them off balance. One broke his grip; Dafydd smashed the other against the wall of the waterwheel pit and butted his face. Spinning round, he picked up the stick and faced his last assailant. No mercy was given, as he laid into his tormenter. The rage took him.

Dafydd winced at the memory. He'd never imagined he could be that violent.

'*Iesu*… Dafydd, what have you done?'

He heard the shout from the engine house and looked down at the body below him. There was no movement. Blood was running from the man's ears. Dafydd ran like he had never run before.

'You've got to keep running, boy,' Mam-gu had shouted, grabbing the jar from the fireplace, tipping out the emergency fund.

'No!'

Dafydd had never heard his mother shout so loud.

'We'll protect him here!'

The old woman shook her head. 'No grandson of mine will be taken for a killer,' she had growled. 'Those vermin had it coming. We should have had Owain sort it long time back.'

'The boy may not be dead,' his mother cried desperately, 'At least wait until we know what happened…'

'I'll not chance it,' Mam-gu snapped. 'Go now boy,' she said, thrusting the money from the jar into his hand. Hastily, she kissed his brow. 'Make a new life for yourself, *cariad*. Get away.'

'Please!' His mother whispered. His little sister, Sioned, whimpered at her skirts.

'There's no time,' Mam-gu said.

'I'll be all right, Mam,' Dafydd tried to reassure his mother. Her shoulders slumped in defeat.

He hugged them all, then ran out into the night. He'd not even had time to thank his father – for teaching him how to fight. For saving his life, perhaps.

Dafydd now felt anything but all right. He thanked God for the moon, which allowed him to make good progress – although it threw the wooded areas into deep shadow, which slowed his flight. He'd passed a few scattered cottages, dark and silent. Nobody disturbed him, though he felt hunted nonetheless. It was a relief when he smelt the salt in the air and he knew he was close to his goal. He would lose himself in Aberystwyth town, perhaps change his name…

Why bother though? No one knew him anyway.

He stumbled down a hill to a crossroads, the gateway to the town. The shadow of a larger hill lay ahead and Dafydd knew it for Pen Dinas, the one with the monument at the top. Its fair slopes went down to the harbour, where Gwen lived in Ropemakers' Way.

The gloom was lifting slowly and Dafydd stopped. Five roads met here, with a small turnpike cottage in the middle. He almost panicked as he saw the white house. He imagined smoke wisping from the chimney and a glimmer of light in the window, but the gates were open, and the house remained silent.

Creeping forward, he crossed into the shadow of the bushes beyond the cottage, then ran as fast as he could past the white gates and down the road. He ran until his legs gave way and he rolled to a stop, gasping, heart pounding. Exhaustion overwhelmed him and he stood and retched, before settling into sobs. He cursed himself for a fool – for what he had done, for running when he had nowhere to go. Most of all for the panic-induced dash that now left him keeled over by the roadside.

'Why scared of a turnpike?' he whispered.

They'd stopped using them before he was born, when his father was a child, and this one remained only as the ghost of a watching presence. Now, a door opened. Someone called out. Dafydd got up and set off down the hill towards the town.

He found himself near a railway bridge. The breeze was picking up and the smells of the port grew stronger; rotting seaweed, fish, and a faint malty aroma from a nearby brewery. He knew where he was now: at Trefechan, across the river from Aberystwyth. The south bank of the harbour. He had reached his destination – and the end of his plan, such as it was.

As he crossed the bridge his legs ached from the night-long flight, his back had stiffened and he began to shiver. He was also hungry, but there was nothing to be done about that for now. He scanned his surroundings for somewhere secluded to rest. He'd try the landward side of the bridge, where it curved slightly from the road. Just a few minutes, out of sight and out of the wind...

'Dafydd?' A voice came through his dreams; light and gentle, musical even – full of humour, faintly familiar.

'Dafydd, is that you?'

He stirred, his shoulder felt on fire. He heard the rustle of a skirt, felt sweet breath as someone gently shook him. He wondered why he couldn't see anything.

He woke. It was morning and the early rays of light showed him a road busy with carts, a path full with people going about their business. And Gwen Jones, the girl of his dreams, the creator of his nightmares.

Men were drawn to her like a magnet. Her fair hair, long eyelashes and dark eyes bewitched them. With her easy smile and happy manner, it was no wonder she was fought over. Now she crouched in front of him, a basket over her arm. She was smiling, but with a look of puzzlement. Her hair curled out of the sides of her lace cap, making Dafydd want to reach out and touch them. There was, he noticed, a smell of warm bread in the air. His hunger made him imagine fresh rolls nestling cosy in her basket all ready to be buttered and eaten.

'Sleeping off a night in The Beehive are you?' she said, then frowned. 'No, you don't look hungover. What you doing here then, run away or something?'

Dafydd nodded. He tried to speak, but only managed an incoherent croak.

'You're parched, boy,' Gwen said. 'Starving too, I'll wager. Right, best have you away from here before the constable has you for a tramp and marches you off to the workhouse. Come with me, I'm off to the baker's and you can tell me all about it as we go.'

He noticed a few folk staring, and curtains twitched in a nearby house. He got up hastily. A seagull landed on the wall of the bridge nearby to laugh at him. Gwen took his arm, and they made off.

Dafydd had been in awe of the girl since he had first met her at the harbour. Frongoch's lead and zinc came down from the hills to Trawscoed, then was taken by rail to the harbour for loading onto ships. Jones had set Dafydd to work checking the loads were secure, and that the bags reached the ships safely. Of course, once Jones was satisfied, he'd want to quench his thirst. On that hot summer's day they had settled themselves in the street in front of the tavern.

Dafydd had never tasted beer in his life. He looked glumly at the mucky brown liquid, as the splashing flagon was thrust in his hand.

'Here, Roberts' best and from the source,' Jones nodded to the brewery behind the tavern. 'Tell you what, we'll have a few here, then why don't you explore for a little while. I have business to attend to.'

Jones didn't say, but Dafydd knew there was a woman he visited. Parry had smirked about it many times before.

Dafydd sipped his ale. Jones was long gone and the noisy and boisterous tavern made him nervous. His head buzzed. He drank the last of the ale, then wandered down the road feeling as if a blanket was stuck on his head. He went down to the river for the cooler air and leant against a wall. After a while, the river's noise and motion made him feel better.

'Well,' a voice rang out. 'You going to be sick or not?'

Dafydd saw a girl, about his age, deftly working at the frayed ends of a large rope with a knife. She grinned as she carried on with her work.

'I'm not going to be sick,' Dafydd grunted, then ran to the riverside and lost the contents of his stomach.

'There now,' the girl said with a gentle smile. 'Feel much better for that, I'm sure. You can give me a hand now.'

Dafydd spat away the taste as best he could and wiped his mouth. Then he stumbled over and sat by her, watching her deft fingers sort the good ends from the bad. He felt grateful that she hadn't mocked him. He joined in the work, and as they talked, he warmed to her the more.

He remembered the day well, for the ale had made him cheeky to his father on the return, and he'd got a sore lip for his trouble. He'd been back a few times to Trefechan since then and always found time to see Gwen, the girl at the river. He looked forward to every visit. In his happiness, he failed to notice how it had only stoked the jealousy within others that would bring him to this wretched moment.

Now, with Gwen's arm linked in his, Dafydd felt warm for the first time in ages. He had never touched her before and his hand tingled with pleasure.

'Seems you're always picking me up at the bridge,' he managed.

She smiled. 'I suppose I'd best let you walk closest to the river then, in case you want to be sick... You're all serious you know,' she added, as her remark failed to raise a smile.

'Oh God, Gwen, I'm in trouble,' he groaned.

'I can see that,' she replied. 'But let's get some food in you and then we'll have a chat, right?'

She bought her bread and then took him down to the river, by the old mills.

'Here,' she said, handing him a roll. 'But I need to talk quick before the bread gets cold and I'm missed.'

'I'll pay,' said Dafydd, his mouth crammed with hot bread.

'Got it extra, Daf, don't you worry. Save your money there.'

Dafydd looked away. 'I think I killed someone, Gwen.'

She arched her eyebrows. 'You think? You'd better tell now.' Dafydd told her the tale. 'So, what you saying is this. You beat someone senseless,' Gwen said. 'Knowing that bully-boy, he deserved it and all.'

'Gwen, I killed him. I'm a murderer.'

Gwen shook her head, squeezing his arm for support. 'How do you know – ask the doctor, did you? He was still alive when you left and, knowing the thick heads of that lot, I'd wager he's still alive now.'

'But he wasn't moving,' Dafydd stammered.

'Proves nothing,' Gwen said, flicking her hand for effect. 'Tell you what though, you probably done them all a favour. That Parry was a right *twll du*. You done womankind a big favour by kicking him where it hurts. There's less chance of children for some poor wife later on.'

'Kept on saying you were his girl,' Dafydd said shyly.

'Him?' Gwen's raised her voice in shock. 'I'd become a nun before I'd lie with him. Besides,' her smile was sweet. 'I'm no-one's girl. Not yet, at any rate, and whoever wins me won't have it so easy neither. Parry's a fool. I'm with who I want and it certainly's never going to be that lump of...'

Dafydd was taken aback by Gwen's cursing and she saw his look and smiled. 'Sorry Daf, forgot you were a bit delicate.'

'I've heard worse, girl,' came the defensive reply. 'Just never from a lady.'

'A lady?' Gwen laughed. 'Well, it's nice to be called that. It's a bit rough round here. What you going to do now, anyway?'

'No idea, Gwen. Thought I could maybe jump a ship or something.'

'No need, Dafydd. This town is big enough to hide you. Besides,' she said, showing the tip of her tongue in a sweet smile. 'I think I'd like you around here for a while.'

Dafydd sighed. 'To do what? I've no trade.'

'Come back with me to Ropemakers' Row. No, listen now. I'll ask around and see if there's anything at the harbour. Plenty of trade here; chandlers, sailmakers, ropes, lime burning. We'll find you somewhere safe.'

Her brown eyes held him in their spell.

'All right, Gwen, I'll try it out. I suppose I'll at least get to find out what's going on. Just let's not try over the Trefechan side, that's all.'

'Had your fill of Frongoch then, have you?'

Dafydd gave a tight grin. 'Well I don't want to be seen around the ore ships, just in case.'

'Wouldn't worry 'bout that,' Gwen replied with a giggle. 'We're pretty tight-lipped around here. I'll make sure no word gets around. Right you are then, I'll hide you from your devils, Dafydd *bach*. Come back with me down

Ropemakers' and meet my father. He'll know what's going on.'

She smiled and stroked his cheek. 'Don't you worry, Daf, I'll look after you now.'

A tingle went down Dafydd's spine. All he wanted now was to be at Gwen's side. He felt safe for the first time in days as he followed her off towards the harbour. 'Your father going to mind you turning up with a strange tramp in tow?' Dafydd asked.

Gwen just laughed. 'He's seen worse tramps in his time. Don't you worry, he's not hit anyone for ages now. Besides, you've learnt to duck, haven't you?'

CHAPTER TWO

The Ropewalk

G WEN TOOK HIM back over the bridge to Trefechan, and steered them through a busy narrow street of terraced houses. A carter at the maltings called a greeting to a coalman offloading into the cellar of the tavern next door. Barrels were being stacked, people bustled to and fro, the sickly smell of ferment from Roberts's brewery wafted over all.

Gwen took the road skirting Pen Dinas hill, above the harbour industries in full flow. Dafydd looked warily for ships loading lead ore, for fear of seeing anyone who might know him.

'What's the matter with you, then?' Gwen asked.

'I can't go this way,' he replied nervously.

'Well, it's where we are,' she replied, giving his hand a squeeze. 'Don't you worry now. You got to trust me, Daf.'

The road took them behind the warehouses, climbing above the harbour chimneys until only the masts and spars of the ships at anchor were visible. Dafydd continued to look nervously for familiar faces.

'Dafydd.' Gwen grabbed his hand to get his attention. 'Nobody knows you here, but they will soon enough if you creep around looking like you done something.'

He nodded, falling back into step with his friend.

'There's three ropewalks in town, you know,' Gwen said, as

they carried on up the road. 'Two here in Trefechan, supplying all them ships and stuff. The other one's behind Capel Seilo, for farmers and the like. Ours is the best, mind.'

They were nearing a large warehouse, longer than a ship.

'That's our ropewalk,' said Gwen. 'Needs to be long, so we can get good lengths of rope. Stronger that way.'

'Who do you make rope for?'

'Anyone who wants it. Boats mostly, but farmers, millers, foundries, breweries…'

'Mines?' Dafydd was still worrying about Frongoch.

'Only if they ask. Daf, I told you, you got to trust me now.'

A big man stood at the open doorway, his arms folded like vices.

Gwen smiled, but the look on his face didn't change.

'Thought I only sent you out for bread there,' he said in a deep voice.

'For sure,' Gwen shouted back, cheerfully. 'This is Dai Morgan from Talybont. He's come to Aber looking for work.'

The man nodded. He tipped his chin suspiciously at Dafydd.

'What's he want, then?'

'Any work – and I need to find lodging,' Dafydd replied. 'Gwen said you might know of somewhere.'

'What's your trade, then?' the man asked.

'Labourer mostly,' Dafydd said with a shrug. 'Done a bit of roofing though.'

'Thatcher or a tiler?'

'Neither, sir,' Dafydd said quickly. 'In truth, I have done some thatching work, but mostly only on the house back home. Helped others too. Tad taught me, he learnt from his father.'

'What's he do, then?'

'Lead miner.'

'Where?'

'Allt y crib.' The lie was easy enough, but the man's eyes hardened.

'You're hiding something.' He looked at Gwen. 'You know what's going on.' It wasn't a question, and Gwen nodded quietly. '…but you want to hide him.'

Again it wasn't a question. Gwen nodded without a word.

'Will it harm us?'

Gwen looked him in the eyes and shook her head.

'Are you lovers, then?'

'No,' the reply from Gwen came quick and like stone.

The man's eyes fixed on Dafydd once more. 'My daughter chooses her friends very carefully, and if she knows what's going on and you're here, that's something to respect. I'll find out eventually boy, don't you worry. Until then, I need someone for the ropewalk and you can sleep in the stores. Rope makes a warm enough bed, at least until you find lodging in Trefechan –' Dafydd could have sworn he hadn't moved, but the man's eyes narrowed and his tone changed. '– or wherever you stay. As long as you're here on time, I don't care. Best check Allt y crib is still a working mine, though.' He turned and went back indoors.

Dafydd slumped. The exchange had sapped his energy. He prayed he would not be found wanting.

'He trusts you,' Gwen said in hushed tones. 'So don't you ever lie to him again and he'll be fair back. Come on.' She stepped inside.

Dafydd's nose was itching straight away. The air was musty and dry, and heavy with the smell of pitch. He was breathing strands of hemp. He had the urge to scratch at his neck.

Gwen's father was waiting for them. 'You a smoker?'

Dafydd shook his head. 'Not regular.'

'You smoke anywhere near here and I'll string you up. Any of this stuff catches light, the whole of Trefechan will be ashes by morning. You can leave your pack there.'

Dafydd put his knapsack in a corner. There wasn't much in it bar a change of clothes. Mam-gu's money was close to his chest and he would not be giving that up without a fight.

He looked around the long narrow shed. It was not well lit, but he could make out a long strand of rope down the middle. It was three strands being twisted together, hooked on a strange turning device at each end. Gwen's father stood close to the far end in between the strands, holding a block that he pulled back slowly with the turning. Dafydd watched as it tightly wove the strands. His eyes on the work, the man shouted to Dafydd, 'You can sweep the floor for starters. Broom's in the store cupboard. Sweep it up to the door. We use the waste on the fire in the house.'

Dafydd sighed quietly. It was basic work, but in time it could lead to a trade. He wondered where Gwen had gone.

The day passed slowly, Dafydd watching closely as rope ends were spliced together and soaked in pitch. Then he learned how to store it in loops that wouldn't just fall apart. His first go was clumsy but with a bit of guidance, he soon learnt to do it right.

They worked through the morning without a break until Dafydd felt the torment of growing hunger. By late afternoon he was flagging, leaning on his broom. A younger man working alongside him disappeared and came back with a steaming tin mug of tea.

Seeing they were alone, he grinned. 'Tea works well for itchy throats, Dai,' he said, proffering the mug.

Dafydd took it gratefully.

'Don't you worry, you get used to the feeling,' he went on.

'And don't worry about Joshua, he's all right, really. I'm Joe.'
He stuck out his hand and Dafydd took it.

'Do you eat?' Dafydd croaked and Joe nodded with a grin.

'Yes, but some days you take breaks when you can. Gwenny'll be in with food for us all, off your wages mind. On a day like this, I'd say we should sit outside.'

'Wouldn't mind sitting outside whatever the weather,' Dafydd muttered.

Joe laughed. 'I know what you mean, but some of them storms would change your mind.'

Gwen arrived with bread, cheese and pickle. Dafydd was given another mug of tea.

'Brewed in heaven,' he grinned.

'It'll be a bit stuffy, sleeping in the rope store,' Joe said. 'It'll not be for long mind, I'll ask in Trefechan tonight. There's bound to be somewhere spare.'

Dafydd thanked him, though there was still the fear of being discovered. Gwen flashed him a calming smile.

The day's work ended and the finished rope was packed away. The spinners were stopped and Dafydd was pleased to shove the broom back in its cupboard. He was delighted to see Gwen walking towards him.

'Hard day?' She asked with a sweet smile.

'Itchy,' Dafydd said with a nod.

She held out some cleaned potatoes.

'Hungry?'

'Starving,' he groaned.

'Come on then.'

He followed her down a winding path to the harbour shore. She made for a strange square building with smoke blowing from it, even in the dusk.

'Lime kiln,' she said happily. 'They're burning the stuff all day long The fires don't go out in a hurry and I like to go on an evening sometimes. Meet up with folk at the end of a working day.'

'Why do they meet there?' Dafydd asked.

'Because it's warm, there's no trouble and you can cook your potatoes for free.'

There were a few people sitting around and Gwen was welcomed. Dafydd got polite nods. Soon they were taking their turn cooking at the kiln fire. The smell of warming potato had Dafydd's stomach going mad, but soon Gwen came back with two blackened, juicy potatoes.

'I put in some butter to make them sweet,' she said. 'Careful, they're hot.'

They sat on a stone slab close to the harbour shore, gazing across the water as they ate.

The water flowed gently under the bridge. A sailing ship appeared to glide effortlessly to the harbourside over in Aberystwyth, a vision of calm only broken by the frantic activity on deck as it neared the quay.

'He's late in,' Dafydd murmured.

'Yes, they'll be drunk in the taverns tonight,' Gwen said. 'Over that side, mind you. No-one would come and mess with us Turks here.'

'Turks?' Dafydd asked.

'Turks or Turkeys. That's what they call Trefechan folk. Heaven knows why.'

Dafydd looked over the harbour at the reddening sky. The sun had gone behind a band of cloud and the sky turned golden below it, tinged with pink above.

Gwen sighed. 'I love it when it does that on a sunset. I could watch it all night.'

Dafydd nodded. 'It is pretty special. It's over the mountain before you know it back home.'

'I can show you some other places,' Gwen said brightly.

23

'We could go up the smelters or even on Tanybwlch beach. Watch the sun go over the end of the horizon there. Sea goes all funny blue, lovely it is.'

'Won't your father mind?' Dafydd asked.

'No, he trusts me and he's got the measure of you too, Daf. He knows we'd not do anything wicked.' Her smile matched her words for a second. 'Not now, at any rate. Besides, he'd have you out before that happens.'

'I don't want to cause no trouble,' Dafydd replied hastily. 'What with him being kind and all.'

'Daf, you take your chances when you can. They may never come round again.'

Her smile was teasing and Dafydd didn't know what to think. As they sat with shoulders virtually touching, he felt as if he wanted the evening to last for as long as he could stay awake.

He woke on the hemp sacks in the ropewalk. He was stiff, but not as bad as he'd been on the bridge the night before. The taste of hemp was still on the back of his throat. He scrambled to his feet, keen to get outside before the day started, to find water, and most of all he hoped to find Gwen arriving with a mug of tea. But it was Joe who appeared, bearing news.

'I've done a bit of asking about and there's a small room for you where I stay if you want it. Back of the brewery, near the riverside. Not too pricey, a bit stuffy, but clean, mind, and close. You get fed and all. I'll take you if you like, after work.'

Dafydd said yes, though he'd as soon eat potatoes at the lime kiln with Gwen. He didn't see her all day, which made him silent and sullen.

In the evening, he followed Joe to the lodging house. It

was not too far from the pub that Jones Foreman had taken him to. The thought made him nervous, though he tried not to show it. 'It's small but it's dry,' grinned Joe. 'In more ways than one, more's the pity – Mrs Owen is a teetotaller. Chapel and Methodist; the worst kind.' He gave a quick frown. 'I mean, you're not, are you?'

'I like a jug,' Dafydd replied. 'Not too many, mind.'

'Oh, well, she's a bit of a Welsh dragon, is Mrs Owen, but there's a heart of gold there. Least, I think so.'

Dafydd laughed. He'd take a room from a dragon if it meant getting out of the ropewalk for a while.

Mrs Owen looked him up and down, then nodded stiffly and went inside, expecting them to follow. She walked badly, stooping over misshapen legs.

Joe gave Dafydd an encouraging smile as they followed her upstairs, then pulled a face behind the old woman's back. Mrs Owen stopped and Dafydd could have sworn she had seen, but she carried on, grumbling. 'I want rent in advance. More if you want feeding.' She was panting with the effort of the stairs.

'I can pay,' Dafydd replied. Another grunt met his attempt at politeness.

'There,' she said, as they reached the top of the house.

Dafydd looked at the old box room and its slanted roof. There was a long, narrow window looking out at the hill behind. The bed looked old, the chest of drawers worse, but he liked how the place felt safe. He pulled out a half sovereign.

'Will this do?' he asked.

Mrs Owen took the coin and held it out in her hand. The world stood still for a while and Dafydd thought he'd offered too little. 'This will keep you here for a while,' she grunted, and shuffled off.

Joe gave Dafydd a smile, but it was less certain now. The coin seemed to have troubled him, too.

'I'll give you a knock when there's food,' he said and was off pretty quickly downstairs, leaving Dafydd to his thoughts.

The next morning, Joe had gone out early and Mrs Owen grumbled about his wasted food, until Dafydd offered to eat it. He made his own way to the ropewalk but knew there was trouble straight away. Joshua stood waiting with Gwen, who looked worried. Joe slipped behind Dafydd and quietly closed the door. Joshua stared at Dafydd. The silence made him want to run, the air felt heavy and it was difficult not to panic.

'It's time to have that talk, whoever you are. David, Dai, Dewi, Dafydd,' Joshua said stiffly. 'Dafydd, is it? You had best tell me how a boy with nothing bar what he is wearing can turn up a half sovereign without thinking. What you been up to, boy?'

Dafydd felt cornered, his eyes darted from side to side as he looked for an escape. His chest tightened with fear and he could almost feel the hangman's noose around his neck.

Gwen put a hand on Dafydd's arm.

'Gwen!' Joshua snapped. 'Come away, he doesn't need no help. You tell me everything now or we're off to the constabulary this morning. Sit down here,' he said, patting a chair.

Dafydd sat down and took a deep nervous breath. He looked at Gwen's frightened, pleading eyes and gave a half nod.

'I'm not from Talybont, mind. I'm from Trisant, up by Pontrhydygroes. I used to work at Frongoch.'

Joshua nodded, arms folded but said nothing.

'I worked for Jones Foreman, we got the ore from the mill

loaded on carts and taken to the wharf here. Been in with him a few times in the past, it's how I met Gwen.'

He glanced up, met Joshua's gaze, caught Gwen's scared smile. Joe looked tense, perhaps waiting for Dafydd to break for it. The idea steeled Dafydd, though. All that was past. No more running.

'I been bullied there, three boys picking on me. One used to come in with Jones to Aber. He got nasty when I got chosen in his place. When he heard I had got to know Gwen, well, it got rough. He reckoned Gwen was his girl.'

'Who's that, then?' Joshua asked.

'Parry,' Gwen said quietly.

'That sack of shit!' Joe hissed from the door. Joshua held up his hand and beckoned Dafydd to continue.

'They had me cornered one night after work. Down by the wheelhouse, where no one could see.' He licked his lips. 'Three of them. I got angry and Tad had taught me how to fight.'

'What happened?' Joshua asked.

'I done them. Hughes was bashed in the head and I may have killed him, I don't know. I ran away.'

'Where did you get the money?' Joe asked.

'My mam-gu. She took it from the jar at home. Said I had the need more, told me to start a new life.'

The sorrow returned like a wave.

'What did your father have to say?'

'He didn't... I mean I never got to say...'

Gwen ran to hug him as he struggled to contain the sobs. It passed with a shudder.

'Do you believe me now?' Gwen said to her father.

'I never didn't believe you,' he replied. 'I just wanted to hear it from him, in case he'd lied. There were gaps in his story. All right Dafydd, you'd best start work... Yes boy,' he gave a grim smile. 'There's been no talk of murders in the newspapers, so I'm guessing you don't hit as hard as you think. Don't flash big coins around though. It makes people talk. Joe, you'd best have a word with Mrs Owen, she may give him some money back.'

Joe nodded and moved away. His face was still clouded as far as Dafydd was concerned. Gwen gave Dafydd's arm a squeeze as she walked past, making him flush.

They met after work and strolled to Tanybwlch beach, south of the harbour. They crossed over the railway line, stopping at the Ystwyth Bridge to look down at the river. It seemed so clear and deep that Dafydd fancied a swim. He thought better than to ask Gwen to come with him.

The beach was long and rugged. A steep shelf of pebbles made the going hard as they walked. He looked at the green plain beyond, which led to sharp cliffs where the land fell away to the south. Dafydd gazed at the shadows of headlands even further down and thought it all beautiful. Having Gwen there made it like heaven.

'There you are, told you it would be fine,' she said. 'You'll be all right with us and you can take me to the beach every night from now on.'

Dafydd stared out to the horizon of the flat, calm sea. There was a boat offshore. It looked so still, like a painting. A group of people gathered below the breakwater, casting lines into the gentle waves below, in the hope of mackerel. The breeze was warm in the face, making Dafydd feel sleepy.

'I could grow to like this place,' he sighed.

The weeks moved on and Dafydd began to enjoy the daily life. It was not a difficult job and after his trouble at Frongoch, it was good to be among friendly faces. At the lodging, Mrs Owen was still as tight-lipped as ever but she didn't grumble as much. Joe was often around to talk to.

They would sit down for bacon and eggs in the morning and Mrs Owen would watch them, finally grunting approval when their plates were emptied.

One Sunday afternoon after chapel, Joe was out and Dafydd had the lodging to himself. Gwen had not said about meeting up and he had been too nervous to ask her. He knew he liked the girl a lot – so much at times that it scared him. Besides, he told himself, as the rain lashed the windows in a summer squall, nobody would be out in this if they could help it.

He went downstairs to cadge a brew of tea. In the narrow hallway, the sideboard caught his eye. It was beautifully polished, so that even the coat hooks were gleaming, the mirror, too.

He looked at his reflection – young, lean and healthy. He had not shaved for a day or two and his top lip was in shadow. He wondered if a moustache would be fitting, then decided to buy a razor for his chin at least. He frowned, seeing the line of the mirror wasn't true. Distracted, he moved the sideboard, noticing the top was loose on one side where it should be tight to the wall.

'Hole's too big,' he muttered.

'What of it?' Mrs Owen said, from the stairs. He was startled – he could normally hear her wheezing from two floors up.

'Sorry, Mrs Owen, didn't hear you. I was thinking of how to fix it, that's all,' Dafydd mumbled quickly. 'You got any matchsticks, if that's all right?'

She stared for a moment, then sighed and turned for the kitchen.

'It's used ones I'm wanting,' he said to her back.

She came back with a box of fresh ones. He chose two of the thinnest, struck them, blew out the flame and clipped off the heads. One fitted in the hole easily. The other was a bit too long, but he took a small knife out and quickly shaved it down. He refitted the screw, using the edge of his knife. The sideboard looked level now, certainly in his eyes.

'I'll need a hammer to finish it,' he said.

'No need,' she replied, taking off her shoe. Two wallops and the matches were snug in place. 'Cup of tea, is it?'

He could have sworn her face had softened, as he followed her to the back room, where the fire was merrily licking a kettle. Mrs Owen took an old dishcloth and lifted the bubbling iron kettle off.

'You're a good boy, Dafydd. I'll be sorry to see you go.'

'I wasn't...' he began, but she smiled.

'Course you're not, *bach*, but I seen your likes before. You've been running from something and the way you look there's some running still to come before you're done.'

'I'm hoping to stay,' he said uncertainly.

'How old are you,' she asked. 'Think she'll wait?'

'I...' Dafydd floundered and flushed. 'I mean, I never...'

'Tongues clock round here, simple as that. She's a lovely girl, but you got to be careful. There's a free spirit in that one and she'll not be tamed by any. All I'm saying is this. You're young and there's a few twists and turns you'll have before you settle. Don't set your heart too early.'

CHAPTER THREE

Ashes

'DAFYDD, THERE'S A man here for you.'
Dafydd looked up from the strands of rope he was
turning. He could just make out the shadow of the man
behind Joshua. For a brief moment, he thought of running
for it. He saw Gwen standing like a statue, her eyes fearful as
if a trap was being sprung.

The visitor was large, right down to the bulging waist. His
hat was clutched in his hands. His balding pate was gleaming
with sweat as he approached Dafydd, who knew him from
old. Jones Foreman.

'Dafydd boy, thank God you're safe! Are you well?' Then
it got the better of him and Dafydd, who a moment before
thought he was about to be arrested, was swept up in an
enormous, sweaty bear hug. 'I was that worried for you,'
exclaimed Jones.

Joshua took them to his office and closed the door.

'Jones and I go back a long time, Dafydd,' he said. 'Where
else do you think Frongoch gets its rope?'

'Yes indeed!' Jones replied, still playing with his hat. 'And
when Joshua told me you were here, well I had to be over as
quick as I could.'

'What happened?' Dafydd asked. 'After the fight, that is.'

'Captain Kitto discharged them,' Jones said frowning.

'Quick as you like. Sorry, *bach*. I let it go on like a fool. That English boy as worked with your father, he sorted them out good and proper a while back. Just walked up to Parry and laid him flat. There was never any more nonsense from them again until the Englishman left. Then they got bolder and I should have seen it, should have done something, fool that I am.'

'It wasn't your fault,' Dafydd said quietly. 'They always waited until your back was turned.'

'Yes but, I'd a feeling it was going on. I suppose I'm one for wishing an easier time.'

'It's not...' Dafydd started, but Jones held up his hand.

'Don't be good about this, son. When Captain Kitto had me and your father up before him, I was only out to save my skin. It was your father who spoke for you – for me and all, for my job was on the line. I'm grateful.'

Jones looked at Joshua, who nodded, before turning back to Dafydd. 'There's a place for you back in Frongoch now, with those three out and two of them still quiet after the beating you gave them. You're welcome back. Your mother's beside herself with worry, your mam-gu also. We'll look after you, Dafydd, I promise.'

Dafydd slowly shook his head. 'I'll be all right, Mr Jones. I don't mean to sound ungrateful and all, but I'm happy here. It's time I walked my own road. Tell my family you seen me and give them my love. Tell them I'm safe and I'll visit when I can.'

There was a long silence. Jones looked like as though sins had come back to haunt him, Joshua sized up the scene in silence, as he always did. Dafydd held up his hands.

'Look, it's nothing bad, I just like it here. The air's fresher than the old mine and I'm wanting to get along on

32

my own. There's so many things I could do here. The mine would have me just stuck on labouring, as before.'

There was Gwen too, but he wasn't going to voice that thought.

'If it's Parry, don't you worry,' said Jones. 'He fled. No-one knows where.'

'I don't care for them and I don't care what happens to them either,' Dafydd said. 'Look, I'm not worried and I don't blame you. What could you have done?'

Jones nodded sadly. 'If you ever need me, leave word in the Fountain.'

Joshua walked Jones to the door. Dafydd smiled at Gwen, feeling the dawning of a new stage in his life. He then managed to walk straight into the rope turner, and the scene ended with Gwen's laughter echoing in his ears.

Back at his lodgings, he was lying on his bed, digesting what had happened, when he heard the window rattle. Another tap and this time he could hear the pebble roll off the roof. He jumped to his feet and saw Gwen standing below, tossing pebbles.

'Dafydd, where did you go after work?' she whispered loudly.

'I didn't know there was anything going on,' he whispered back. 'Why don't you come up?'

'She won't let me,' came the hissed reply. 'Says you're not allowed women guests. Gave me a right look and all.'

'Oh,'

'You coming down or what, then?'

'Where?'

Gwen held up two large potatoes and beamed back. 'Lime kiln. I thought we'd celebrate. Come on, you,' she said with a smile. 'You got to be celebrating. It's not every day you get cleared of murder.'

'You want me to celebrate with potatoes?' Dafydd asked, and she laughed.

'*Twpsyn*, I want you to celebrate with me.'

He needed no second asking. Mrs Owen had taken to leaving a key on a string and you could reach through the letterbox, so he had no worries about returning safely. He was soon out on the street, Gwen giggling prettily as he linked his arm with hers and she steered him to the river.

'Let's go under the arches, it's quicker by far,' she whispered.

Under the bridge, she suddenly stopped and curled her arm around his waist, pulling him close. Before Dafydd could even think, he felt the pressure of her lips on his.

The kiss was long and full, and left him gasping. He felt a tingle all over his body. Gwen broke away, looking at his lips. Then her beautiful dark eyes raised to meet his.

'I'm so glad you're safe,' she whispered.

Dafydd only managed a grunt in reply, drawing a beaming smile from her. She pulled him towards the lime kiln.

They talked with the people there, for it seemed only polite to do so. An old sailor regaled them with tales of his adventures on an Aberystwyth brig, and they warmed to the stories. After a while, the potatoes were ready to eat. Gwen nudged Dafydd.

'We were going to catch the sunset,' she said.

They traced their steps along the shore, as they had done on that first night a few weeks previously, until they found the path that led up past the wharves. There was a smell of dust in the air that had Dafydd thinking of Frongoch. Bags of lead and zinc ore that he had loaded on cart after cart. He felt sad for the events that had sent him running, but now there was a warmth inside him for where he had ended up.

He was happy as they walked along the railway siding on

the wharf and followed its track up to the link across the Ystwyth and Tanybwlch beach beyond.

The sea was green, with white lines that rose and fell. The sun was bright and yellow on the horizon. Breakers were being driven along the shoreline by the gentle breeze that warmed his face.

'Let's go down to the sea,' Gwen whispered in his ear, making him thrill to the sound.

'Not too close, mind,' Dafydd murmured, and he saw her flush.

They walked along as best they could on the shingle, the pebbles getting smaller as they got closer to the sea. There wasn't much to say. Dafydd's senses took in the drama around them; the waves, the breeze, the gulls overhead and Gwen by his side.

'How about we do this every night?' he said.

'What about when it's raining?' she asked, her voice soft as silk.

'It's only water, mind,' he replied quickly.

'Come on,' she said. 'Let's move up the beach. It's cold I am now.'

Dafydd put his jacket around her and she took hold of his hand as it rested on her shoulder. He made to offer his cap, but she shook her head.

'How would I look?' she asked gently. 'Let's sit further up.'

They were halfway along the beach now and far from prying eyes and wagging tongues. The beach was steep here, making their steps more laboured, until Gwen sat down and rubbed her legs. 'It's hard after a long day of fetching and carrying.'

Dafydd sat by her side and gently put his arm around her waist. She glanced sideways at him, but didn't speak. They sat and looked out to sea. The sun made the sky blush around it. Dafydd realised she had pressed against him once more. He squeezed her waist and she gave him a lazy smile.

'Trying to tickle me then, are you?' Gwen murmured.

He looked at her and wondered what to do next. Then finally, making a bold decision, he moved towards her. Her lips opened to greet his.

Gwen lay back on the pebbles and Dafydd kissed her once more. He moved his hand up and cupped a breast. He felt her tense. She took his hand.

'Dafydd *bach*, you're going too fast. We're not ready now.'

'I love you,' he whispered.

She smiled and stroked his cheek. 'We're too young Dafydd, now's not the time. Just a kiss and a *cwtch* is all we should do.'

Dafydd turned red and she leant forward to catch his waist as he sat up.

'Don't be shamed now, it's only natural. I don't mind. Come on, give us a *cwtch*, won't you? It's your special day after all.'

He gave her a quick kiss and lay back, then she put her arms over him and he drew her close on top.

'I love being with you,' she muttered as he gently stroked her hair. The talk died as they just enjoyed the contact in the evening sun. The tingling in his back was there, but this time he closed his eyes and enjoyed it. It felt good, with her head on his chest. The warm breeze had begun to make him sleepy and he began to doze.

Dafydd woke again slowly and then remembered Gwen was asleep in his arms. He didn't want to wake her. Indeed, he wished the moment could last forever and took in a deep breath to release a sigh of happiness. There was smoke in the air, faintly hanging there. It felt out of place.

'Someone's lit a fire,' he murmured.

Gwen raised her head. The light was fading now, but they could still see the trail in the evening gloom. Her eyes narrowed, then widened in fear and surprise. She jumped up.

'The ropewalk!' she shrieked, and rushed off, leaving Dafydd floundering to get up.

Smoke was pouring from a window in the shed when they arrived. Joe was out with a bucket of water, and others had arrived to do the same. Dafydd had seen this all before at the mine and knew what to do.

'Form a chain!' he shouted. 'Pass the buckets along; else you'll all be in each other's way.'

'Do it!' Joe shouted and they began to move.

'Where's Joshua?' Dafydd shouted over the noise. There was a crackling now as some wood had taken.

'Inside, he's trying to save the spinners.'

Dafydd looked through the doorway, now clouded with thick smoke. It was simple – like the fight with Parry – straight in or never. He took a deep breath and ran inside. The storeroom was ablaze and the heat had begun to blacken the door at the top. Joshua was on his knees by the rope spinner, trying to unbolt the device from the floor. Dafydd's eyes began to sting and his lungs drew in the black smoke. Joshua struggled on.

'Get down, boy,' he shouted. 'Air is clearer down here.'

Dafydd got to his knees and crawled to him.

'Damn store's gone,' Joshua wheezed. 'Rope's a slow burner, that'll go for hours and the shed is lost. I'll live with that, but if the spinners go, I'm finished.'

'What if I shut the door?' Dafydd shouted.

'Door'll burn down anyway,' Joshua replied.

'Yes, but it'll take time. I'll damp the beams near to it.'

'Do it,' mouthed Joshua, between coughs.

The smoke was thickening. Dafydd crawled to the door. Inside the store, flames were licking as far as the frame. His eyes were raw and weeping from the smoke. He dived forward, grabbed the bottom of the door. Something hit his neck. He flicked the door towards him and dived back out.

For an instant, he'd seen the piles of coiled rope, one corner of the room blazing like a fireplace, the other side smouldering. Dafydd grabbed the door latch and lifted it to slam into place. He yelled. The iron was very hot and he had to drop it. He recovered and tried again, thanking God when the latch clicked shut, his fingers pulsing with burns.

He turned to find Joe coming in with a bucket.

'Throw it on the door,' Dafydd shouted.

'Where's Joshua?' Joe coughed. Dafydd couldn't stop coughing now. He wanted to fall to his knees, but Joshua was slumped on the floor by the spinner. Joe helped him haul the stricken man a through the door. Once outside, Dafydd collapsed, coughing and wheezing. He desperately tried to speak between gasps.

'Keep... door... wet. Save spinner. Door will keep fire... douse beams.'

A crash, and Dafydd saw the roof falling in by the store. The top of the wall went with it. He could see the spinner now, standing proud in the rubble.

He pointed. 'Must keep...' he fell forward and all went dark. He heard Joe's voice, fading into the background.

'Come on boys, collapse will make a firebreak. Let's get the spinner. If we lose the store we'll still have a living.'

His voice faded to a buzz. Dafydd's eyes flickered, and he saw people standing around. One of them looked too damn much like Siôn Parry.

He was sleeping on a bed. He could still smell the cold ghost of smoke on him. His throat hurt. There was a rustle of skirt nearby. He thought of Gwen and how he met her on the bridge. He thought of the way his heart lifted whenever she was near. He heard a rustle in the background and a thrill of anticipation went through him.

'Gwen?' he croaked.

'She's not here, *cariad*,' came the reply. It was Mrs Owen.

He opened his eyes. He was in the lodging room. A cup of water was placed to his lips and he sipped it gratefully. His hand felt on fire and there were points of pain on his neck and back.

'She's not here,' Mrs Owen said again. 'Though she's been here. You rest, *cariad*, you've had a bad time of it all.'

'The ropewalk…' Dafydd lurched upright.

Mrs Owen moved to stop him. 'It's all right now, everything's done. All are safe, thanks to you – and they'll rebuild it. Even managed to save some of the rope. You got a few burns from the pitch and took in a lot of smoke. Doctor says rest and I've some *cawl* in the pot and bread for you when you're ready. Joe will be back later, I'll get him to bring it then.'

Dafydd drifted off back to sleep and never saw Joe, though when he woke the soup was by his bed and still warm. He realised he was hungry, and ate as quickly as he could. As he finished off the bread, he started longing for Gwen to be with him. *Perhaps when I wake up*, he thought as weariness crept up on him once more.

He woke again as sunlight made shadows on the wall. Was it the same day? What day was it? He pulled himself up and out of bed. He sat back down, head spinning, then stood up again more slowly, and opened the window. The air was cool and fresh, with a faint smell of salt. There was no malt in the air, so he guessed it was a Sunday.

How many days? Two, maybe three? He closed his eyes and saw the fire, heard the echo of Joshua calling. His head felt light again and his breathing laboured. The floor rose up to meet him.

He woke back in bed. Joe had just put a mug of tea on the bedside table.

'Looks like you'll need it more than me,' Joe said cheerfully.

'How long have I been like this?' Dafydd asked.

'Three days,' came the reply. 'Mrs Owen's been fussing over you something awful. You're not related by any chance?'

He smiled at his own words, but Dafydd wasn't paying attention. Mrs Owen, Joe said, not Gwen?

'What's happening then?'

'Well, we've a spot of building to do, that's for sure,' Joe replied. 'I expect it will take a few weeks to put the wall up and roof the whole thing.' He stopped. 'That was a tidy spot of work you done there and no mistake. We'll be poor for a while, but at least we can still make rope.'

'You said "we".'

'Well, Joshua's the master, but I'm a cousin, so I always say it's in the family.'

'How is Joshua?' Dafydd asked.

'As bad as you,' Joe made a face. 'Worse perhaps, but he'll be all right. He's an ox that one.'

'Where's Gwen?'

Joe grinned like a wolf. 'Safe, don't you worry. She'll be along to visit soon enough.'

The days went past and Gwen did not come. Dafydd had plenty of fuss from Mrs Owen, and Joe visited his bedside many times, but Gwen did not.

When Dafydd was strong enough to walk without holding onto something, he was straight down the stairs, out and over to the riverside. He sat for a while then, to catch his breath and watch the world. The air was fresh and he'd never welcomed it before as he did then. Joe saw him from the house and waved a greeting.

A few days later, Dafydd suggested they both went back to the ropewalk. Joe agreed, but with a strange look on his face.

They found Joshua in bed, pale and sweating, coughing up muck. He looked a shadow of his former self. 'Sit down boy,' Joshua said with a grim smile. 'Sit down. I hope you're well. It's thanks to you I still have a business, you know. You and your sweeping. A dirty floor would have had the whole place up in flames.'

Dafydd nodded: at that moment, *thanks for sweeping the floor* was not what he needed to hear.

'Are you better now?' Dafydd asked.

'As much as can be expected,' Joshua said. 'You saved my life, boy, and my business. Saved my family from the workhouse even. I'm going to reward you, though I wonder if you'll feel that way.'

Dafydd, puzzled, could only stare back as he sipped some water.

'You saw Parry,' Joshua whispered.

Dafydd went white, a memory of Parry's face in the crowd, flickering in the firelight like a demon.

'Then again everyone looked like that at the time to me, and I wasn't sure it was him anyway,' he said out loud.

'You were shouting his name, Dafydd,' Joe said quietly. 'I been doing some asking and he was seen hanging around Trefechan.'

'I think he's following you,' Joshua said. 'I think he wants revenge. It wasn't the ropewalk he was after. It was you.'

Dafydd couldn't think what to say. Joshua looked to Joe. 'Leave us.'

Joe slipped out the door and Joshua drank more water.

'Dafydd, this man's after you. You can't stay here.'

'But you need me now,' Dafydd stammered.

'Dafydd,' Joshua sighed. 'I need you, but life just got harder. I can't afford you.'

'I'll wait then,' Dafydd said, desperate not to be sent away from Gwen. 'I'll find another job and wait until you need me.'

Joshua shook his head. 'It's an expensive town, Dafydd. It's also a hard place to get onto a decent trade, especially at your age. There's another thing and all. You're a young man, Dafydd, a fine one too. But you're going too fast with Gwen. You're not old enough yet. Give it a few years and you'll both be ready, but now you're running before you can walk.'

Dafydd flushed and made to answer, but Joshua's gaze still bore into him. 'I've found you work, Dafydd. One of the firms that take my rope up in Talybont. They need men to help build a new railway up there. This is the address; I've already spoken to him.'

'Talybont?' Dafydd whispered. It felt like exile.

'Yes, go and help. Then when that work's done, perhaps a few years, you can come back and – who knows?'

'But I want to stay...'

'I advise you to go,' Joshua said firmly. 'Get a train to Llanfihangel, then a few miles' walk. I said you'd be there tomorrow.' He sighed. 'I know how you're feeling, Dafydd. But it's for your own good.'

Dafydd stumbled out of the room. He was in shock and could only think of one person. When he saw her walking away from him, he broke into a sprint. His heart was in his mouth as Gwen turned and he saw her eyes.

'You know?' he asked.

Gwen nodded, but didn't speak.

'Can't you talk to him? Make him see?'

She sighed. 'It was my decision and all.'

'Why?'

Gwen looked away and Dafydd gripped her arm, letting go quick before he hurt her.

'Because I must.'

His mind went numb. 'I want to stay with you.'

She looked sadly at him. Perhaps there were tears there, although Dafydd couldn't see them through his own.

'It's not right. Not now,' she whispered. Dafydd stood there helpless, for there was nothing to say, the decision was made. In the end, she asked, 'What did he say?'

'For me to come back in a few years. Will you wait?' Dafydd asked. His heart was aching with dread for the answer.

'If there's a chance,' she started to speak and then stopped to breathe. 'If there's someone out there you find... Someone who's really... If there's a chance. Don't think of the past.'

'Will you wait?' Dafydd asked again. 'I love you,' he pleaded desperately.

She turned then, stood on tiptoe and kissed his brow and he held her close.

'God willing,' he murmured, in resignation. Then she was gone, leaving him staring into nothing.

Dafydd shuffled back to the house, the world blurred with tears. Joe saw him go and looked away; there was nothing to be said. Dafydd went into Mrs Owen's kitchen, where she was preparing tea.

'Joe told me,' she said quietly. 'What you going to do?'

Dafydd shrugged. 'I have to go, he made it clear.' He bit his lip.

'The girl, I can see it in your eyes. Listen, *cariad*, I'm one for fate and if it's not happened, it's for a reason. It could be it's not the right time. There is much tying her to her father. She has been his world since her mother was lost in childbirth. She is his, as he is hers. She has been allowed to be a free spirit, but her loyalty remains to him. Whilst he is poorly, there can be no other. You have to carry on, Dafydd *bach*. Someone will be there for you, and it might even be Gwen. Just not today.'

The gruff old lady let him hug her then and softly sang a *cwtch*ing song as he wept like a babe in her arms.

CHAPTER FOUR

Talybont

'YOU DON'T HAVE to go, Daf,' Joe said as they walked over Trefechan Bridge. 'Just because Joshua is telling you. You could find work in town.'

'It's finding work that pays,' Dafydd replied. 'Besides…'

'Gwen,' Joe said.

Dafydd had to nod. 'I just need to get away.'

'Well, they do say Talybont is a rough place, them country folk and all. Best watch your back, especially with that Parry looking for you.'

'Well, let him come,' Dafydd snapped. 'I'm one of them rough country folk and all, ent I?'

'No offence,' Joe's hands rose in defence.

Dafydd shook his head, it was just words.

'Will you come back, do you think?'

Dafydd shrugged. 'Look, Joe, you been a good friend when I had none. Just… Thanks, that's all.'

Joe beamed back. 'No problem at all, boy. You're all right yourself. Come on then, if your mind's made up, we'd best get you to the station.'

They shook hands at the barrier. Then Dafydd was off down the platform. This was his first journey on a train and he was surprised by the bustle of the station. Anxious passengers calling to and fro, porters wheeling luggage, chatting eagerly to their patrons in the hope of a bigger tip, trolleys wielded like weapons, people jumping out of the way. Dafydd found a seat on the train and watched a young couple being seen off on their honeymoon: crying women, excited children, men shaking hands with the groom. One girl started to throw confetti, setting off a cheer. A porter rushed in to stop her, polite but firm. A man in overalls speckled with grease shouted as he walked by, armed with an oil-can. The woman blew him a kiss, and he responded with a roar of laughter.

The guard gave the all clear, the engine whistle sounded and the train lurched forward. The whistle shrieked on as they gained speed.

'Don't worry, ma'am,' an elderly gentleman was saying to a rather flustered lady. 'They always do that for newlyweds. Only as far as Llanbadarn Crossing, that's a mile away or so. Then they'll be stopping.'

Dafydd sank into his seat. The merry scene left him all the more isolated. He just wanted to get to Llanfihangel, find the way to Talybont and start work. Wherever he looked, he saw echoes of Gwen's fair hair and teasing smile.

On the platform at Llanfihangel, he watched the train roll away in a wall of noise. He watched it until the red painted back of the last coach was out of sight, and he was left with his thoughts.

'Where's the road to Talybont?' he asked a porter.

'Off to your right,' came the reply. 'But you may as well walk the embankment of that new toy railway line. He pointed out the line of soil and light grey stone curving away. 'At least it's dry.'

Dafydd wondered if this was the work of his new employer. He followed it across the Borth road and past a few cottages. There were no rails laid, which surprised him. The stone was lighter than the surrounding rock, so bright

Dafydd reckoned you could follow it in the dark. The stones soon made his feet hot and tired, for all his boots were still whole and the stones looked flat. At least it was dry. Dafydd plodded on. A farm boy working in a field stopped and gave him such a stare that he wondered what feud he was walking into.

The line passed on through fields, running parallel to a cart road, then swung away towards some woods and a large bridge over a dip in the land. He stopped midway across a bridge to peer into the deep gully and wonder: if they had managed this already, how much work was left? He carried on out of the wood, through a village and, to its left, the workings and wheels of a large mine. Talybont. Where now?

He had been given the name of Morgan as the man to look for, but the line crossed the cart road above the village. In doubt, Dafydd decided to carry on along the track bed until he found someone who worked for the railway.

At length, the road dropped down the valley, and Dafydd saw a few small buildings ahead with a small water tower. Two men were standing there, and he made his way to them. The larger of the two was clearly in charge. His barrel-like frame bulged beneath a waistcoat. His reddened cheeks spoke of a liking for drink.

'Mr Morgan?' asked Dafydd.

'Aye, aye,' Morgan said, blowing angrily through a bushy moustache. 'And who might you be, then?'

'I been sent by Joshua Jones, ropemaker, to find a man named Morgan.'

'Well, you found him right enough. Thomas, is it? I was expecting you earlier.'

'I was on the first train out from Aber, sir.'

'See you're ahead of yourself, walking the trackbed like a lord. We just got that settled and level.'

'I meant no disrespect, sir,' Dafydd replied carefully. 'But the road is fairly poor and I wanted to get here quickly.'

'Well, you'd best get started, then,' snapped Morgan. 'Boys are on the incline. Best hurry if you want half day's pay today. Do you read and write?'

'Some,' Dafydd replied. 'English and Welsh.'

'What are you? Grammar school or something?' Morgan scoffed.

'No sir, Lisburne Mines School and chapel.'

'Makes no difference when you're shifting rock,' the other put in.

'Good one, Philips,' Morgan laughed. 'Off you go, then,' he jerked his thumb in the general direction Dafydd should take.

'How do I find lodging?' Dafydd asked.

'Do I look like your mother?' Morgan shouted, squaring up as if to strike him. 'Philips, take him with you, the farm is on the way.'

'Come on then,' Philips said, leading the way. 'I've to get the farmer to stop his bloody sheep grazing on our trackside. They start now, it will happen all the time – and it'll be us to blame, you'll see, if they're run down…' He paused, and gave Dafydd half a smile. 'Don't you worry about Morgan. It's nothing personal. Things have not gone well of late and we're way behind. Should have rails on and engines running up and down by now. Don't you worry about you being a reader and all. One day it'll stand you in good stead. Probably not here, mind.'

Dafydd grinned wryly, and trudged on.

'We need every good man now for the last push,' Philips added. 'Ask the men about lodgings, they'll find you something. They're a good bunch here – now that Parry's gone, at any rate.'

'Parry?'

'Troublemaker, he was. Glad to see the back of him.'

They parted at the farm and Dafydd returned to his own thoughts, plodding alone along the grey trackbed. Dipping through a small cutting, the line dropped down level with the river. Dafydd stopped to drink and look about him. It was a pleasant walk, if a little eerie. There wasn't a soul in sight. He was still stunned by the events of recent weeks. During his walk, he'd played them over and over in his mind – the fight, the flight to Aber, Gwen, the ropemaking job, the fire – then the farewell to Gwen, the job, and Aber in one catastrophic event. He'd asked himself when his life had last been "normal", and why he was still running – if running he was. But he had no answers yet. He shrugged, shouldered his small sack of belongings and moved on, munching the cheese sandwich Mrs Owen had slipped into his sack. *Heart of gold, that one*, he thought.

There was a small chapel in the valley, but few other signs of life. Farmhouses were far-off spots further down below the trackbed. Dafydd spotted a cluster of larger buildings that the line seemed to be carving a path to. It looked like a mine.

As he drew closer, he saw that the waterwheels were idle, the spoil heaps old and grassy, the buildings empty. Dafydd's thoughts drifted to Frongoch, and the larger wheels and chimneys of his childhood.

He thought of his family: Tad, level and honest with all; Mam, her beauty hiding a will of iron; Sioned, his sister, caring and kind; Angharad, the baby he hardly knew, and Mam-gu, the captain of the family, though quieter since the loss of his tad-cu. She'd always looked out for Dafydd, but she was old now. He'd like to be there, to look out for her. If only it had all been different, and he hadn't had to run.

Dafydd moved on past the mine, beginning to wonder if he would ever reach the work party.

Around another curve, and the line dipped down again. A group of men came into view far off at the foot of a long steep slope. Did they mean to take the line up and over the lip of the valley end? Dafydd's mind was racing. Surely nothing would get up a hill like that?

He approached the bottom of the incline. At the foot was the imposing form of a large spoked waterwheel. Dafydd decided it was sixty or seventy feet in diameter. He could hear the rushing of water echoing through the wheelpit, and from the stream bounding down the side of the hill opposite. The remains of a small mine hung next to the incline. Broken walls and small grey spoil-heaps. Wherever he went, Dafydd decided, he would never be far from his past.

The men were packing ballast at the foot of the hill, throwing up an earthwork parallel to a jagged cliff. Dafydd groaned inside as he saw the work to be done, but he took off his cap and made for the foreman, as meek as he could. The men stopped and stared.

'Grab a shovel, young man,' the foreman said. 'Hope you're used to hard work. It's uphill all the way now.'

He's not joking neither, Dafydd thought, as he stared up the incline of the cliff.

In minutes he was one of a line of men, building up the ballast at the base of the incline. All around him the sound of tools against rock, the heavy breathing of labouring men and occasional snorts and stamps from a group of horses with carts stood by. Dafydd did his best to get stuck in. Pretty soon, however, hunger and thirst took their toll.

50

When break was finally called, he was almost out on his feet. He sat a bit away from the others and tried to rest his aching limbs.

'Hey, you not with us or what?' A voice broke through Dafydd's thoughts. *English, north at a guess*, Dafydd thought, remembering the English miners at Frongoch.

'Probably doesn't understand you, John, mate,' said another with a Midlands tinge to his sing-song voice. He was the one Dafydd had heard addressed as Jim.

'I do, sir,' Dafydd replied, polite enough. 'I worked with English before.'

'Where you from?'

'Trisant,' Dafydd replied, then seeing their blank looks. 'It's by Frongoch, one of the big lead mines. That's where I was learning my English.'

'Lead miner, then? You'll be used to them holes in the ground,' said Jim, nodding towards the spoil heap of an abandoned working nearby. 'Like ghosts, they were. Come here, dig holes, then vanish like the wind.'

Dafydd thought of the dark hole, promising an end to all struggles.

'Like us, when this line is done,' John was saying.

Dafydd shook his head gamely. At least his companions were being polite, despite being a rough bunch. 'Why have you come over here?' he asked.

John shrugged. 'Building railways, it's what we do. You not eating or drinking?'

'I have nothing,'

'Expecting us to give you charity, are ye?' John grunted.

'No sir, I got told of this job only yesterday. I came from Aberystwyth this morning. No food, or lodging for that matter.'

John shook his head. 'I've had to sleep in a barn before.'

'How old are you, son?' put in Jim.

'Sixteen now.'

'You been out of this land? Seen a big city?'

'I been working in Aber for a few months,' Dafydd replied.

John snorted in his derision. Jim perhaps hid a smile, as he stood to go to the fire, on which a kettle boiled. He threw the tea from his cup and refilled it.

'You remind me of my boy in Dudley,' he said softly. 'Take this, there's a hunk of bread for you also. Be quick now, break's nearly done.'

'Are we charity?' John asked.

'No, Pendle John, but if we don't look after our own, there's more for us to do, in my mind. I'm James, son. They call me Lucky Jim. That's Pendle John, he's a bit wary of the Welsh. We had a man here and he was a menace. Got us in no end of trouble.'

'Parry,' Dafydd said, without thinking.

'How do you know him, son?' Lucky Jim asked.

'Man at the station told me,' Dafydd said hastily, then wished he hadn't. 'But I met Parry before. He tried to kill me.' And with that, he found himself telling his tale.

'That's Parry all right,' Pendle John said.

Jim frowned. 'Didn't think he were one of the locals.'

A whistle was blown and the men rose as one. 'Right, we'll be back on this later. Come with us and we'll sort you lodging, I'm sure.'

Dafydd ended up in a lodging house full of railway workers in Talybont village. He was sharing a room with three others. At first he couldn't sleep for the snoring and the reek of sweat. Very soon though, tiredness took over. It was just good to feel safe once more.

He paid the rent, chipped in to the food kitty, and a week went slowly by. The team were up and out at dawn, loading the carts with tools and leading the horses down the strange path that was soon to become an iron way.

The incline was developing, leading up to the lip of the valley, where stone was being quarried and which was to be the final destination for the railway. 'Soon the train will take the stone west,' Lucky Jim said. 'There's talk of a new promenade in Aberystwyth, you know. Then there's a great big dam they're building over in the Elan Valley' (he pronounced it "eelan", which made Dafydd wince). 'Many of the lads came over for that alone. So, who knows after that?'

'What brought you here?' Dafydd asked.

'I heard of work on the Rheidol railway.'

'They can't stop arguing on that one,' Dafydd said.

Pendle John nodded. 'Or changing the route. Which side of the valley? How far up? I came to try and get work on the original plan, when it was supposed to run to Aberaeron.'

'And so we ended up here,' Jim said. 'For what it's worth.'

'What's the problem?' Dafydd asked.

'Look around you boy,' John snapped. 'What do you see? Nothing. Empty shells of mines and empty hills. The quarry's fine, I grant you, but who's going to come here for stone?'

'There are other mines,' Dafydd protested.

'All over the hill, boy,' Pendle John jabbed with his pipe to make the point. 'All dead and gone, in the main. And who's going to come up and down this with an engine?'

'So what are we building it for?'

John rubbed his fingers together and Jim chuckled.

'Money, and that's what coming to us Saturday.'

'Come with us,' Jim said. 'We'll have a jug in the Black Lion. If you can put up with John Pendle's harmonica.'

Dafydd hesitated. 'I'm a chapel boy too, you know,' he grinned. 'I don't take to the harmonica. I won't be staying long if it gets rough.'

'You Welsh are bloody soft,' John muttered.

Two inns stood side by side at the bottom of the village, nestling between the hills in a sharp dip.

'Why you choose the Black Lion from the White Lion?' Dafydd asked, nursing a jug of strong ale.

'Stands to reason,' Jim replied. 'It's owned by the Squire of Gogerddan, the White by his neighbour. Seeing as Mr Pryse Pryse,' he stopped to belch, 'Pryse is sponsoring the railway, we have to be seen in the right places.'

'And Mr Pryse is?'

'Mr Pryse Pryse Pryse is squire.'

'Oh. You don't like him?'

'Don't know him. I'm sure he's a good man at heart. We work on his land, so there's always respect there.'

'What you running from, boy?' John asked suddenly.

Dafydd spat a mouthful of beer in his eagerness to say, 'Nothing, why?'

'Look at you. You read, you speak English and Welsh. You're handy with a shovel, but there's more you could be doing.'

Dafydd shrugged. 'I've not been one for moving unless I've had to.' Perhaps they thought he was some sort of scholar. He wondered if he should tell them more of his story.

John and Jim were good company and Dafydd needed that the more after all the things that had happened. With the two men, he felt he could at last relax. He looked at them, sitting at ease with their jugs of ale. Jim had a clay pipe lit, puffing away in one side of his mouth as he talked. John, left thumb in waistcoat pocket, smiled away the work of the week. He held his harmonica, tapping the table to music already being played in the inn. Both were old enough to be Dafydd's father, but they treated him as equal. He decided he had no intention of letting them think he was a lost boy on the run.

He threw himself into conversation and song, which went on long into the night, until Dafydd began to grow weary and got up to go. Jim clapped his arm fondly.

'You keep yourself safe, boy. I'll see you in chapel.'

'In that, at least, Jim will be true to his word.' John said 'He may not know the language, but he hums a good tune and knows his Bible by heart.'

Dafydd got up, swaying a bit, and left. He might take up a pipe, he thought, it looked pleasant. He eyed up other people's sideburns and beards. *Perhaps a small moustache*, he mused.

'Hey – come here, you,' a rough voice shouted and someone squared up to him. 'You been spreading bad words about me, en' you.'

'No... I don't...' Dafydd started to say, but the stranger launched a punch at his head. Dafydd ducked, but the beer in him slowed him down and the man's fist grazed the side of his head, adding nausea to pain. Dafydd just managed to push him away.

The man came back faster than he looked capable of. Dafydd stumbled under his weight and went down. The man was on him like a rabid animal. Dafydd kicked and pushed as much as he could, but couldn't shift him until his groin came within range and Dafydd lashed out. He could have crippled him, but he pulled the kick. Somewhere inside, Dafydd remembered how it felt to think himself a murderer.

Meanwhile, the kick made the man angrier still. He snarled and grabbed for Dafydd's throat, his full weight behind his hands. Dafydd began to wonder if this was the end of him. But then other hands pulled the stranger off. Someone bashed the man's head and he lay still. A burly man pulled Dafydd to his feet. He blinked, and registered the blue uniform of the local constabulary.

'Right, off to the station with you,' grunted the policeman.

'I done nothing,' Dafydd cried. 'He attacked me.'

'Tell it to the judge,' the policeman growled. Dafydd was marched up the hill, protesting his innocence fiercely, until it was suggested a truncheon could be used to silence him.

'Throw you in the cells, and charge you with breach of the peace, that's what we'll be doing. We'll have the judge in petty session here Thursday. He'll sort you out. All right, go sleep it off.'

Dafydd was pushed into a cell. He caught a momentary vision of a flat slab of a bed with a grubby grey blanket, a bucket in a corner, and grey desolation. Then it went dark as the pit. He stood, swaying slightly, then felt his way to the bed and pulled the blanket round him, hunching into its meagre warmth and praying the world would stop spinning. The ale helped him slide through misery to sleep.

He awoke with a start to the sound of grating metal. It was cold and the light of a grey morning shafted down from a small window. The door swung open, and he realised the sound had been a key in the lock. His head throbbed as he clambered to his feet. 'Am I supposed to come out?' he huskily asked the waiting policeman.

'Well, I'm hardly here to offer you breakfast,' came the reply. 'There's a man vouching for your parole.'

Dafydd didn't know what that meant, so he followed the

policeman out to find Lucky Jim waiting.

'Thought I'd get pick you up in time for chapel,' he said with a smile.

'He's in your charge now,' the policeman said. 'Your word that he comes to court on Thursday.' Jim nodded quickly and steered Dafydd to the door.

'It's not my fault,' Dafydd said breathlessly as Jim rushed to the house. 'The man just went for me, no warning.'

'Yes, well, he's one for that. Nothing but trouble, that bastard. You said you had crossed him before, didn't you?'

Dafydd frowned. It hurt. 'What do you mean?'

'You said he gave you trouble at Frongoch. Stirring it, bullying you and that. And then the fight you had? No wonder he came for you. He's a bitter man, that Parry.'

'That's not Parry!' Dafydd spluttered. 'I never seen him before in my life.'

'Well, that's the Parry we sacked last month.'

Dafydd was lost for words.

The sermon in the chapel was about the error of those who fell prey to the evils of alcohol. Dafydd felt fully chastised and hoped the minister would finish soon, so he could go off and be sick somewhere.

On the day of the hearing, The foreman turned a blind eye as Dafydd stayed in Talybont to attend. Parry was fined a pound for disturbing the peace, and Dafydd six shillings for not restraining himself. Dafydd could not wait to pay and get back to the incline.

'All all right?' John asked.

'Well, my beer money's gone for a month,' Dafydd said.

'That'll learn yer.'

'Yes, yes. Good view here,' Dafydd said, changing the subject.

'Aye, only two more inclines to sort in the quarry.'

Jim came over, holding a piece of paper.

'This came for you, from Aberystwyth.'

Dafydd's heart leapt as a flood of old thoughts came back to him. A letter from Aber? Could it be Gwen?

CHAPTER FIVE

Redemption

IN THE WEEKS that Dafydd had been at Talybont, he had heard nothing of Gwen. His adventure with the law and the hard labour had kept him busy, but the memory was always there, waiting to spring up in waves of hope or misery.

Now, as he stuffed the letter in his waistcoat pocket, he found he could feel both at once. He had no idea how long it was until the next break, but he put all his energy into digging and kept his head down.

'What's up wi' you?' John asked him. 'I nearly put my pick through your foot and you don't even blink.'

'Huh? Nothing, just thinking, I was, that's all.' Dafydd replied, still not meeting the man's eyes.

'Thinking? Is that what you do?' John teased, fishing for a response.

'I think the young fellow is distracted, Pendle John,' Jim bounced back.

'Aye, I think you may be right, Lucky Jim. Why is this?'

'I think that letter be to blame, Pendle John.'

'Why on earth would he be so distracted, Lucky Jim?'

'Perhaps there is a woman, Pendle John?'

'I dare say, Lucky Jim.'

Dafydd flushed at the Punch and Judy act.

'Should we let him open it, Pendle John?'

'At break, yes, Lucky Jim. The only question that then remains,' John said, launching his pick near to Dafydd's feet once more. 'Is how many toes shall he have by then.'

They were both chuckling unashamedly now. The whistle finally blew and they put down their tools. Most went to sit on the valley lip with food and tea. Dafydd made for a place away from them all. His hands were tingling with excitement, but his throat dry with fear. He looked at the writing on the envelope. There was no clue there.

Dafydd Thomas, Plynlimon & Hafan Tramway, Talybont

He had never had a letter before. He opened the envelope clumsily. Excitement quickened as he took out the pages. He sat and read it, then read it again. Slowly and carefully, he folded it and placed it in his pocket. He sat and looked down the valley, thinking of broken dreams.

'Pretending to read, are you?' A voice sneered from nearby. One of the Welsh labourers had gone for a piss and was using the opportunity to leer over Dafydd's shoulder.

'You think you're better than us, don't you?' He grabbed Dafydd's hair and tugged. 'You're nothing but a common English-loving *bradwr*.'

He pushed Dafydd's head back and walked away. Dafydd scrambled to his feet and grabbed the man's throat. John and Jim moved just as fast to pull him away. 'I'll kill him,' Dafydd growled. 'Let go, he's a dead man.'

Jim had grabbed him.

'Let it pass. He's baiting you, Dafydd. Stop, listen to me!'

Then Jim slapped Dafydd's face, stopping him dead.

'Right,' Jim said. 'John'll let you go now and you got two choices. Come back with us or go and sort him out. If you sort him, I tell you now, you'll be out on your ear. Just like Parry.'

John released Dafydd, who stumbled and stared, anger turned to shock and doubt.

'He called me a traitor, because I am with you English boys.'

'Fool,' said Jim. 'We're all here to work, that's all.'

They all turned at the sound of a scuffle.

'Seems he's not popular,' said John.

The man's gaffer had cuffed him to the floor.

'There's enough problems working this damned incline without the likes of him to deal with,' Dafydd muttered darkly.

'It's the letter, i'n't it,' Jim said. 'Trouble with your woman?'

Dafydd shook his head. 'It's from my old foreman at Frongoch. It's not about my woman, who is not my woman anyway,' he sighed. 'My mam-gu – my grandmother, is dead. The funeral's on Saturday. Jones Foreman wanted me to know.'

'Well, we should see to it that you're there, my boy,' Jim said, 'if she means enough for you to knock the head off a wastrel.'

Dafydd stared into the distance. 'When I was young,' he said, 'I wouldn't listen, not even to Tad. Just the one person got through, my mam-gu. I helped her grow stuff in the garden. I...'

Jim put his hand on his shoulder. 'Leave it to me.'

He went to talk to the foreman. John Pendle watched him go, fishing for his pipe all the while.

'Don't you worry on those hotheads, son,' he said as he lit up. 'You're in good company with us. Foreman has our respect. When the main job's done, we'll have the pick of what's left, you'll see. Stick with us, you'll learn more.'

Dafydd watched Jim and the foreman for what seemed

a long time, with the foreman doing much head shaking, Jim pointing at the incline, and the gang. In the end, the foreman shook his head but laughed and they shook hands. Jim came back, all smiles.

'That's that sorted. You lose a day's pay, go off and come back for Monday morning.'

'How? What?' Dafydd spluttered.

'Easy. I agreed to sort out a problem for him next week.'

John spat on his palms. 'Now I do like a challenge.'

'More than that. If we do our bit in a timely fashion, we'll be on rails straight after. Then when everything to Talybont's in place, we'll help put the engine on the line.'

'Jim,' Dafydd said, 'you're a good man.'

'So are you, mate,' Jim replied. 'Don't forget it.'

Dafydd flushed and turned away, not sure whether to feel comforted or alarmed that the man knew him so well.

One of the local men told Dafydd how to get to Ponterwyd. Over the lip, straight for Bryn-yr-Afr mine, then right, following the Nant-y-Moch stream. Apparently, he couldn't miss it. Dafydd was grateful, he knew the path from that town, but the mountains of Plynlimon made a bleak and weary route. Fearing he would miss the village in this wilderness, he resolved to stop at a farm and ask on the way. Scanning the windswept brown hills, he wondered if there would be a farm out there at all.

The railway was only in the foothills of Plynlimon, so it felt like pure guesswork when Dafydd found a junction of three streams and decided where south lay by the sun. At length, he caught sight of the roof of Ponterwyd chapel. He could have run to the steps and kissed them.

From the village, he knew the road to Devils Bridge and from there to Trisant. He was soon on the road he remembered from the old horse fairs. The way put him in mind of his flight from Frongoch. There had been no morning sun then, just cold silver beams of moonlight and the sound of his own feet as he had run for his life.

He was ashamed for the disgrace to his family and the sorrow he had brought them, ashamed at the lack of courage he had shown in not waiting for his father that dreadful night. With nobody on the road to see, he let the tears stream down his face.

The green land ahead was a sharp contrast to the barren hills of Plynlimon. It should have been welcoming, but when he saw the first cottages of Trisant, he felt denied, and sought to reach the chapel through the neighbouring fields.

In the lane alongside the chapel wall he crouched quietly, for the burial was already in progress. He watched as they lowered the body into a grave and sang a hymn. Dafydd recognised it well; the music filled his ears. He mouthed the words from his hiding place.

Arglwydd dyma fi!
Ar Dy alwad Di
Golch fi'n burlan yn y gwaed
A gaed ar Galfari

His mam looked small and his father grey and old. His sister Sioned was sobbing without restraint. His tad's butty, the Cornishman David Treveglos, stood tall, smiling sadly as he went around with his wife, comforting those who needed it most. Dafydd's gaze lingered on David's sister Mary. She was blooming, as ever. He had fallen for her as a boy, though she hardly returned the affection. Now he knew his heart was still only for Gwen. He looked on Mary with only distant admiration. He wondered why she looked slyly at his father, though.

For a moment, his father looked up and Dafydd ducked his head. Had their eyes met? It was like a spark through his body that left him shaking. There was no way he could face his family like this. He sat down below the wall rim, breathing shallow breaths. After a while he risked another look. The gathering was leaving the churchyard through the gate opposite

Now, Dafydd felt foolish. He should have been with them. Perhaps he would go to them later, after the guests were gone. The desire to go home and feel his mam's kiss on his brow coursed through him.

He watched carefully as they all made for the house, to take tea. Whilst people were paying their respects to his tad, Dafydd sat by the new grave and hugged his knees.

'Mam-gu,' he whispered gently. 'I'm sorry I let you down. I promise you I'll turn out all right. I'll do better. I'll make you proud of me.'

He became aware of someone approaching and jumped back over the wall again, to wait for the man to pass. There was only silence.

The light was fading and Dafydd began to doze. After a few minutes he awoke, and shivered with cold. To warm himself up, he elected to walk to the village. He turned up his collar and pulled his hat forward. Moving swiftly through the village, he walked to the lakeside of Llyn Frongoch. His father had once thrown him in for giving him lip. Dafydd's tad-cu had done the same when Dafydd's father had returned after a mudfight. Dafydd smiled. It was a family tradition.

Would he ever do the same with a son? His spirits sank again. It all depended on Gwen. He thought of the best and worst day of his life: first, lying on the beach with Gwen

6 4

in his arms, then watching flames leap, destroying the ropewalk and his life with it. He stared into the lake, looking for answers, but the water was not clear. The sky was grey and the wind sent ripples on the surface.

With a deep sigh, Dafydd headed off. The road dipped beyond the dam and then rose up sharply to a high point he had once loved to look out from. As he stood there, the grey of the land below him matched the grey sky and a cold wind blew from Frongoch. The ghosts of his past life rose up and came to life in the mine, now idle for the Saturday afternoon, and Dafydd watched the cameo in a daydream:

It would be the end of the dayshift soon. Time for Dafydd to make himself scarce. The mine sprawled in front of him, a scar in the green surrounding hills. The pumping houses, shafts and wheels stood firm in the sea of spoil and broken rock.

He could hear the crashing of ore being loaded into trams. The slosh and splash of water coming from the wheel below. He could only ever marvel at the Cardi way. How their one great resource was harnessed – water. The wheel would use it and then send it on to the great Wemyss wheel over the hill. That would then throw the water down the valley for Graig Goch mine. No waste, no wanting, as his mam would say.

Sill in his Frongoch daydream, he looked down on the wheel shed, where his three enemies had set him up for a beating. Dafydd closed his eyes as that scene again played in his mind. The anger and fear were still raw. All had gone bad from that point, and he still hated them for that.

Miners were coming up to the surface at the Vaughan shaft. Soon the top would be busy with men and blazing with lamps. He didn't want to be around for that. Some would feel sorry for him, others would think badly of him, in spite of what Jones Foreman had said. Either way, there would be a fuss of questions.

He retraced his steps up the road, his heart like Frongoch lead. The dream had passed, but a cold wind blew down the valley and through his bones. He didn't really want to imagine what his family must think of him for his desertion.

He felt fated. Bad that he had never stuck up for himself before, like his father had taught him. Bad that the first time he did, he'd gone over the top and proved himself capable of murder. Bad that he'd run, and the longer he'd stayed away, the worse that had become. Dafydd thought of running again there and then, far away from the accusing eyes that would fall on him, and laughed grimly at the irony of it.

Trisant was dark when he got back. The faint light from the houses lit nothing, told him no more than that he was shut out. He had left his childhood home under a bright moon. This time, he could not even see the road. He thought of the space by the hen coop at the house, where he used to hide as a child. It was dry, sheltered and out of sight – just what he needed.

He was safely hidden when the voices of miners returning home filled the air. From his hide-out, he watched them pass. Grey-faced men covered in the muck of a day's toil, but full of spirit. A few mentioned Dafydd's mam-gu as they passed. The words were respectful, even if one made light of her sharp tongue. Soon they were gone...

Dafydd shook his daydream out of his head and settled down to rough it for the night. After a while he heard a door open and a single pair of footsteps went out a short way. There was a sound, faint in the breeze. It was a man, sobbing.

The door opened again and this time Dafydd chanced a look. His mam was holding his father in a hug. He couldn't see their faces. They stood together a while, then they quietly kissed.

Like a small boy, Dafydd ached to run and join them, but his body would not move. He could only watch helplessly. They stared around into the night, as if willing the darkness to reveal something, hugged again, and went inside. Dafydd felt more alone than ever before, and cursed himself for being born. He settled down, biting his hand to still his emotion. In time, he heard the click of the door opening again. Was someone in need of the *tŷ bach*? He held his breath and waited.

'Dafydd?'

It was his father's voice.

'Dafydd?' He called again. This time Dafydd's foot slipped and the sound was like thunder to his ears.

'I know you're there, Dafydd.'

That gave Dafydd the resolve needed. He got up slowly.

'Tad.'

'Diolch, *Iesu*,' his father said. 'Come in quick, you must be frozen.'

Dafydd stood still and shook his head, even though he didn't know if his father could see him. He tried to speak, but his throat was dry from long silence.

'I done wrong,' he croaked. 'I shamed you all.'

His father stepped forward and Dafydd saw his face in the dim light from the house. It still looked full of tears.

'It's all right, boy, that's past. Captain Kitto said you can have your old job back. He knows how it was.'

Dafydd shook his head. His words were still slow, as he was desperate not to start crying in front of his father.

'It's too late, I got work.' Dafydd tried to sound brave about it. 'Good rates and all.'

'Where's that, then?'

'Talybont way. They're building a railway there and I'm helping out. I hope to stay on when it's done, I'm in good favour with some of them.' He thought of Jim and John. It wasn't too much of a lie.

His father smiled. Dafydd could see it was hard to do so.

'That's good news.'

'I can't come back now, Tad. Not after what I done. Mam and Sioned, what do they think of me?'

'Look, son,' his father said quickly. 'Them buggers had it coming. Mam and Sioned as sorry to lose you as they are to lose your mam-gu.' He grabbed Dafydd gently by the arm. 'Dafydd, please come with me. It's a bad day for us and we're all beside ourselves. Best tonic for us all would be you back in the house. That's for me included.'

Dafydd gripped his hand and his voice trembled. 'It'll be just for one night.'

His father breathed a sob and they hugged, father and son.

'One night will be a blessing,' he whispered.

'Know this, Tad,' Dafydd said as they began to walk in. 'If you ever need me, I'll find out and I'll be running back before you can blink.'

His father gasped and then recovered himself.

'How did you know of your mam-gu?'

'One of the men at the mine sent word,' Dafydd replied.

'But no-one knows where you are. Unless... Jones Foreman? Well I never, the old bugger. I think I owe him an apology.'

He opened the door and Dafydd went in. His mam was asking what was wrong. They'd been outside a while, Dafydd guessed. It had felt like hours.

'Where's Sioned?' His father asked asked, ignoring her question.

'She's sleeping now.'

'Wake her.' His father's voice was like stone.

'What, *cariad*...'

'I said, wake her.'

His mother's beautiful face looked tired and drawn. Her brows raised high as her gaze fell upon her son. Years seemed to fall away as her face changed through anger and surprise to one of great joy.

'Sioned,' she whispered, then stronger. 'Sioned! Here, now.'

'*Beth sy'n bod?*' Dafydd heard Sioned mutter sleepily and the sound of shuffling upstairs. He saw her head coming into view, her dark curls, just like her mam's, untidy now as she rubbed her eyes.

'Come down here now, sweet sister, and there's a *cwtch* in it for you,' Dafydd said.

Her mouth formed a perfect 'O'. Dafydd wondered if the baby would scream, but Angharad seemed not worried by the noise at all. Sioned was fair running down the ladder, but Dafydd didn't see much, for Mam had got the *cwtch* in first.

'Your mam-gu's last gift to us,' she whispered. 'Bless you, Mam, you brought my boy home.'

'You grown up quick,' Sioned said cheekily, when Dafydd had told her how lovely she was.

'One for the ladies, my boy is,' Mam said, coming over to give him yet another hug.

His father handed Dafydd a piece of paper he'd been working on.

'What's this then?' Dafydd asked.

'For your Aunt Myfanwy. I reckon you'll be passing their farm. I need to tell her about Mam.'

'You sure? I passed few farms on my way.'

'I'll tell you how to get there. But stay here the night, go back Sunday. Then you'll catch them in chapel instead.'

'Think they'd let me stay?' Dafydd asked. 'Then I'm nearer work than my lodgings for the morning.'

'You short?' His father asked suddenly, making Dafydd flush. He didn't want any more of their savings.

'You not been spending it on drink?' His father said with a gleam in his eye. 'Only I hear them navvies live on beer and beef.'

Dafydd thought of Jim and John and tried to remember when he saw them with anything else. Probably drunk all the time, but still gentlemen with it.

'Not much else, Tad. There's not much else in Talybont besides work and chapel. Thing is, I was rather wanting to hold back on spending for a while, so I can give you this.'

He held out a gold sovereign. It was all he had left from what his mam-gu had given him. His father shook his head straight away, but Dafydd pressed it into his hand.

'Please, take it. For me.' Dafydd chuckled then. 'Besides, it will keep me from the tavern for a while. If you take this, I'll stay and I'll give you a hand with the roof tomorrow.'

'Why do you think I need a hand?'

'Tad, there's always problems with the roof,' Dafydd grinned.

'Well now, happen there's nothing wrong. However, I do have a problem with the inside. I could do with help there and no chapel watching us.'

'Done then.'

He nodded, his eyes sparkling.

'Just like old times, isn't it? It'll make your mam think she's in heaven. Sioned too, for that matter. Tell me you'll go to Myfanwy's? I don't think the letter's good – you can say the rest.'

'I'll try, Tad, honest I will. I don't know what to say, mind.'

'Just tell them what you saw and what Mam-gu meant to you. They'll be happy with that.'

'All right, I will.'

His father sighed. 'They're your nearest family now and if you need anyone, well, they're nearer to you, that's all.'

'Tad, I'll go. They won't know me though.'

'Better you do it now before you learn how to grow a moustache proper,' Sioned chimed in from behind him.

Dafydd had to laugh. 'It's good to be back.'

His mam came over to sit with him and started peeling potatoes, dropping them into a pan. 'Can't you get him a job underground now, Owain? Prospects are better than they have been in a while, after all.'

'Ceri, I'm sorry, *bach*,' his father replied sadly. 'There's still more miners than jobs and I got a partnership with old Ben Treveglos and his son David. Besides, Dafydd's worth more than spending a lifetime under the grass. There's a brain in that head of his and I hope one day he'll get to use it.'

The Sunday morning was grey and damp. After a slow start, the heavens opened.

'God obviously don't want me to go,' Dafydd joked, reaching for his coat.

'We don't want you to go neither,' his father said.

'When I get to Devils Bridge road, I might get a lift,' Dafydd said.

'Take care of yourself,' his mam whispered, fussing at his jacket. Then Sioned came to weep on his shoulder and, finally, Dafydd was left facing his father.

'I feel as if I've lived a lifetime of goodbyes,' he grumbled.

Dafydd gripped his shoulder. 'It's just goodbye for now, I promise,' he said, and then was off before he could cave in and stay.

He did get a lift on a cart, to Ponterwyd, and then strode out for Plynlimon. He eventually found his aunt's farm but when he arrived, his heart sank, for nobody was home.

He thought about waiting in the barn but the sky was dark and the mist was already closing in. He didn't know if it would clear overnight and he knew if he wasn't at Hafan for the morning, he'd be out of a job. With a heavy heart, he left the letter under the door and made for the road. Perhaps one day he would get to meet them after all.

By the time he reached Hafan, the light was poor and the chill of evening had set in. There was a store in the quarry and a careless hand had left it open. Gratefully, Dafydd ducked inside, pulling the door to and feeling warm for the first time in ages. The wooden frames kept the weather out and he stripped to his smalls and hung his clothes up to dry, found some sacks and fashioned a bed.

He felt like a tramp, and the sacks made his body itch, but he was too tired to care. Exhausted by the journey and the events of the past few days, he slept.

CHAPTER SIX

I'll Be Your Gwen (1897)

'BRIGHT AND BREEZY, Mr Thomas,' Lucky Jim called, struggling up the incline.

'Damp and dreary, more like,' Dafydd called back from his perch on the top. 'I been waiting for you. I sheltered here last night, the weather was that bad.'

'Well, that answers it,' Pendle John rumbled. 'We had you down for a dalliance, did we not, Lucky Jim?'

'We did indeed, Pendle John. With a woman, no less.'

Dafydd flushed, thinking of his night with Gwen on the beach. 'Don't talk nonsense now.'

'We have news, young Dafydd,' John said. 'We're done here.'

Dafydd gasped, thinking of the coin he'd left in Trisant.

'Don't fret, young un,' Jim added. 'The rails have arrived. We've been told to work in Llanfihangel. I just asked for today to tidy up – and fetch you, of course.'

'Course we'll have to come back here in time, but we have a plan.' John added.

'What's that?' Dafydd asked, but Jim just tapped his nose with a grin. 'And we have a new recruit to our gang, do we not, Pendle John?'

'We do indeed, Lucky Jim.'

Their constant Punch and Judy act told Dafydd he'd come home. He laughed, but stopped short when he saw the new arrival. It was the Welsh boy that had insulted him at work a few days before.

'This is Huw Rees. I believe he has something to say,' Jim said, clapping the young man on the shoulder with enough force to make him step forward.

'Sorry about my scrapping last week,' Huw muttered, with blazing eyes.

'It's all right,' Dafydd said wearily.

'See, we spoke to the gaffer and thought it best he come with us,' Jim said. 'Given the danger of trouble between Welsh and English that was brewing.' He chuckled. 'This way, any problem is kept to ourselves. You two go and get the picks and shovels and we'll put in a solid day's work. Then we'll say goodbye for now over a pint of ale this evening.'

Dafydd walked off with a surly Huw. By the time they started loading up with tools, he'd had enough. 'What's your problem, then?'

Huw didn't reply or look up. Dafydd dropped the tools at Huw's feet.

'If you've got a problem, you have the guts to share it, boy. If it's a fight you want, we'll sort it out after work. I tell you now, I'll not spare you.'

'Like you done with Parry?'

'Parry?' Dafydd rolled his eyes. 'It's always bloody Parry. I walked out of the Black and he jumped me, right?'

Huw frowned. 'Not that one, he was a drunk and a troublemaker. I'm talking of Siôn Parry, the one you beat up. He's my cousin and you got him thrown out of Frongoch.'

'Iesu Grist!' Dafydd muttered. 'Three of them jumped me with sticks and I got lucky, that's all. What would you have done?' Dafydd bent to pick up the tools. 'And another thing, Parry was lucky. He only got his manhood bruised.'

Dafydd moved off but the anger was still burning within him and he had to let it out. 'You're on a good thing here. Them English boys have looked after me and they're in favour with the gaffer. You cause any problems and I'll sort you out worse than your cousin.'

With that between them, there wasn't much else to say. At the end of the day, they all made off for Talybont and the ale that awaited. Without thinking, Dafydd found himself in step with Huw. They walked in silence until they reached Bwlch Glas mine, situated two thirds of the way along the line.

'I heard different,' Huw mumbled, without looking up.

'What did you say?'

'I heard different 'bout you and Parry. He said you'd got him fired.'

'Well, that's true at least. What he don't ever tell is that him and his two butties made my life hell for years before. Chopsing about me, hitting me, and then I got friendly with a girl and your cousin just got jealous. They came to give me a good beating. I got in first, that's all.'

Huw went quiet for a long time as they made for the village. 'I only met him a few times. Thought he was rough then.' He muttered and then cursed. 'Well, they say you gotta be loyal to family, but you don't have to like them.'

Dafydd had to laugh out loud then.

'What now, then?' Huw asked.

'We go off to the Black with Jim and John. Sink a few ales and try to leave early before we get too involved in a drinking night. We'll be bright for the new work tomorrow.'

'And you won't wake up in jail,' Huw replied, with a wicked grin. He was bold as his tongue was tart, yet they were beginning to warm to each other.

'So where's your cousin now?' Dafydd asked.

Huw shook his head. 'In truth, I don't care. I heard he'd gone to south Wales.'

It was a load off Dafydd's mind, but he still wondered if Huw was lying. Parry had burned down the ropewalk, so perhaps he'd only *said* he was off south. The way things always seemed to turn out, Dafydd couldn't be sure.

In the morning, Dafydd was woken by the smell of sausages. And a sore head. The two English navvies had a tradition of celebrating with sausages and Jim had got in some of Talybont's finest. Dafydd made for the kitchen, to find John dishing out food and Jim holding out a mug of tea.

'Get that down you, young 'un. It's an early start we have today.'

'Them sausages are not as fine as we are used to, Lucky Jim. Perhaps we should have a word with the butcher?'

'I think we should, Pendle John. Finest we asked for and finest we should have.'

'I don't understand why you are making such a fuss,' said Dafydd. 'We're moving to another job, but it's just fetching and carrying in the end. All the same.'

'He's a young one at heart, Pendle John.'

'He is indeed, Lucky Jim.'

John wagged his knife at Dafydd to make his point. 'What he doesn't understand is that we are asked to do something different. We're a team as can be trusted with different work. It makes us high up the order.'

'And the more we're asked to do, the more likely we'll be kept at the end,' Jim added. 'Railways aren't built every day. Staying on saves miles of boot leather, looking for work.'

They set off for Llanfihangel, and for Dafydd it was a pleasure not to see the incline again. A few large railway trucks with

CAM RYS painted on their sides sat in a siding at the station, looking like big grey beasts in comparison to the smaller trucks of the tramway. As Dafydd and the others approached, he saw the wagons were loaded with rails.

'They want us to take all of them off today,' Jim said. 'The Cambrian's threatened to take them back to Aberdyfi. That's why there are so many of us here.'

Dafydd looked at the gathering groups of men and took off his jacket to start what was clearly going to be a hard day. They levered each of the heavy rails off the trucks by hand and then carried them over to a pile.

'Put them here,' Jim wheezed. 'We've run a siding up to the side of the Cambrian line to allow transfer of goods. Interchange they call it.'

'Hey, them rails are different,' Huw grumbled, looking at the ones being loaded onto carts by others. 'Simpler ones, lighter too, I bet.'

'He's right,' Dafydd added. 'Smaller "n" shape than our "I" ones.'

'Them's for the quarry,' said Jim. 'Don't need them so smooth, as they won't be used by passengers. Ours are for the real tramway. The lighter ones give a bumpier ride.'

Dafydd made a face. 'Strikes me we should start here, lay the track. Then get a truck, put rails on it and push it along with an engine, laying in front as we go. We'd be past Talybont no time.'

Jim smiled. 'You're a waste doing this, young man. It would be faster, right enough, but they want some rails for some do in the station and that's what we're told to do. Besides,' Jim chewed his pipe. 'There's no trucks, or an engine either, yet.'

'This lot for us, this for the quarry, this for the run from Talybont,' John told Dafydd, but he got no response. Dafydd was watching a cart making its creaky way along from the

Borth road. It was plain and open with a board for the driver to sit on front, and a single horse in harness. An old man was at the reins. All Dafydd could see of his face was big grey sideburns between coat and cap. He looked straight ahead, not caring about anything else. But in the back sat a slender girl, her long hair tied back. With a sudden rush of excitement, suspicion turned to certainty and Dafydd was off after the cart for all he was worth.

'Gwen! Gwen!' he yelled as he ran.

The cart was slowed by the hill leading to Rhydypennau and Dafydd, running as fast as he could, managed to grab the tailgate and made to climb in.

'Gwen!' yelled Dafydd, even as he saw the brown mocking eyes of a stranger laughing back.

'I'll be your Gwen if you like,' she laughed, looking Dafydd up and down.

The old man began to scramble into the back, whip in hand.

'What the...? Get off my cart, you bloody navvy...'

'I'm sorry,' said Dafydd, tumbling into the cart. 'I thought...'

He was pushed off and hit the ground hard.

'Bloody Irish,' the man snarled, smacking the girl's head as he climbed back to his place. 'You behave yourself.'

She scowled, then gave Dafydd a wicked smile. The cart rolled on and he got to his feet, rubbing his backside. He made his way back to the others, wishing there was somewhere to hide.

'Now there's a tale worth telling, Lucky Jim.'

'What will the rest of the year bring?'

'What indeed?' Dafydd muttered sourly. He didn't want any part of their play.

'Come on, boys,' Jim said. 'A few rails to load for the *in-*

org-you-ray-shun. Mr Molyneux is to lay the first track at Talybont before we can start.'

'Who's he, then?' Huw asked. 'He's going to be doing it by himself, is he?'

'Mr Molyneux is the chairman, young Huw, and he's not. We'll put the rail down and he'll put a quick tap on a pin and the world will know that he laid the first track on the Plynlimon and Hafan.'

'There's no justice,' Dafydd grumbled.

'There is, as long as we know we've done well,' Jim replied. 'Come on you, less thinking of farm girls and more earning your keep.'

Huw was right: the rails were too heavy for one man, and even hard going for two or three. Their arms were burning when they were done for the day. The four of them walked steadily back, Pendle John rubbing his back.

'I'm no young 'un,' he complained. 'Soon as we have rails on, mind you, I'll show you.'

Dafydd raised an eyebrow but no explanation was forthcoming. 'I'll not join you boys tonight,' he said.

'No need to play the Jessie because you're lovesick,' John replied.

'Call it what you will, I'm tired.'

'All right, son,' said John and then, his tone lowered, 'just don't be harsh on yourself. Thinking too much don't make it happen and moping around won't make you any happier.'

Dafydd knew Pendle John was right, but he was not in the mood to hear it. He was weary of the day, and of the life that appeared to have chosen him. All he wanted to do was go back to the room and be on his own. Even so, his sleep was troubled.

Dafydd was walking back to Trisant. It was dark as he

reached his family home. He opened the door and saw Gwen. Then she drifted to the back of the room and Parry and his cronies were at the door, barring the way. Dafydd turned and ran, and the road was like a silver line in the ground, lit by a bright moon. He was back on the road to Aber and rounding a corner. The path ended at the old mine shaft. This time he was sucked right into it, as if pulled by a vortex.

He was falling, falling. Gwen appeared at the lip of one of the levels. She reached out to grab Dafydd, then she was pulled back. It was Siôn Parry and he laughed as Dafydd fell past them. Their voices grew fainter, Gwen calling, Siôn laughing. Then Dafydd hit the ground and the breath was knocked from him. He felt the gravel under his body, it was round pebbles.

He could hear the sea, rising and falling up the beach. He realised someone was with him, by his side. She turned over and lay on Dafydd's stomach. Her head raised so she could look at him with her mocking grin. The waves grew louder in the background.

'I'll be your Gwen,' the farm girl said, and Dafydd woke in a panic.

There was nothing moving in the room, save the rise and fall of Pendle John's chest in the bunk nearby. His snores gently rose and fell like the tide of the sea. Dafydd lay back and wiped tears from his eyes.

CHAPTER SEVEN

Muddy Waters

FOR FOUR MONTHS they laid sleepers and rails. Dafydd came to know every twist and turn of the way from Llanfihangel to Talybont. Other groups worked with them, whilst many more passed through, working on the rest of the line.

'It's not fair,' Huw grumbled. 'Them in the quarry only have to pin their damned bridge rails down. Light things too. We got this heavy stuff and two pins and two bolts per sleeper. They've got it easy.'

'Just say the word and I'll let you go back up the incline,' Jim replied.

'Put that way, I'm preferring the hard work,' Huw muttered.

There was a scraping sound behind them and they turned to look at Pendle John, who was trying to lever something onto the rails.

'A wooden frame on wheels?' Dafydd said. 'What use is that?'

'Well, young Dafydd. If you keep yourself on my right side, you can join us. We'll be sitting on this trolley and legging our way along the track. Save time and effort.'

'But we're building to Talybont, not from it.'

John just tapped his nose. 'Don't you worry, there'll be plenty of times when we'll need it.'

Dafydd kept quiet. He'd learnt to wait and see with John.

With the line laid all the way to Talybont, a small locomotive shed was built, with a water tank beside it at the station. An inspection pit was then dug at the shed entrance. Dafydd was fed up with the daily toil, but at least he was not out in the wilds at the incline. He could see their lodgings from where he worked and looked forward to the quick return there at day's end.

'Wednesday is the big day,' Jim said. 'Twelfth of May. We're to go to Llanfihangel and put the new engine on the rails. Told you we'd have the top jobs.'

'Told you the trolley would come useful,' said John. Huw rolled his eyes at Dafydd.

They were off on the trolley in the evening. After a sunny dawn, the clouds had grown and a cool breeze was in the air as they walked the trolley down the line.

It may not have been far, but they enjoyed themselves, waving like gentry to those slogging it on foot, laughing back at the resulting curses. There was a final rise, past the row of cottages known as Glebe Inn, then they coasted gently down to the Cambrian goods siding. A low truck with a strange-shaped load lay ahead, and a large crowd had gathered.

'I hope you brought your gold watch chains to parade in front of this lot,' said John. 'We'll be famous for this.'

They took the trolley off the rails and went to look at the new beast.

'What, do we have to put it together and all?' Huw asked.

'No, that's the engine,' John replied.

'It's like a boiler on wheels'

'That's what a railway engine is. Is it not, Lucky Jim?'

'Always was in my day, Pendle John.'

'*Victoria*,' Dafydd said, looking at the name. 'Well, it's black, like what she wears, and it's large and round…'

Dafydd stopped when Jim gave him a look. The engine was like nothing he had ever seen. Shaped like a mail carriage without its horses. Two wheels linked by a rod on each side, the boiler upright and squeezed into a cab with big spyglass portholes.

'Where's the driver go then?' Dafydd asked.

'Well, they got slim men,' John said doubtfully. 'An engine's an engine and I'm sure she'll sound sweet when she's fixed up. They all do.'

The crowd was watching every move as the engine was prepared. There was a buzz of excitement in the air.

'How they going to get the train off?'

'Won't it be special to go to Talybont on the train?'

'What, on the wagons?'

'No, there's a coach, they do say.'

'You Welsh boys look lively,' Jim said. 'And tell us if anyone's nasty with their language to us.'

Dafydd ignored the vague insecurity people have on hearing what to them is a strange tongue. Besides, the locals were too busy admiring the engine.

At length, they decided to rope *Victoria* up and guide her down on rails, slowly, to the track. A team of horses were ready nearby for extra pulling power, but most of the work would fall on the gangers.

Dafydd joined one of the teams holding the ropes to balance the engine as it was shuffled forward. From the platform, the Cambrian staff cast looks of disbelief and muttered mocking remarks, but they appeared more worried about how the wagon would hold up to the operation.

The crowd gasped as the engine slid to one side. Some

sounded as if they wanted it to topple. More ropes were lashed over and the men tried again.

'I always wanted to join the circus,' Huw muttered, making his fellows laugh.

They awaited the result of a long discussion between the foremen and the supervisor in his bowler hat, then Dafydd's gang got sent to pack more timber under the guide rails, and they were off again. The engine shuffled over inch by inch, until it was gently moved onto the sloping rails leading to the ground. It wobbled briefly in protest before starting its downward journey. Slower now, with gangers behind holding on for their lives, the engine was lowered to the ground to great applause. Some of the gang bowed in mocking reply, others cursed. Dafydd just rolled his eyes.

'You'd think they never seen a train before.'

It was a long time before she sat on the tramway rails. The horses were lathered and exhausted and the teams weren't much better. They pulled and pushed the engine until she stood proud, and the air filled with what Dafydd felt were more idiotic questions.

'When's it going, then?'

'What now, then?'

'Who's the driver?'

The gangs ignored them and went to sit, rest and eat. Coal was delivered by cart to start the fire and a chain of buckets from a water cart to fill the boiler. Then *Victoria* slowly bubbled into life.

'We're to wait here, in case,' Huw said, coming back to sit on the grass with Dafydd.

'Where's Jim and John?' Dafydd asked.

Huw shrugged. 'Tell you what,' he said with a grin. 'I reckon we should hitch our trolley on the back and let the damn thing pull us to Talybont. Baccy?'

Dafydd shook his head. 'No thanks. What I'd do for some ale, though.'

'Hey, you'd best watch it or you'll be a true navvy – red-faced and potbellied, just like our English boys.'

Dafydd ignored that. 'How long does it take that old kettle to brew?' he said, jerking a thumb at *Victoria*.

'There's smoke coming out the chimney.'

'That's dust.'

Huw chuckled. 'No offence, *bach*. I didn't mean to be sharp. Just thinking, a navvy's life is not for me. I'll make a few shillings then I'm off to town. I'll get a trade in Aber and settle down.'

'Why not go now?'

'Well... when you have a family like mine, you need to get the world to see past the name. What about you?'

'I don't know,' Dafydd said. 'I might even fancy a go on one of them engines. Them boys seem to get all the attention.'

'From the girls, for sure,' Huw added, nodding to the side. Dafydd followed his gaze. The girl from the cart he'd chased was watching the drivers. He sat back quickly when her gaze moved in his direction.

'You two tramway gentlemen go and laze about somewhere else,' came a voice. 'This is Cambrian Railways property and you're trespassing.'

It was the local station master, clearly out of patience. 'We've let you take your freight away, but if you want to skive, you can do so on tramway land. And another thing,' he added as they scrambled to their feet, 'I want that trolley off the embankment.'

'What?'

'Beyond the road bridge. Smart to it now, if you're so short of work.'

'Come on,' muttered Dafydd to Huw. 'Let's not get any bother here.'

'All right, man,' said Huw, 'but let's stop at the top of the bridge first. *Victoria's* looking ready to go, then we'll pick up whatever after.'

They joined a crowd of gangers waiting for the great event. It seemed to take forever. Occasional chuffs and wisps of steam from the engine teased them. Then suddenly the beast gave a sharp toot. A great cheer went up as the pistons hissed into motion, and the first blast of smoke came from the chimney.

The engine lurched into a slip and the chimney rang with quick blasts before it settled into a slow ramble towards them.

'There we are now boys,' Jim said, appearing by Dafydd's side. 'All our work for the good.'

'Where's John?' Dafydd asked.

'Looking for his trolley, like he's lost his pet. Here he is. A bit of bad driving, Pendle John?'

'Indeed, Lucky Jim. That smoke's as black as pitch. Bad engineering, I calls it.'

The engine belched closer with another flurry of steam.

'He'll have me to answer for if he damages them rails with his slipping,' John grumbled. 'That's my work he's ruining.'

As the engine drew level with them, Dafydd peered into the cab. One man stared at a glass with water inside, the other looked just as upset with the firebox. The engine glided slowly up the gradient towards Glebe Inn Cottages, by the side of the Cambrian railway bridge, and then hissed to a standstill.

'Like a bloody funeral,' Huw muttered.

'She'd make a fine cup of tea for us,' Dafydd offered.

The engine drifted back down the line, with little show of

steam, then screeched as the wheels ground their way round the curve.

'They saving it?' Huw asked, as Dafydd wondered if all their work had been for nothing.

He'd heard an anxious voice from the cab – something about "muddy water".

'There'll be some unhappy folk at Talybont,' Jim moaned. 'All the nobs are waiting for the grand opening of the line.'

'John,' Dafydd said. 'I think I found your trolley.'

He took them over the railway bridge and they looked down the embankment. The little trolley was upside down at the bottom.

'How do we get it back?' Huw asked.

'Easy,' John snapped, and climbed over the fence.

'The station master said we were to...' Dafydd began

'Well, he can go to hell,' John suggested. 'If he wants it done, we'll do it our way. Tell you what though, what with muddy water and this, either the tramway is cursed or someone's trying to stop it.'

They all hopped over the fence after John, aiming to walk on the rails to the tramway siding.

CHAPTER EIGHT

The Deadly Sleeper

B Y THE NEXT day, with a lot of hard work, *Victoria* was in steam and off to Talybont. This time, there was no crowd.

Dafydd looked around sadly at Talybont station, which had now been named Pen-Rhiw after the farm and its surrounding land. The bunting hung out the day before for the grand opening now looked old and forlorn as it fluttered in the wind, no band playing rousing music to it below. Nobody was around now to greet the train that would save the village and reopen the mines.

'*Victoria's* boiler needed a complete clean out.' Dafydd told Huw. 'The steam pipes were that clogged with mud, they had to drop the fire for fear the engine would blow.'

'No idea what that means,' Huw replied. 'All I know is that box doesn't look half as smart as the Cambrian ones on the line to town. People are starting to whisper dark thoughts,'

'Do you blame them?' Dafydd replied.

Huw nudged him. 'Who's that?'

Dafydd watched a barrel-shaped man approach. He waved and increased his pace, his huge hands swinging as he walked. His plain face was split by a wide grin and Dafydd knew him, though he'd not seen him since he was a child.

'Uncle Idris?'

'Dafydd boy, *Duw*! There's like your father you are. Younger, mind. How is it? When you coming to see us then?'

'I don't know,' Dafydd said. 'I'm working six days a week. Perhaps if we're over at the quarry on a Saturday, I could come over?'

'And come to chapel with us Sunday,' Idris boomed. 'Excellent, just whenever you can boy. That would be good.'

'How'd you know where I was?' Dafydd asked.

'The letter, boy. Your father wrote that you worked on the railway and there's only one here now, isn't there? Now they talk as if it's going all the way to Bryn-yr-afr – that's on my doorstep, give or take.'

'I don't expect they'll get that far,' Dafydd replied, remembering the mine's waterwheels deserted on the steep valley side. 'We're only told to go as far as the quarry – it's a steep incline to that as it is.'

'Oh well, there you are. Hafan quarry's not that far neither. What you going to do when the railway's built?'

'Well, I was hoping I'd stay on, like.'

'Well, if you don't, come to us. We can always use a hand. Married yet?'

Dafydd thought of Gwen, felt stupid, and shook his head. Work kept her out of his mind increasingly but, sometimes, he knew it was still all about her.

'All in good time, Dafydd,' Idris was saying, 'you're young yet. Come to us when you can and meet all your cousins.'

'I'd like to – I'll be here a while yet,' said Dafydd. 'There is still work on the line, but now there is *Victoria* to move the trolleys and trucks to get there. Still places that we need to pack in the ballast and firm the embankment...'

He felt he was convincing, at least to most of his conscience.

A few weeks on, they were riding on a train of trucks from Llanfihangel back to Talybont. Dafydd's gang were sitting on a flat truck in front of *Victoria* with some others, and a few more were on a truck behind. For them, the main benefit of rails to Talybont was that they didn't have to walk home at the end of the day.

'What do you think?' Jim shouted, nodding at *Victoria*, as they approached the woodland near Glan Fraed.

'She's a noisy beast,' Dafydd shouted back. 'Dirty with it. What I want to know is how the driver is supposed to see past that tea urn of a boiler? They're hanging halfway out of the cab as it is.'

Jim smiled. 'Still, she does have a crisp voice.'

'What's that?' Huw shouted, pointing ahead. 'Something on the line?'

Jim leaned out and waved the driver to stop. After what felt like miles of steaming and screeching wheels, they came up just short of a broad piece of wood, thrown across the line. John got off and threw it into a bush with a snort of contempt. 'There's some tomfoolery here, Lucky Jim,' he shouted.

'You're right there, Pendle John.'

John threw his hands up to shrug at the driver, who nodded back. Dafydd glared at the piece of wood, stuck in the branches of the bush, as they rumbled past. Every time he saw a problem, all he could think of was Parry. It made his mood that much darker. He thought of the fire at the ropewalk, and his coming to the tramway. He had been sent here to stop him being with Gwen, Joshua had said. What had been the man's mind, really? After all, he sent Dafydd packing, but found him work. A reward for saving the ropewalk? And who started the fire? Was it Parry, and was that to stop him being with Gwen also? Surely there was never anything so complicated in his life, he thought. Then he stopped. As complicated as nearly killing someone in self defence? And now someone was trying to sabotage the tramway? What was going on?

That night, he had another dream.

He was alone on a trolley, pushing it along the rails. It was a fine day as he passed the fields of Glan-Fraed. He was over the cart road and making for Pen-Rhiw. As he drew closer to the station he saw a figure and knew it was Gwen. She smiled and beckoned him, though he couldn't hear her. He tried to speed up, but couldn't.

Suddenly, Siôn Parry rose from the bankside, carrying a railway sleeper. He slammed it down on the rails.

The trolley hit the sleeper and stopped. No matter how Dafydd pushed, it wouldn't move. Gwen smiled and shook her head. She turned to walk away, leaving him calling, calling, calling…

Dafydd woke reluctantly the next day. He was stiff, as if bruised, and the bad mood lingered. The coming day's work and another bumpy ride on the flat trolleys were not welcome. The novelty of being pushed by a real engine had worn off. The closer he got to *Victoria*, the louder and smokier the world became.

He arrived at Pen-Rhiw to find two flat trucks on the front, one on back.

'More men today?' he asked John, who took off his hat and scratched his balding head.

'Not that, young Dafydd. Just it gives us distance from that smoky boiler.'

'Looking miserable today, Huw,' Dafydd said, trying to hand his mood over.

'You're a fine one to talk, Dafydd,' came the blunt reply.

They loaded their tools and got on the trolley at the end, Jim giving the "right away" to the driver.

'Not fast enough by half,' Dafydd grumbled. 'We could have got front.'

'We're better off here,' Jim replied. 'They can catch flies for us.'

The train set off slowly from Talybont, Dafydd grumbling disapproval with each wheel slip and spray of smut. The soon-to-be station master stood on the ground, where there should have been a platform, and Dafydd grumbled about that, too. It was a sign, he said, that money was running short. No grand station building, just a wooden hut and a shed for the engine. That was Pen-Rhiw. It looked unfinished. It was never going to rival the Cambrian, for certain.

'We'll be making the branch down there next,' said Huw pointing at a cart road to the west. 'For when Elgar mine re-opens for mining. Then we'll tunnel to Bryn-yr-afr.'

'Steady, Huw,' John muttered. 'Best not go ahead of ourselves. Tramway's got to bring in the brass first. Besides, if we tunnel, are we putting the station in the mine itself?'

Dafydd rolled his eyes. A few sidings called a station, and a strange engine to limp around on. People were more likely to compliment *Victoria* when she ran with empties, not when she was struggling with a train full of lead ore. As for going up the incline, God was being called on for his mercy. Weeks were going by and still nothing was running for profit. Dafydd began to wonder where he would look for his next job.

After a morning of work at Llanfihangel, they headed back to the train at Pen-Rhiw. Dafydd wished again he'd got the front trolley, but three were already there, forcing his team to sit amid *Victoria*'s sooty exhaust. As always, she struggled up past the Glebe Inn cottages, before heading up towards Glan Fraed farm. They were getting close to where the piece of wood had been dropped on the track the day before, when one of the gangers pointed and cursed.

'That bloody plank's back!' yelled Huw.

'Keep going,' one of the men shouted, and lay down at the front of the wagon.

'He'll flip it away, Pendle John,' said Jim approvingly.

'He's a bright lad, that Richard Roberts is, Lucky Jim. I'm more than hoping to keep going meself.'

They approached the obstruction and Richard dropped his hand to track level. Dafydd yelled, seeing loops of wire glinting around the log, pinning it to the rails. The wagon shuddered, the men scrambled to brace themselves. Dafydd saw arms and legs flail around him as he was thrown into the field below.

His ears rang with the screech of iron and the crashing of trolleys. His breath whooshed from his lungs. He saw stars. Struggling for breath, he watched the mist clear from his vision, revealing the wreckage nearby, where there had once been a train.

Victoria had derailed. The front trolleys hung down the small embankment. Only the rear wagons were still standing on the track. Dafydd spotted Jim and John in the field. John was rubbing his shoulder, being helped up by Jim, whose face was covered in blood. Huw was on the track on his hands and knees. A few men were gathered around the front trolley. Dafydd gave Huw a hand up, they moved towards the group and saw a pair of legs, like those of a rag doll.

'Wired to the track,' Huw muttered in a daze. 'Who the hell would fix wood to the track?"

'Dafydd, get you to Pen-Rhiw,' said Jim. 'Get the doctor. Get help.'

Dafydd lurched off along the track. For the first time he thanked the Lord there were no other engines on this line. He had not got too far before he saw the doctor riding along the nearby Aberystwyth road in his trap. Dafydd shouted, waved his hands and ran to meet him. He was silenced by the doctor's first words.

'Where's the crash?'

'Train…' Dafydd stammered.

'I know son, I've been told. Hop in, you can guide me to the spot.'

'Over by Glan Fraed farm. If we take the Llanfihangel road, it's by the entrance. Not fifteen yards away,' Dafydd gabbled, through the pain pounding in his head. 'There's a man under the train.'

'Well, he's the most important, then.'

At the crossing, the doctor jumped down, grabbed his bag and hurried to the stricken engine. Dafydd sat and watched him in a daze. How had the doctor known?

The Black Lion was subdued that evening, as the men sat around a table of flagons. The beer stood long enough for its head to subside before anyone wanted to speak. They stared at the beer without any appetite, until Pendle John slowly reached forward, daintily picked up his flagon, took a sip and cleared his throat.

'Cuts and bruises – and poor Richard,' he said.

'He was a good one for the Chapel choir, all told,' Huw replied. 'There will be crowds at his funeral.'

'We have to take it on the chin and move on,' said Jim grimly.

'I suppose you're right,' said Dafydd. 'John, go show the doctor that shoulder.'

'Never you mind me, son,' came the gruff reply. 'Happy enough not to waste doctor's time. Nowt a bit of hard work won't fix.'

'Maybe you should be under the doctor yourself,' said Huw. 'You're quiet as a mouse these days.'

'I'm wanting to go and all,' Dafydd said. 'If only to ask him how he got the alarm before I reached him.'

Jim raised his eyebrows and looked at John, who tapped his pipe to his teeth.

'You know, Lucky Jim, the young 'un's right. I'd best see to me shoulder.'

Dafydd heard nothing more of it until a few nights later in the Black Lion. Dafydd had had a few drinks and set off to relieve himself. As he made his mark on the wall, he heard voices the other side of it. One was John's.

'Don't play the mute bugger with me, taffy. I know you understand me.'

There was a muttered reply followed by a thump, and someone gasped for air.

'And don't you curse neither. I'm not daft enough to learn how to speak sweetly in Welsh.'

'What do you want?' came a wheezed reply, as if there was a hand to the speaker's throat.

'I want to talk to you of logs and how they get bolted to railway sleepers.'

'What of it?' The man sounded bold now. It was rewarded with a slap that made him grunt.

'Don't test my patience, son. A good Welshman's dead because someone's trying to stop this tramway.'

'I don't know nothing of that.'

'Yet you could alert the doctor? Well in advance of anyone at the crash? I sent someone for him and he was met halfway. Who do you think told him?'

There was a silence then. Dafydd made himself respectable as quietly as he could.

'I never touched no log!' The voice now was almost begging. 'I never done nothing wrong. It wasn't me, I just got told to...'

'All right,' John muttered, but so low as Dafydd had to strain to hear. 'Know this. If it weren't you, you know who it were. There's more than a few men relying on this tram running. I'll not turn this place into a battleground, so we'll keep off for now. Damage has been done, and the man were killed. What I'll say is this: any more tinkering on our tramway and me and the boys will torch this village to find them that are against us. You don't want to see us angry, lad, you don't want that.'

There was another grunt of pain as a punch was thrown.

'Now if you know nowt, then I think you'd best make sure that them that DO know are aware of my words. For if another of them accidents happen, I'll know where to start looking.'

Dafydd heard footsteps coming from the bar. He nodded at the approaching man, and tried to think of a way to drown out John's noise.

'Lovely evening for it,' he said loudly.

The man frowned, and glared. 'What you talking about?'

'Only making conversation,' Dafydd shouted. 'No harm in it, is there?'

He could still hear John's voice over the wall.

'What are you, one of them funny boys?'

'No, I just made talk, that's all. No need to get all angry.'

'If I were you, I'd shut up and push off before you lose your teeth.'

'Get out of it, you're just spoiling for a fight, that's all.'

'Right enough,' the man said, squaring up as he buttoned his trousers.

Huw appeared at that moment. 'Come on boy, easy now. Don't want us all thrown out.'

The man lunged, but Huw blocked him.

'Dafydd, get out of here. You're making it worse.'

Dafydd moved away smartly and found to his relief John was back, pipe in hand, drinking with Jim.

'Where've you been?' John asked.

'Covering your back,' Dafydd snapped.

'Sound lad.'

Huw came back looking angry. 'You owe me a flagon, that's what it took to pay off that bastard. What's with you?'

'I didn't want anyone to hear John talking, that's all.'

Huw frowned. 'Well, you could have picked a better place. Make folk think you're one of them, you know... you're not, are you?'

'No,' Dafydd said.

Jim smiled like a kindly grandfather. 'Young man's got his heart set on a girl in town. That right, Pendle John?'

'Indeed, Lucky Jim,' came the inevitable reply.

'Well, maybe you should do something about it then, rather than hang around by cess-pits,' said Huw.

Dafydd watched the man he'd nearly fought come back in. They eyed each other warily, though nothing else was said as he passed.

'Don't worry,' said Huw. 'You won't get no problems from him no more. I just told him you were *twp*.'

'Thanks.'

'Well, what else was I to say? You never gave me much choice of excuses there.'

Dafydd looked over at his English friends. Their faces were beetroot red. Jim had his beer to his lips, but he didn't seem able to drink. Tears rolled down his face. John moved sharply, taking away his clay pipe and spitting out the end. Then he roared with laughter and they all joined in. Dafydd scowled and turned away.

'Last time I do you any bloody favours,' he muttered.

'I'm glad you did it,' said John. 'It's just, well... never mind now. Huw's right, boy, you should get yourself to Aberystwyth. Go on a Sunday, dress up a bit and show off to this girl. Take young Huw, he could do with a visit to the outside world.'

Dafydd thought of baked potatoes at the old lime kiln in the harbour.

'I'll not be around for your courting,' Huw said with a snigger. 'I'm not your father now.'

'Maybe I will go, payday,' Dafydd replied. 'And maybe you will come to regret them words.' He put it off, always finding a reason not to go.

A few weeks later, Dafydd and Huw were busy plugging a leak in the water tank at Pen-Rhiw when Jim and John were hailed by the foreman and after a brief talk, set off together down towards a ridge called Braich Garw.

'Nice of them to say what theyr'e up to,' Huw said.

'Come on boy,' Dafydd suppressed a sigh. 'Let's plug this bloody leak. I'm fed up of standing in mud here.'

'What do you make of the new engine?'

'What?'

'They bought a new engine, didn't they? Where've you been? *Victoria's* not going to last the year at this rate and she's not got enough puff to get close to the incline. It's coming with a coach, the new engine. They got it on the cheap.'

'Why am I not surprised?'

'Tell you what, boy. We should get on the job unloading that lot. Then we can get a lift back in the coach like true *crachach*.'

Jim and John came back later, pushing an open truck. Jim stopped to speak to the foreman, while John sat on the frame, gazing at nothing, and mopped his brow with his sleeve.

'You all right, Pendle John?' asked Dafydd.

John nodded but didn't speak. His legs pushed the trolley a few inches back and forth as they stood there. He bit his lip and sighed. 'There's been another death, boys.'

John put a hand on Dafydd's arm and shook his head. 'No boy, this is an accident. A real one. There were four people on the trolley. Three gangers and a mother holding her bairn wrapped in a shawl. As they pushed the trolley with their feet, the shawl got caught in the wheel and...' He put his hand over his eyes. 'A bairn. Not old enough to talk.'

Dafydd looked down, and saw the splashes of red on one of the wheels. He pulled at a piece of cloth clogged in the axle. John stood up, grabbed the trolley and with a snarl, flipped it off the rails. 'We'll not be having any of these on the rails again,' he growled. 'That's it, take a lift on the trucks or bloody walk from now on. I tell you what, this bloody place is cursed. This whole bloody tramway – and we're cursed with it, the longer we stay.'

He stormed off towards the village, wiping his eyes as he went.

'Some people take it harder,' said Jim as he walked to the pair. 'Especially when they've lived through summat similar.'

They helped Jim tidy up in silence. He wasn't in the mood for talking further.

Dafydd wondered what to do with the long, August night ahead. He felt the need for a walk alone, to get away from the stifling sorrow. From the bottom of the village, close by the bridge, a path ran towards the hills to the west. On the side of the hill were the dark shadows of the abandoned Allt y crib mine, and Dafydd made for it. Somehow the feeling of being at a mine again filled him with calm.

He walked up the hill, past the still waterwheels and cold empty buildings, while his mind went back to the ropewalk. Simple work, but he'd enjoyed being part of somewhere.

The mine was spread out on levels up the hill and he made for an entrance with a mound of spoil tipped below it. The entrance was solid stone, crafted even. No fancy carvings or figures, but you could see the pride taken in the stonework.

Water still flowed from the mine tunnels and Dafydd watched the strands of weeds gently swaying in the stream. His mind wandered again back to his childhood in Trisant, the family around him. He conjured a vision of himself wearing nothing but breeches, working underground in the flickering candlelight, his father holding the drill as Dafydd hammered it into the rock. His uncles, David and Matt, stood below them, shovelling the fallen rock into the trap. All were covered in dust and gleaming with sweat. It was what might have happened, years back, if not for the fight, if not for Aber, and the railway.

Dafydd sighed, and pressed on up the hill until he could look back on the village in the red rays of the sinking sun. A layer of smoke hung on the roofs, a sign that the air was cooling. Night would presently cloak the small square of neat houses and the two taverns.

Dafydd smiled fondly at the village, which now felt like

home. He ambled on, to peer into an old shaft. Leaning against the pulley supports, he looked down, counting each level below him until they faded into blackness. Each had tunnels off, one level on top of the other, like a cake, a nice slice of *teisen lap*.

Dafydd thought about his life and its many paths, each moving into the darkness of not knowing what lay ahead. Then a sudden loneliness chilled him – or was it the cold of sundown? He pushed himself away from the supports, and set off back to their lodgings, eager for food and a fire.

'I'm off to Aber Sunday,' he said, as soon as he saw Huw. 'You coming?'

'What? This Sunday? It's a bit soon, *bach*.'

'It's up to you. There's someone I got to see.'

CHAPTER NINE

Bridge of Lost Dreams

THE TRAIN MOVED slowly out from Llanfihangel station, with Huw and Dafydd perched on bench seats in third class. It gathered speed past the small signal box, overtaking the people thronging the road that ran level with the line. Men in suits, women in black dresses and bonnets, busy and solemn, chapel bound and proud. Dafydd knew he would be missed in Talybont. As for chapel, well, the deacons could have his soul later. God would forgive him for this weekend. Huw lit up his pipe, making a large cloud of blue smoke, which had Dafydd longing for the cool air outside.

'Don't you worry now; I'll be done by the next station.'

'Well, that's just round the corner, Huw *bach*. Bow Street, we're slowing down already to it.'

'Funny name that, isn't it – Bow Street?'

'Well, big joke. It's where the circuit judge used to go, that and one a bit south they call Chancery. Named after London courts, they are.'

'You know a lot of things, don't you?'

Dafydd gave a thin smile.

'Only what I'm told, Huw *bach*.'

'Never travel much, me. I'm happy where I am.'

Dafydd looked out of the window; he had no mind for small talk today. His mind was taken up with where to go and what to say when he got to Aber.

The train stopped for a few door slams at Bow Street, then launched itself up a hill, the speed and the noise from the engine making Dafydd think the driver was missing his lunch. A maze of cuttings and bridges followed and then the line curved and the valley opened up. Aberystwyth lay before them. Dafydd's stomach knotted. The search was on.

'I never seen so many houses in my life,' Huw muttered in surprise as the flashing image of the village of Llanbadarn gave way to the town's varied roofs.

They rumbled past the square tower of Plascrug castle on one side, the bustling, smoke-shrouded engine shed on the other. Then, with a great flourish of steam, whistles and shouts, the train arrived. They clambered out, rubbing their stiff limbs.

'What now? Fancy a drink?' Huw asked.

'Fat chance on a Sunday.' Dafydd grimaced. 'Look, I got business, can I...?'

Huw tapped his nose. 'Why don't we say we'll meet at two by the castle tower?'

Dafydd nodded, though he had no intention of keeping to it. He wanted the time to go back to his days in Trefechan. He'd been away far too long.

He headed off down Mill Street at a lively pace. It felt unchanged from nearly a year past. His throat went dry with the sweet, hoppy aroma coming from Roberts' brewery. He wanted to run. He wanted to shout her name, but there was a big chapel overlooking the road. He remembered being clipped around the ear as a boy, for running on Sundays. Trefechan Bridge was empty of the weekday bustle of carts and carriages. A few people drifted by on the narrow footpath, perhaps returning from the chapels in Aberystwyth. Dafydd nodded to a few of them, and matched their ponderous pace. Finally, he veered off at the square and took the path alongside Pen Dinas to the ropewalk, where he would be free to stride out towards his past.

He came to a startled halt when he found the ropewalk was a ruin. Between the blackened beams, nothing had changed since the day of the fire. The sun came out of the clouds and for a second, metal glinted in the rubble. Joshua's spinner.

A breeze cooled Dafydd's flushed face, and he shivered. He'd expected to see the old shed restored, Joshua and Joe's work stored inside. He stared, and amid the silence wondered, what now? There was one place he could try. Mrs Owen's house. She would have the answers. He set off past the brewery and the neat terraced rows behind it. The street seemed longer than before, made worse by the silence of the place. He would have to wait for her return from chapel.

When he turned the corner of her street, he saw a figure at the far end. Breathin a prayer of thanks, he shouted, 'Joe!'

Joe looked up, turned on his heel and walked off into another street. Dafydd called out in bafflement and ran after him. Joe broke into a run also, past the terraces and over towards the river, as if the devil was after him. He made for the arches of Trefechan Bridge. Dafydd was gaining and in his panic, Joe slipped and fell. His trousers ripped and his knee grazed, he scrambled up and made off again. Dafydd kept running, arms flailing, and managed to grab Joe at the lime kilns. They rolled to the ground where Joe pushed

Dafydd away and tried to be up and running. Dafydd grabbed his arm.

'Joe – it's me, Dafydd!'

'Don't kill me,' yelled Joe.

Daffyd was baffled by the panic. 'Joe, I'm not going to hurt you. What's happened? Where's Joshua and Gwen?'

Joe looked like a trapped animal, his eyes darting to and fro, desperate for a bolthole.

'I didn't mean to do it,' he blurted out. 'I didn't mean to. Just a small spark, not enough to cause much damage.'

'What you on about?' Dafydd said. The way Joe flinched, he must have shouted.

'Just wanted you out the way, that's all. Gwen, she'd never look at me with you there.' Then light seemed to dawn. 'You really don't know nothing, do you? The ignorant country boy come to the big town. The world at your feet and you never knew it.' Joe squared up, a mocking smile on his face. 'You know what, country boy? I feared this meeting every day since. Now we're here, I don't care no more. That was my ropewalk. Mine after Joshua, I built it up with him and I damn well deserved my share. That and Gwen – she was for me. Always had been. Things were working out well, then you came along, a poor little lost boy and Gwen finding you a home in the rope shed.'

'Joe, I never came to take the ropewalk,' Dafydd said slowly.

'Joshua took a shine to you though, didn't he? Treated you like a prodigal son, and he approved of you seeing Gwen. Approved! You, a common miner's son. I had to get you out. A small fire, nothing more. A little bit of evidence to blame you for it. I didn't know the whole place would go up. I didn't think Joshua would go back in.'

Joe looked away.

'Joe, what have you done?'

'What have I done? What have *you* done, more like. Why did I fear you?'

He rushed at Dafydd without warning, a hysterical light in his eye.

In one movement, he shoved Dafydd to the ground, lined up a kick, thought better of it, turned and made off into town.

Dafydd got to his feet, new ideas hitting home. He had blamed Siôn Parry, blamed the violence in his own heart, blamed fate... Joe started the fire. Joe had pretended to be friends with him. Fear and jealousy had made Joe plot to get rid of him. He'd been successful, Dafydd thought bitterly. Banished to the hills, out of the way.

Dazed, Dafydd made his way back to the bridge, dusting himself down as best he could, waiting for the story of his life to re-adjust itself to this shape. He could probably find out where Joe was. Mrs Owen would know, but Dafydd no longer had the taste for any chase. He crossed back to Aberystwyth and headed for the castle to wait for Huw.

As he crossed the bridge, Dafydd heard an argument going on in the arches by the old mill. A man had another by his lapels and gave him a slap on the face. Dafydd felt contempt for the bully, growing to anger as he approached and recognised both men. The man against the wall was Huw and Dafydd rushed to his aid. His lip curled with contempt as he saw who faced him.

'Siôn Parry,' Dafydd said sweetly. 'Didn't expect you this side of Cardiff. Lost your way, have you?'

Parry licked his lips, his eyes started darting, looking for an escape route.

'No one with you now, Siôn. And you're bothering a friend of mine. Best you let go.'

Dafydd backhanded a slap across Parry's face that made him stagger back, then hit him square in the stomach. Parry doubled up, wheezing for breath.

Dafydd froze, catching sight of a woman looking on. It was Gwen. He looked back at Parry, who grinned.

'Talk your way out of that one, bastard!' he whispered.

Then he flinched as if Dafydd was going to hit him again and, with a wretched cry of 'Mercy, don't hit me!' he scuttled away like a crab.

Dafydd looked at Huw, whose face flushed in embarrassment. Gwen had gone. Dafydd ran back to the bridge glancing around wildly. She stopped and turned halfway along the bridge, and he knew nothing had changed in his heart. He called her name as he ran. She smiled, but wanly, as if close to tears.

'Gwen, please wait. We need to talk.'

'Hello, Dafydd.' Her eyes were on the river below, her voice uncertain.

'I been looking for you.'

'You found me.' Her reply was distant and she looked up the street.

'I...' Dafydd stopped, for his mind had frozen by the wild flow of events. First Joe, then Siôn, now Gwen. He reached out a hand. 'Why are you like this?'

'I never had you for a bully.' Her eyes followed the river Rheidol, searching for nothing on its banks.

'He was hurting my friend.' She made no reply. 'Gwen, for God's sake, it was *Siôn Parry*. He tried to kill me once. Tonight, I gave him a slap and sent him on his way. He deserved worse.'

'Some things should be left in the past.'

Dafydd looked away. The river suddenly appealed to both of them.

'I saw Joe.' Dafydd saw her stiffen slightly, though she did not reply. He took a deep breath. 'He started the fire.'

'He said you done it.' Her words were like a whisper in the wind from a statue. They both stood and watched a gull swoop to land on the water. A few ducks quacked in disgust.

'Joshua?'

'Is dead.'

The reply was like a door slam. And then suddenly, the tension broke and Dafydd held her as she cried. She clutched his shoulder as if he alone could stop her falling, then she took a deep breath.

'He's dead. Only a month back. All because of a fool. I wished you were there. I prayed you would come back, but Joshua had sent you from us. All because of a fool. Joshua found out it was Joe all along.'

'I'm here now.' He gently wiped the tears from her cheek.

'In Talybont?' she said.

'I can move tomorrow.'

She shook her head and moved away. 'Not now, Dafydd. I'm not ready to see you, honest now. I don't want to see anyone, now just. I want to be by myself, I'm sorry.'

'When?'

'I don't know. Come and see me in a month.'

'A month!'

'Maybe two. I just need to grieve on my own for now.'

She reached up and kissed Dafydd on the cheek. Her body was so close, it made his soul cry with pain.

'Take care, Dafydd Thomas. We will see each other soon.'

She walked off and Dafydd called after her.

'How do I find you?'

She stopped again and looked back. There was the old Gwen standing there like in those happier days that Dafydd craved to rediscover. Though her eyes were sadder and her smile a bit tight, it was still the look that made him yearn for her.

'Ask Mrs Owen, you should know that by now.'

He watched her go, his mind screaming for the words to keep her. He cursed himself for the helplessness he felt. When she was at last out of sight he turned and made back for town. Huw was still down by the river. Dafydd didn't feel the need to say anything, for he must have heard it all.

'I'm sorry, boy. I hope I haven't made it worse,' Huw said.

Dafydd shook his head.

'No, you haven't. The damage was already done by others.'

'I'm sorry, Daf. Siôn is nothing, but when we were younger and he were bigger than me – bigger and stronger and all...'

'You're right there, he's nothing. If he does that to you again, you give him hell. You're a tough boy and he's not a brave one.'

'I will, Dafydd. What will we do now?'

'Go home. There's nothing else left, is there?'

'She said to come back, Daf. Isn't that worth waiting for?'

'Yes, I suppose. Was she just saying it, though?'

'Well, I wouldn't say that if I didn't mean it. I'd be too worried they would take me at my word.'

Dafydd wanted to laugh, but got no further than a snort.

'Some things you fight for because they are meant, others you don't. In the end, Daf, you choose your battles. You want to walk across the fields?'

Dafydd looked towards the station. The meat market, the candle works, all were dark and grim.

'We'll take the road, and be civilised with it.'

'If you don't mind me saying, this town's not civilised. Thinks too much of itself, what with the college and all. I prefer it in Talybont. At least you know where you stand.'

'Perhaps,' Dafydd said with a sigh. 'Perhaps.'

They made for the railway station. The single storey building looked so fragile, as if one good storm would blow it away. The long rows of grey slate on the roof matched Dafydd's mood and it was made no better by the reception.

'Train's not due out for another hour,' the ticket collector grumbled at Dafydd. 'You can come back later. I'll not have you loitering on the platform.'

'I have no interest in loitering,' said Dafydd, coldly. 'I am forced to wait for the Cambrian Railways Company to provide me with a train home and I wish to wait for it on the platform. I'll speak with the Station Master about it if you wish.'

Dafydd heard Huw gasp at the tone.

'Station Master's far too busy for the likes of you.' came the reply. 'Perhaps you should do something useful instead, like attending chapel.'

'In that manner, so should you, my friend. Now, here are our tickets. Either let us through or bring me the Station Master.'

The man held Dafydd's eye for a moment, then sighed and stepped back.

'Keep to the benches, don't go in the waiting rooms. If you have to stretch your legs, go on the Milford platform.'

'You're too kind.' Dafydd muttered.

'What's the Milford platform, anyway?' Huw asked, as they walked up past the buildings.

'The railway south, that bay there. It's run by the Manchester and Milford Railway. God knows why it's called that, it doesn't go to neither. He's just trying to get rid of us.'

Huw slumped down on a bench. Dafydd carried on up the platform. He saw a flash of white sleeves in the signal box, as the signalman busied himself with his levers. Dafydd walked up to a signal post. It stood tall and proud, like oak. Its many arms jutted out to the left. On each of the arms, a metal signal rested, glimmers of red from an oil lamp shining through a spectacle of painted glass at each side.

Dafydd studied the bars and wires, trying to work out the curious set-up. The signals were different colours. One or two had rings circling a black spot at the end of the arm. He decided they were for lesser tracks, like sidings. Large wooden beams set upwards and across on the frame. Cables ran along each arm and down and off to the box. Each cable had its own path, like different paths in life that led you to different places. Dafydd wondered if he was on the right path yet. Where would it end?

'It's no use; you can't force them to move on your own. God knows I've tried.'

Dafydd turned to see a railwayman dressed in greasy overalls, carrying a lamp. Soot smudged a face broken white by a big smile. 'In the end, it's your butty in the box over there that makes it happen for you.'

'You're right, I suppose. Our destiny isn't our own; it's made with the help of others.'

'Destiny, is it?' The man roared with laughter. 'Signalman's important enough, but if he hears that, he'll start thinking he's God.'

He walked down a ramp at the end of the platform, put his lamp on the back of an engine that was gently smoking and hissing away at the entrance to the shed, and climbed into the cab. Dafydd heard the metallic knocking of tools being used, then the scuffing of coal onto the shovel. He wondered how easy it was to drive one of those beasts. Surely it was a fine skilled trade. With a sigh, he spun on his heel and rejoined Huw.

'Man's been gracious enough to allow us on the coach,'

said Huw, puffing on his pipe. 'Soon as I'm done smoking, at any rate.'

'That's fine,' said Dafydd. 'I'm feeling the cold now.'

'Did you do what you needed to do in Aber then, Dafydd?'

'Not sure – I'll wait a few months and see how I feel. There's plenty to do and it will give me time to think.'

'Good plan, my friend.'

They were soon on their way. The coach wheels complained all the way to Plascrug. Dafydd's gaze lingered on Trefechan Bridge as they left. He was an age away from that troubled boy Gwen had adopted in Aber... was he leaving her behind for ever?

An evening gloom lay over the land by the time they stepped down from the train at Llanfihangel. Dafydd glanced at the station clock on the front of the building and sighed. Very soon it would be time to start work again.

Huw was still by Dafydd's side. He'd put up with his friend's mood all day, even taken a punch along the way. Dafydd gave him a friendly nudge and nodded to the other platform.

'That boy's a long wait until the next train to Aber. There's not one until morning now.'

'You missed the last train,' Huw called across.

The man stroked his moustaches and looked back. He was a working man, but his dress and bearing told of an artisan with a good trade.

'Do you speak English?' the man shouted over to them, Lucky Jim's accent in his voice.

'Some,' Dafydd said. 'There were miners from the Midlands at Frongoch.'

'Midlands, you say?'

'Yes, my Uncle Matt was from Cannock.'

'Cannock! Why, that's near my home. I've been sent here

by Bagnall's – the engine builders. They wanted someone to train the men on the new engine.'

'On the Hafan? Well, that's where we work.'

The man smiled broadly. 'Oh, you gents are a welcome meeting then. I'm lodging at Talybont, but I haven't found anyone to tell me where it is.'

'Follow the rails,' Huw muttered.

'I didn't know you had the English,' said Dafydd, surprised.

'I keep my talents to myself.'

'Come with us, we're going on the railway.' Dafydd called to the man.

'Is that safe?'

'Nothing runs on a Sunday. Nothing ever happens here.'

The man grabbed his bag and joined Dafydd and Huw.

'Keep to the sleepers and it's level going,' Dafydd said. 'The track is more direct and, well, it rains here a bit.'

The man laughed. 'So I understand.'

'Perhaps you could get Dafydd work on them beasts?' Huw asked quietly. 'He's always on about them engines.'

'Well, we'll see what I can do. They have a driving team, but they must need cover. I'd be happy to ask. The *Treze de Maio* is a beauty. A little wonder, she's a joy to drive.'

'The what?'

'Oh, it's the engine's name. Brazil she was bound for, but – well, she's here now. Do you boys know this line well?'

Dafydd chuckled. 'We laid virtually every sleeper.'

'Well, I have landed on my feet then. Tom Long is the name. Very pleased to make your acquaintance. Yes, the engine. She's a little beauty, you'll see. We've given her a new lick of paint and called her *Tal-ee-Bont*.'

There was a long silence then and he coughed a bit.

'You know, you gents have been champion. I didn't know

what to expect, being English and that. I've met so many people who won't talk to me. I'm in a foreign country. Just thanks, that's all.'

'You're a very trusting man,' Dafydd said. 'Given you don't know us.'

'I'm a good judge.'

'You're right then, you'll be all right with us. Just as soon as we teach you how to say "Talybont".'

CHAPTER TEN

Talybont's Journey

H UW WAS VERY much against anything to do with engines after *Victoria's* accident. He was even worse with Tom's arrival, but someone English *and* a new engine?

Dafydd, however, was drawn to the new locomotive. After *Victoria's* squat ugliness, the new engine was a little marvel. Its round boiler and square tanks, the small cab at the end and little wheels with driving rods made it look like a proper engine. What pleased Dafydd most was that the little black engine had the name *Talybont* on its side in cheerful letters.

'Not like a tea urn, this one,' he said.

'More like a coffee pot,' came Huw's grumbling reply.

Behind *Talybont* was a new coach, with steps and a hand-rail at the end, leading to an open covered platform.

'Yes, Daf. Why don't you go and look at your new kettle and I'll go sit inside the coach and wait for you.'

Dafydd gave up on him and walked on, watching wisps of steam coming from around the wheels as the little engine gently hissed to itself. He reached the cab, and peered in. There was a crash of metal on coal and Tom Long appeared in the doorway. A bucket was lobbed out onto the ground.

'Morning!' he shouted with a smile.

'She looks excellent!' Dafydd replied.

'She is. I'm taking her to the quarry today to train the crew.

Though the Hafan crew have gone on *Victoria* the other way. I'll end up having to run the engine down the line on my own if they aren't back soon.'

'They're probably pushing their engine by now.'

Tom smiled grimly. 'You're probably right. Whoever built that heap of junk had never seen a railway.'

'It was the railway's owner.'

Tom roared with laughter. 'Tell you what, I need a hand. You busy?'

'We're awaiting our orders.'

'Well, here's your orders: you're working for me. Fill that bucket with coal and bring it here. I'm trying to build up a big fire. You can come down the line with me.'

Dafydd went to tell Huw, who curled his lip. 'No way I'd be working for him.'

Dafydd ignored him and went back to the engine. 'My friend is worried we'll get into trouble.'

'All right, well, your friend can tell them where you've gone. Sound good? I wouldn't ask, but the driver and fireman should have been with me. I have to run her in and I'm damned if I can wait. What do you say?'

Dafydd offered his hand with a grin. 'I never said my name,' he said. 'Dafydd Thomas – David.'

'David. Grab a few more bucketfuls then come on board. Try to keep the lumps hand size, they burn better.'

Dafydd did a few runs to the coal stack while Huw stood sulking. 'You in service now with the English?'

'The English own the bloody tramway anyway, you idiot.' With that, Dafydd jumped into the cab. It was strange seeing the mass of wheels and pipes on the rounded end of the boiler. The cab was small and hot, and he daren't move a finger for fear of being burned. The boiler emitted a series of echoing plops reminiscent of a great kettle. Tom climbed in and opened the firebox door, producing a wave of heat that had Dafydd sweating in seconds.

'Look inside,' said Tom, peering at the raging orange storm. 'Normally, I'd have it nice and level. Not too high, raise a lot of heat, no mess – but I want to do this trip in one go, so I've built it up like a haycock, high and dropping off back. We can't carry much coal here, except on the top of the engine, so I've given her a lot up front....

'There's the regulator. Forward, reverse, easy enough. That is the water feed...' Dafydd listened eagerly as Tom demonstrated the levers. Tom nodded and winked. 'Don't worry son, I'm not wanting you to drive, but you'd best know. Anything happens, pull the regulator back and put the brake on. All I really need you to do today is watch that side and tell me if you see anything ahead. We should be all right. I'll carry one bucket of coal, in case.'

He couldn't have wiped the grin from Dafydd's face with a brush.

'Be back later,' Dafydd shouted to Huw.

'Where will you be working after they sack you?' came the reply.

Dafydd laughed. 'On the railway.'

Huw turned and walked away, shaking his head in mock despair.

'You can see why I filled the fire,' shouted Tom, once they were both squeezed into the cab. 'No room to really swing a shovel.' He looked out, and made a swift adjustment as they were lost in a cloud of steam.

'Smoke's a bit black, I'm adding some water.'

Dafydd looked out, watching the blur of land rush past as *Talybont* wobbled along the line. If he fell out... He tightened his grip on the hand-rail, just in case.

Tom's hand rested on a small handle in the centre. Every

time he moved it away from him, the little engine responded with a slow surge. 'Track is bad,' he shouted.

'We done our best,' Dafydd shouted back.

'Not your fault – I'd say the track is old and worn, the way she's rolling all over the place.'

'I thought that was normal... There's sheep on the track!'

Tom peered out on Dafydd's side of the cab, grabbed a chain and pulled. *Talybont* blew a toot from her whistle, sending the animals scuttling away to the fences in a bleating panic. 'Good girl,' he shouted, and they rolled onward. The engine slowed as it began to climb and Tom pulled his trusty handle. 'Ease the regulator gently to give her more or she'll slip on the track.'

The engine responded with a throaty chuffing as it sought to accelerate.

Tom started whistling a tune as he gazed ahead. Dafydd looked back at the coach riding behind. It was rocking away, echoing the action of the little engine. Dafydd thought how much space there was on the platform of the carriage. There was even more comfort on those padded benches inside, where passengers could sit and watch the land passing the window at speed – but he would not have swapped places. In the dark world of the engine cab, with its hiss of steam and roar of fire, Dafydd felt more alive than he had in years.

The wheels screeched in complaint as they rounded a tight curve. Dafydd was lurched forward and caught a blast of hot air in his face. Though the firebox door was shut, a small jet of flame spat out as the engine moved on through a tiny gap. The world was full of clunking and banging as the engine lurched forward and the carriage behind complained.

'You enjoying it?' Tom shouted.

'*Ardderchog*!' Dafydd shouted back, forgetting his English.

Tom saw Dafydd's face and nodded. 'Good lad. Looks like she's shook up the coal a bit with her wobbling and we've lost a bit on the grate. Have to be careful now. This one will need to be fired little and often.'

Already, Dafydd felt more at home than he had in any other work. He'd fumbled from one job to another, never feeling a part of it. Now, he wondered how he could make this new experience last.

They were down the track in no time. Farms, quarries and mines appeared, passed in a blur, and were gone. Soon, they were looking down the valley to the incline cut by the side of the jagged rock face. It looked very steep. Dafydd wondered if Tom was accelerating to run up to the top. Could the little engine do that? If that was the case, surely the coal would fall out of the firebox and they would be dancing on hot coals.

'I'm letting her go, so I can get speed up,' Tom shouted. 'I want to give her a good run and see what she's capable of.'

'You think she'll get up the incline?'

Tom laughed. 'No, not even this one would get up there without being winched and even then the couplings would lock with the coach behind. Hold on, we'll race down to the end.'

Dafydd did as he was told; there seemed little else to do. He trusted Tom's belief that the little beast wouldn't let them down.

At the bottom of the incline, Tom eased off. The approach was flanked by two old waterwheels from long-abandoned mines, looking like silent sentinels.

Tom cursed.

'What's the matter?'

'The track's not level. If we hit that at speed, the couplings will crack – or worse, the carriage or us will go off.'

'I'll take your word for it,' said Dafydd.

Tom just nodded and closed the regulator. They approached the end, where a loop allowed a run around, and slowed to a stop. 'Come on, my friend,' he said. 'Let's take a walk up to the top and see what's what.'

Dafydd followed meekly. He looked up again at the incline he had laboured on for so long. The line of rock to the left was like an imposing cliff. They gazed on it in silence at first, then Tom spoke. 'You boys done this?'

Dafydd nodded. About halfway up, a mine shaft opened to the side, empty and forlorn. Tom jumped off the incline and stood back to admire the view.

'You boys done some work here. That embankment is like one large wall. That's dry stone walling at its best.'

He smiled and moved back to meet the incline and continue the walk up. 'Oh, it gets a bit steeper up this way, David.'

He continued the walk and as they reached the top, they were both panting and stopped to breathe. Dafydd looked back and was struck by the view of the valley. The sun was high now and the grass sparkled with what was left of the dew. Small buildings were grey specks on the land. A few old lead mines looked on in peace. He wondered what the sunset would be like. He'd been too busy to notice scenery when he was working on the incline.

'Nice place to work,' Tom said.

'I'm not so romantic,' Dafydd replied, and Tom chuckled.

'It's all opinion, David.'

They turned to look at a small quarry. The men there had stopped work and were staring. Tom gave them a cheery wave. There was a nod of response and they were back to work. Their surprise and respect made Dafydd feel proud. He wanted a trade that would have people always look at him that way. He wondered how Gwen would react if she saw him now. 'The main quarry is up that other tall incline and round the corner,' he said.

'Lovely... well, we'd best get back, but thank you for showing me this, young man.'

Dafydd wondered what he had done, as they made their way slowly back down. It was nice to revisit the site. The view was wonderful, but it made Talybont seem like a big town in comparison and Dafydd did not miss the bleakness of the quarry.

Tom showed Dafydd how to uncouple the engine, then pointed to a lever close to the end of the loop nearest the incline. 'Go down there and when I'm past, pull the lever over. We'll get the points shifted and I'll run the lady around on the loop.'

Dafydd did this with all the importance of a Cambrian porter. *Talybont* came past slowly, with Tom leaning out, pointing and shouting. Dafydd saw the point that ended the loop and ran to it. A bit less dignified in his rush, he threw the point, jogged up to the coach, re-coupled the engine and hopped back onto the cab.

'I'll coal up here if I have to,' Tom said. 'Stand back, I'll just check if the fire has shifted. The boiler pressure's down, because we were up the top too long. It's a delicate balance. Flood too much water in and the boiler will cool down. Shove in a load of fresh coal at once and it'll do the same. We'll do it gradually as we go and it'll see her right.'

Dafydd tapped the shovel hard on the firebox door, then held it at an angle in front as he opened it. A bit of burning coal fell out onto the shovel and he threw it straight back in.

'You're a natural, son,' Tom said. He eased open the regulator once more and Dafydd looked on with concern as the engine began to move. The coach roof appeared lower and lower in the small round cab window. Dafydd waited for the crash of buffers locking once more, but this time Tom had the measure of it. Dafydd grabbed the sides, expecting the coach to break free or the engine to be lifted up. Neither happened.

He leaned out of the cab and began to smile. This was truly the way he wanted to live! Master of power, able to look out over God's land, marking it for its beauty. They coupled the coach to the engine and Tom reached to open the firebox door. 'Now we can stoke her up as we should. Look in the fire. Do you see there are darker patches? Back to the left, middle on the right. That's where we need the coal: it's where the fire's at its coolest. '

Dafydd reached for a coal bucket and asked, as he worked the lumps into the right places with a small shovel, 'How do you get to be a driver?'

'Bit you, has it? Well, being an apprentice is the start. Learning the engine and how she breathes. Cleaning every bit of metal until it shines, firing her, taking out the clinker after. Checking the brick arch for damage. Then, when you're ready and shown yourself able...'

'You're a driver.'

'You'll be passed as an occasional fireman. Make no bones about this, it's a long road and a lot to learn. Many don't make it.'

'How do I ever get that in Talybont?'

'Well, there's a shed in Aberystwyth. One in Mac... Mac... Mac-in-cleth. You could ask. You got family here, boy?'

'Yes, they are out in the hills.'

'No, I mean wife and bairns?'

'I'm only just turned eighteen. I never really known anyone that well.' Dafydd desperately tried to push Gwen from his mind. She still hovered in the background, like a siren, luring him to the rocks.

'Well son, you're a bit old, but I could ask at Bagnall's.'

'In England?'

'It's not so rough son, trust me. You have the language all right, already. I'm getting on a bit now and won't be around forever. They could do with a young 'un to take my place in time.'

'You would ask?'

'Well, why not? You've took me at face value and I can only do the same. You've shown me trust and friendship. I've seen you work and you're quick with your wits. You could always lodge with us. Me and the wife.'

'I don't know what to say.'

'Think on it and tell me before I go.'

'I will, thanks.'

For the rest of the journey, Dafydd looked on in near silence as Tom operated the regulator. He looked out at the land he loved so much and wondered if he could leave it. He thought of what there was left and what he would lose. Now, it seemed he'd run from home as a child. He'd hardly had a chance to notice himself growing up – who was he now? What was there left to lose? The love of a girl who appeared to have grown cold to him? One who had asked him to go away for months? The back of his neck tingled with the thought of a new start, a proper one this time. He had not made anything of his life so far – perhaps now he could start anew.

When they got back, *Victoria* was standing in a siding, the engine crew glowering at the approaching *Talybont*. Dafydd saw his gang standing by the station with the gaffer, who stood with his hands on his hips. Wisps of smoke from a rubbish fire behind them made as if the man was smoking in fury. 'There's a welcome for me,' he said.

Tom looked out. 'Get over the other side, son. Let me do the talking.'

'What the hell you been doing? Who gave you authority to go off there?' yelled the gaffer.

'Tom doesn't speak Welsh,' Dafydd offered.

The gaffer looked away, and then gathered himself. He repeated himself in English.

Tom shrugged. 'We had arranged to meet here this morning and do the run. When I got here, there was no-one around and I was left waiting.'

'I said, who gave you authority?' repeated the gaffer.

Tom tensed. 'I did, mate and I'll tell you why. I'm here for a reason. To do a job, delivering your new locomotive.'

'We were busy.'

'Fine. Go off and be busy. Just remember this place is paying for me on a by-the-day basis.' Tom took off his gloves and tipped his cap back. 'Or you give me your people for the rest of today and I'll be gone by evening.'

He gave Dafydd a wink as he turned back to see to the engine. 'You remember what I said, son.'

Dafydd walked off as quickly as he could and found Huw approaching. 'Let's go over the hill a bit,' he said. 'There's some work needs doing up the cutting and we can lose ourselves there. The English boys will cover, as always.'

'Thanks, Huw. I expect I shouldn't be surprised it was a risk to go with him.'

'Risk and more if you ask me. The drivers had words when they came back on that old kettle. They were most put out. Still, don't blame them – working that piece of shit every day. They were looking forward to a real engine. Then some country trackboy comes, jumps on and steams off when their back is turned.'

Dafydd had to smile at the thought. There was an edge to Huw's words, but they were aimed at the tramway, not at his friend. There was also more than a hint of jealousy that he hadn't done the same.

'This is for you,' Huw said, and gave Dafydd a letter from his waistcoat pocket. Dafydd stared. 'Can't you read, Daf? You want I do it for you?'

Dafydd grabbed the letter and tore it open, but he read slowly, feeling Huw's impatient eyes on him. Huw let him read it in silence though, showing more understanding than ever before.

'You know what's in this, right? You open it or something?'

'Didn't have to, Daf. The girl that brought it was damn keen to get it to you. She came around here looking for you and picked up on me soon enough. Remember, she saw you duff Parry up for me that Sunday a few weeks back?'

'She was so different then, distant and cold.'

'And now she's sorry, right enough. Said how sad she was that her father had died and all. She was so full of how nice you were. I sure as hell didn't recognise you from her words, Dafydd.'

Dafydd's mind was back on the beach below Pen Dinas. He was unsure now if it was a memory or just a dream. The grin on Huw's face suggested he could all but see the memory.

'Good upbringing, that one,' blustered Dafydd. 'I wouldn't mess with her.'

'Well, seems as if she's forgiven you. For what, I've no idea. She was wanting to see you. Like old times, she said.'

'Baked potatoes at the lime kiln.'

It was only a whisper, but Huw grunted agreement.

'Well, whatever it was all about, I thought she meant – you know...'

'Know what happened just now, Huw? I been working a steam engine. '

'Well, I saw you go so sort of guessed that's what you were doing, Daf. In the cab and all. What of it?'

'I just… well, I loved every moment of it. I been a labourer all my life. Tad had me down for doing figures, but I didn't care for the learning. I was loading and unloading carts at the mine. When I got to the ropewalk, they had me sweeping floors. I come here and I been carrying rock, lifting rock. Hammering, picks, shovels, like some bloody convict. None of it's ever been a trade, yet when I'm faced with the chance of one for the first time; I can see the pride of doing a good job. Being the one who does things and power at your hands…'

Dafydd tensed his hand and the letter crumpled. He looked down at it and tried to smooth the paper as best he could. 'You know, Tom said he'd try and find me a job at the railway works. Reckons I could apprentice over there and learn to drive proper trains. None of this tramway nonsense. I could go all the way to England and learn a proper trade, for the first time in my life, have a purpose and respect myself for what I could always have done but never been given the chance before.' Dafydd shook his head in frustration. 'And at the very same moment I get this message. The one desire that has burned in my heart, that I prayed for this whole past year in chapel. The one thing that has happened, that…'

Huw picked up a stone and flung it at the stream far below the track-bed. 'Well, you never been one for long speeches,' said Huw. 'I'm thinking now perhaps a revivalist preacher is what you should be and all.'

'Have you never thought of moving on, Huw? Going to Aber or further on to find a better way of living?'

'Can't say I ever done, Daf. I'm happy where I am. Where I know folk and they know me.'

'Don't stick around, Huw. This old line won't last. There's nothing going to change here. You look at how it's run and how that stationmaster on the Cambrian runs his place at Llanfihangel. It's chalk and cheese, and the Cambrian are known for bad service and all, if you listen enough.'

'What you saying, then?'

'I need more than this. I need a bigger town, I need more again.'

'I was thinking of going to Aber on Sunday. What say you go meet this girl and talk her sweet?'

Dafydd shook his head. 'It'll not come to that. I want the love of Gwen, yes. But I want to like myself and all.'

'So what? You'll stay and write to her?'

'I don't think you're hearing me, friend, but then I don't think I'm that clear myself. I'm all abuzz now. What I want is there, but to take it all would tear me apart.'

'So what you saying then? You going after this girl or not?' Huw's face softened and he gave a wry smile. 'She's not a bad one, that. Say I'd fancy my chances if you weren't. I mean, well, you know. She's a pretty face and looks after herself. Look, I can understand you being shy, I can. I'll go into Aber Sunday and I'll find her. You give me a message and I'll pass it on and take you back the reply. Then you can meet the next time, right?'

Dafydd nodded and he sighed.

'Got there in the end now. So what you going to say, then?'

Dafydd shivered. The world had gone cold around him. 'Tell her I'm off to Bagnall's.'

CHAPTER ELEVEN

The Promise

'SPECIAL DUTIES?' HUW grumbled. 'Don't talk to me about special duties.'

Dafydd was quiet. Many weeks had passed, but there had been no word from Tom or Bagnall's. It was like living in a dream, where he could see the road, but the harder he tried to get his feet on it, the further away it was. Huw raged on. 'Look I know the tramway's been busier since *Talybont* arrived, but special duties?'

A special train had been provided for local tradesmen to travel on the line, and the railway had invited the local White Lion pub to offer refreshments at the incline base.

'Oh, stop complaining, Huw *bach*,' Dafydd grumbled. 'We're to go along and be useful.'

'Strikes me it's all a bit of a do for nothing,' Huw replied. 'We had to walk the line. The Lion folk have come by horse and cart. All to wait the arrival of the train what should have brought us here in the first place! I mean, what's the point?'

'Keep folk happy. Make them feel important. Make the line look important, more like.'

'Right you are, Daf. So what are we going there for again, pouring lemonade?'

'I forgot my pinafore,' Dafydd replied, and Huw laughed.

'The things you do say.' Huw sat a while in silence and then said: 'Only I do wonder sometimes what we are here for. There's not much more for us to do but sit around these days, waiting for the quarry to take off. We been told they need the stone for Aberystwyth promenade. There's that new dam over Rhayader way. We haven't seen anything of the business, like. Then all them lead mines that were going to start back up again? Well, what's all that about then?'

'These things take time, Huw.'

'Time we don't have, I'm thinking. How's this tramway going to save Talybont village if no-one's doing nothing about it?'

The special train arrived and the guests were more than happy. They had clearly enjoyed the thrill of a ride out into the hills. They'd marvelled at the incline and the old waterwheels. They'd earned their free refreshments.

Dafydd and Huw were lucky enough to get a lift back. The guard let them sit on the generous stairs of the coach – on the promise they would make themselves scarce on arrival at Pen-Rhiw, of course.

Jim and John were at the station and waved them over as the train came to a halt.

'Smooth enough ride, boys?' Jim had a gleam in his eye.

'Bit bumpy for my liking,' Dafydd replied. 'It's all well and good these people coming along to feel important. Where they going to be when the train runs to Llanfihangel on a cold October Wednesday morning in the rain?'

'Not on this train,' John added. 'She's running on Mondays only. Isn't that the truth, Lucky Jim?'

''Tis indeed, Pendle John. Them's decided to run the coach from Talybont to Llanfihangel on market day only.'

'What's the point of that?'

'Both of you come down the Black tonight, young Dafydd. We have much to talk of.'

John sat back in his seat, nursing his ale. Jim handed flagons out to the others, before taking a long draught himself. 'We've been doing some long talking, John and me.'

Dafydd smiled. 'Well, that's obvious, isn't it?'

'It's got to be serious, boys,' Huw said between sips. 'You're not doing the Punch and Judy act.'

'No one's going to pay for a ride when they can walk the three miles to Llanfihangel,' stated John, by way of an opener.

'It's not just the folk, it's the quarry,' Jim added. 'We've heard they've lost the contract for the new promenade in Aberystwyth.'

'We reckon someone switched the samples,' said John. 'It's good rock up there.'

'They lost the dams and all. Looks as if that old mountain will be there a while longer. Thing is, Jim and I been thinking and we reckon this place is doomed.'

'So what you going to do?' Dafydd asked.

'We're going to the Elan Valley, where the dams are being built for Birmingham. There's work there for a few years at least.'

'We want you to come with us, Huw.' Jim said.

'Why me?'

'We're a good team here and work well together. You need to get around a bit.'

'What about Daf?' Huw said.

Jim reached into his waistcoat pocket and brought out a letter.

'This came yesterday.'

Dafydd raised a questioning eyebrow.

'Read it.'

'I'm not so good with English writing.'

'No, and the writer's not so good with Welsh words, which is why it's taken so long to come here.'

'You scared?' Huw asked.

'I don't know,' Dafydd said, trembling.

'All right son,' Jim said gently. 'I'll read it. You can study it when you have time.'

He carefully opened the letter and squinted at it. His lips moved in silence as he went through the pages. Everyone else sat spellbound, watching him.

'He says he's found you an apprenticeship at Bagnall's foundry in Stafford. You're to learn how to drive locomotives for testing once made. He says that you can lodge with him and his family and to be there at the month end. Why, that's only a few days. I expect he thought you would get this earlier.'

It was what Dafydd had hoped for and also feared. There was a long silence. Jim cleared his throat.

'Come on, Huw, let's go find some more ale for us.'

Dafydd was left with John, struggling to find something to say.

'What's wrong, son?'

'I don't know. I thought I wanted this and now it's here, I don't know any more. It's just... I feel I spent my whole life running away from something or other. Is this any different?'

'What you running from then?'

'I don't know.'

'The girl?' Dafydd nodded. John sighed. 'So why don't you stay with her?'

Dafydd snorted in response.

'I'm nothing, look at me: a monkey digging ditches and

shovelling rock. I'm not good enough for her. She needs someone who can look after her. Money, like. She needs a man with a trade.'

'I suppose so, but how will she know that? Have you thought about going to tell her?'

Dafydd picked up his flagon and drained it. 'I thought about it. What do I say?'

'Tell her the truth; let her know you're doing it for the good of both of you.'

'What happens if she won't wait for me?'

'Then at least you'll know, and can move on. Don't waste this opportunity, lad. You may never get another.'

Dafydd sat back and took in his words. Why hadn't he spoken to Gwen before? What had he been scared of? A 'no', or a 'yes'?

Talybont pulled the carriage slowly out of Pen-y-Rhiw and Dafydd settled back in his seat.

Huw had come along for the ride, as far as Aber. 'After all that work, it's as well we get to sit in it once,' said Huw.

They rattled over the road to Elgar Farm. 'Once there was talk of a branch to the old mine there.' Dafydd said. 'They said it would produce huge loads of silver-lead and the area would be rich. Come to nothing of course, like the whole of this damned tramway.'

He watched the few people sitting in the carriage grasp their belongings as it swayed a bit more. 'That's the bit you boys did when I was away,' he said.

Huw smiled. 'Do you think this would have fared better if they hadn't started with that tin tub?' He jerked his thumb back to the station, where *Victoria* stood cold and abandoned.

'I doubt it,' Dafydd sighed. 'Never was meant to be.' He

stared at the hated engine, perched uselessly on its sleepers. 'Huw, am I doing the right thing?'

'Without a doubt. You have a chance to do something with your life. What about me? Am I doing the right thing?'

'Course you are. Jim and John will look after you proper. You'll be fine, English boys and all. They know when to stay and when to run.'

'Well, here we are then,' he said, as the train shuddered to a halt.

'Are you staying in town today?'

'No. The coach will stay here till the end of the day, anyway. I'll walk back. Dafydd *bach*, I wanted to say thank you, for being a friend. You've been fair and you taught me to think before I act. You're a good man and you deserve all the luck, boy. With the woman, that is. Oh, and give them English boys hell.'

'You too, my friend,'

They parted, and Dafydd's world became bigger and lonelier. It was a relief when he saw the bustle of Aberystwyth's locomotive shed, and he could set off on foot for Trefechan.

Find Mrs Owen, she had said.

The town was full and busy in the way that marks early mornings, when people don't say much and move about their business. The different smells of the day began to rise and Dafydd was tempted by the aroma of fresh bread from a bakery. He peered through the dark doorway and froze. Gwen stood behind the counter, hair swept up, sleeves rolled back, busy with customers.

What to do? His stomach made the decision for him. He was hungry, having missed even Pendle John's stewed tea that day. He went in. Gwen was tidying the counter, wreathed in shadow except for the moments when the fire from the oven flashed round the grill, making her faint smile seem to dance on her face as she worked.

Dafydd's almost felt the glow of it. Her smile would never dim in his eyes.

'Best give him some bread love, he's looking on like a starving puppy.' A snigger answered the words. Dafydd glanced at the two older women looking on. His cheeks flushed.

Gwen's cheeks were rosy, but perhaps from the heat.

'I'll have a penny loaf,' said Dafydd and, voice lowered, 'I need to see you.'

'Walk her home,' he was advised. 'Big strapping lad like you would see her safe to Turkey Town and I'd get my bread.'

'When do you finish work?' Dafydd muttered.

She looked up. The sun came out again in her smile of surprise. She nodded, whispered her answer, and Dafydd bowed. 'I'll be here,' he said, and made his escape. Pleasure mixed with worry as he wondered what to do next.

Dafydd walked to the sea. His tad-cu had been born of a Barmouth farmer's wife and a Spanish sea captain, so his father always said, though why Dafydd thought of it now, he'd no idea. Dafydd had worked close to the sea before, at the ropemakers', and had never thought anything of it. Now salt air filled his lungs and the sound of the waves drew him, carrying hints of unknown family memories.

He walked by the old castle and looked towards the harbour and the old wooden slips of the forgotten shipyard. It was deserted, although the sea was busy, rolling breakers bouncing endlessly on the grey shingle. He looked out at the white crests of the waves and wondered if a man could survive such a pounding. He lobbed a few of the grey, disc-like pebbles down the beach and tried to think of the future.

He couldn't see beyond the end of the day at the baker's.

He'd sleep rough and take the morning train to Whitchurch, and on to Stafford. Deep down, he had known that he would end up doing so. The wind was warm, blowing straight at him. Soon enough his eyes grew heavy and he dozed.

He woke up shivering, with pebble-shaped complaints down his back. He upped and made for the promenade. A police constable watched him struggle up the shingle.

'Not at work, young man?' he said.

'I'm waiting for my train,' Dafydd replied. 'Got an apprenticeship, I have. In England.'

'See you catch it,' came the curt reply, and he was away.

So there it was, one day off work and he was a vagrant in the eyes of the law. He shrugged angrily. The sleep had done him good, but he had no desire to slack. He went back into town with his bag and waited for the shop to close. He was back on time, and Gwen was soon out, all sunny smiles. She linked her arm with his and pulled him close.

'Where we going, then? Is it potatoes at the lime kiln once more?'

He smiled, but didn't feel like it. He felt a wave of sadness for all the times they should have had.

'Come on,' said Gwen, showing Dafydd a handful of bread rolls. 'They were unsold.'

'I'm full of bread already,' Dafydd said, which only made her smile the more.

'No silly, we'll barter them for some hot potatoes.'

He followed her over Trefechan Bridge and down to the shore where the river met the harbour. He waited while Gwen did her piece of trade at the kilns. The scene was still lovely, the ships majestic. Now though, Dafydd saw memories around him. Ghosts stirred in shadowy corners, around the arches of the bridge and the ruined ropewalk.

'Here,' said Gwen, who reappeared holding two potatoes on sticks. I got some butter in there and all.'

'I was thinking of Joe,' Dafydd said, before he could stop himself. 'I caught him in the arches there and he told me everything.'

'Joe's gone now. He's never coming back.'

'I've got to go too, Gwen.'

There was a long silence, as they ate the potatoes and watched the river. The sun had gone in.

'You going for good?'

'I hope not. Look, I tried my best, honest I did. The tramway's going nowhere, but I've got a chance. An engineer came down and he offered me an apprenticeship in England. I can learn to be an engine driver. It's better for me to have a trade and then I can make a decent living. Better than a common labourer. I can feed...' *our family* – he stopped himself from saying the words.

'Good for you.'

Was her smile tinged with sadness?

'You deserve better,' she said, 'always did. Life's been unkind to you and you deserve a chance.'

Come with me. The words stuck in Dafydd's throat, unsaid. His chest ached with the weight.

She sat, hugging her knees. 'You came to say goodbye?'

'Yes... no... I mean... I don't know what I mean any more.'

'You going to whisk me off to England, are you?'

'If you'd come.'

She smiled, and in the sunset glow her voice was sad. 'I can't do it, *cariad*. I wish I could. Mam and Tad are at rest here and I'll not leave them.'

The shadows grew longer, darker, colder. She shivered.

'It's getting dark here. Let's go to the beach and watch the sunset. Better still, we can go up the hill. You never been up Pen Dinas...?' She watched him gravely. 'It's where wicked people go. I love a good sunset and it's your last night here. I want you to share it with me. You came into my life and out of it so fast! I'd like a time we can just sit down together and let the rest go on around us.' Her smile came back. 'But we have to be quick, *cariad*, before we're noticed.'

They climbed up a path that took them past the smelting works and on towards the top with its strange pillar. Gwen took his hand as she guided him and he tingled at her touch. As the path turned away from the beach, she took him to sit on a small ridge, looking straight down to Tanybwlch beach, past a mass of yellow gorse. Beyond the railway, a large flat area lay between them and the sea cliffs further on.

It was all so green and rich against the grey beach, and the sea of ever changing blue. He started to speak, but she stopped him.

'Not now – just sit, all right?'

They sat and watched the world. Swallows swooped low after late meals. A butterfly came in search of the yellow flowers. A cloud of small midge-flies bobbed around the bushes below.

'Lovely, ent it,' Gwen breathed. 'I come here for peace.'

'Best we leave before sun sets.'

'Don't you worry now, for the sky's so clear we'll have the stars to see by.'

Dafydd could hear the rigging of many ships tapping against the masts in the evening breeze.

'The sea's a lovely blue now,' he said

'Couldn't you just sit here for ever? I know I could.'

Dafydd nodded. 'All the way up here, away from them down there.'

'Tell you what, let's try and get the engineer to come here and teach you. Then you won't have to go to silly England.'

'You know what? Back when he offered it me, I felt there was nothing I wanted more. I got a brain – never used it, mind.'

'It's good for you, Daf. You need to do more and be your own man. Look at the sea now, that's my favourite blue.'

'It's like a pond, with paper boats and stick-men fishing on the shore. Gwen, I got to ask, I just came here to... well...'

'Well, Dafydd *bach*, we've got all night, haven't we?'

'I loved you since first day I met you, Gwen. It's never changed and never going to change. I thought I'd try and forget you, but I can't and I won't, simple as that. If you tell me to stay, I'll do it and be done with England.'

'How do you know you love me, *bach*?'

'When I close my eyes, you're there with me.'

Gwen looked away. Even so, he sensed a sad smile. Her voice was a whisper then. 'You've got to go, *bach*, you're never going to stick being a labourer for long and there's a chafing you'll have for the life you deserve. Go and get a trade, Dafydd.'

'All right Gwen. If you won't come with me and I can't move Bagnall's to Aber, will you wait for me? As soon as I'm driver or fireman, we could... I mean I could write and tell you, then get work in Aber or nearby. There's a few railways around hereabouts.'

Like Plynlimon and Hafan, he thought sourly. Gwen looked out to sea and Dafydd only knew she was still with him by the rise and fall of her shoulders as she sighed.

'It's something I can't ask, I'm sorry,' Dafydd said. 'Perhaps I'll say this. If it's worked out for me, I'll come back and find you. Then I'll ask you again and if you're not taken, you can decide if you'll have me or not.'

'Sit down with me and just *hisht* for now,' she said softly. 'The sun's a red ball and we should see it go down together.'

It took hours, he felt. Even the hairs on his arm could feel how close Gwen sat and, as the touch became firmer, the rush of excitement was difficult to stop. She shivered and he put his arm around her.

'I'm glad you're here.' Dafydd didn't know if she said it or his mind said it for her. He looked at her then and her smile was honest and warm. Mouth slightly open, tongue delicately balanced on her lower teeth. It was enough to spur him and he leant forward and began to breathe once more as she didn't move away.

The kiss was gentle, on the lips, and she gasped at its ending, before another small smile. Her hand came up to gently stroke the back of his head, then she drew him close once more and their tongues touched.

Dafydd's hand moved to her breast and this time she did not stop him. Slowly, their breathing became faster and their caresses urgent. Clothes were loosened and struggled with, and then he was on her, as his friends had always said in the playground. She moaned with pleasure, guiding his hands, her mouth reaching for his.

In the back of his brain, the sermons of chapel droned unheeded, a ghostly Tabernacle full to the rafters of disapproving, God-fearing folk. Dafydd did not flinch, for it felt so right and when he gasped in pleasure, his head spun and he could have sung for them all.

In the end he lay, wasted, and she held him like there was no end. Sobbing and panting, sobbing and panting, until she could whisper the words he had only ever dreamt before.

'I will wait, Dafydd. I promise, I will wait.'

CHAPTER TWELVE

Bully (1898)

WATCHING EVERY TREE and every field fly past, Dafydd sat out his journey to England, ever asking the same question. Was he right to go? Why was he leaving the only girl who had claimed his heart? He felt weary, but he gradually settled on one desire: to return as a true railwayman.

As the train pulled into the first of the English stations, Dafydd started to worry about the names and words of a tongue he spoke a bit, but understood little and read even worse. It was a language harsh to his ear, nothing like the musical tongue of his own land. He wondered how he would find his lodging, and a man he had met only a few times, in this strange land. Would he even recognise Tom if he weren't standing beside little *Talybont?*

Dafydd's luck was in. Tom was waiting for him at Stafford station.

'Thought I was a day late,' Dafydd said shyly.

'Nonsense, son, last day of the month, we said. Come on, it's not far.'

They were soon in a maze of terraces, making up an area many times bigger than Trefechan. The sky was dark and the air thick with the smell of coal fires. Gas lights spluttered on street corners and a dog barked somewhere close by. There was a shout, a curse and a yelp, quickly swallowed up by the noise of a passing train. Tom led him into one of the houses, to its back room, where linen hung from the ceiling, drying in the warmth of the kitchen stove.

'Oh, there you are, me dove.' A round, heavily-lined face appeared through the linen. The woman Dafydd would learn to call "Mrs Tom" limped out with a basket of laundry under her arm.

'Come in, love, and get warm. You need a cup of tea, for starters.'

Dafydd was ushered to a small chair by the fire. A cup of tea was thrust into his hands. He sipped at what tasted like a ladleful of sugar. Tingling warmth coursed through his body. He looked up to thank Mrs Tom – but was met by the sullen stare of a girl of about his own age with dirty cheeks and curly hair, roughly tied back. He tried a greeting but she sniffed and turned away.

By the time the whole family was in the room, Dafydd knew he was lucky to have the chair. Smaller children sat crammed together on a box seat, chatting happily as their parents fussed over them. The sullen girl was alone in her mood, face chiselled out of mud-white stone.

'We've given you your own room, as befits a lodger,' said the woman.

'Oh, I don't want to cause trouble.'

'It's no trouble,' came the cheerful reply. 'You're paying us for it.'

Dafydd stifled a laugh when he found they had divided one of the two rooms upstairs. A large linen cloth hung from the rafters. Eight children would be sharing the other half of the room. At least his own Mam and Tad had only the three, his two sisters and himself.

He sat down to a bowl of stew that evening, served with bread and cheese and a prayer of thanksgiving. It was like being back in Trisant, but for the language, and the constant noise of the town. Tom asked lots of questions as they ate. How was the trip? What did Dafydd think of Stafford? Was he looking forward to the new day? All the while calling him "David", whilst the children looked on shyly, except the sullen girl, who scowled at nothing in particular.

'Josiah Smith and me'll look after you, don't you worry,' Tom said, as he filled Dafydd's bowl with more of the watery stew. 'And the Castle Works will treat you well. She's a fine mistress if you do your job, you'll see.'

Dafydd lay on his bed that evening and thought of it all. A cat screamed and someone cursed, until the scrabble of claws on slates told of the cat leaving. Even the interruption of noise could not stop him thinking of the slopes of Pen Dinas and Gwen in his arms.

Next morning, Dafydd followed Tom out of the house, to be swept on his way amongst a mass of workers, men in their coats, caps and mufflers, women with shawls gathered over their heads. Some talked, others just looked straight ahead purposefully. Many converged on the grand gates of the Castle Works. Dafydd had seen places like it in Aber. Green's Foundry, by the station, was one. But Castle Works was ten times the size, at least. 'We'll be off to find Josiah and he'll get you started,' said Tom.

'You're a bit shabby, Taff,' were Josiah's first words to Dafydd, as he looked him up and down.

'Them's my working clothes,' Dafydd said.

'Well, you'd better start working, then,' Josiah replied, shoving an oily rag into Dafydd's hands and brushing past him. Dafydd guessed Josiah expected him to follow. The man strode off purposefully to an old engine in a corner of the yard. It looked to be held together by mud and rust. The track was heavy with grass and it was obvious the hulk had not moved for a while.

Josiah was watching Dafydd for a reaction so Dafydd made none. He'd had a lifetime of having grimy work thrown at him. He shrugged. 'I take it you want me to work down from the top.'

'Better start with the frame, son,' came the gruff reply. He picked up a can and threw it at Dafydd's feet. 'Use oil and paraffin rags, work the muck clear from the metal rods.'

'Tell you what, I'll know the engine inside out by the time I'm done.'

'That's the point,' Josiah snapped, and was off.

Dafydd looked again at his charge. Perhaps it wasn't so bad. There was rust, but mud caked the beast more. There could be good metal there, somewhere. In a way, the engine reminded him of little *Talybont*. Dafydd stood in the cab and closed his eyes, remembering the time he had fired the little black engine to the incline, and the thrill of standing on its noisy footplate. The motion of the engine was pleasing to him, but the most important thing was the feeling of its power. It spoke to him. Every hiss of steam, every belch of smoke, it all conjured up a living beast. One that responded to each touch like a wild horse, now tamed; one eager and ready for the task ahead.

An engine whistle blew nearby and he watched puffs of smoke bloom behind a shed. He reached a decision. He would bring this hulk back to life. She would ride the rails again, her spirit renewed.

He thought of Gwen as he worked, letting his mind go back to Pen Dinas and the sun setting as they made love. When he stopped to breathe, he grabbed the regulator and gazed ahead down an imaginary line. It was a long road for him to travel, but if he could keep busy, he would be a railwayman, not a common labourer. Then he would go back to Aber, and Gwen would…

'You'll never shift that lever until you've done with unseizing the motion,' Josiah said disapprovingly from the cab door.

'Sorry, I was trying to remember what bits went where and then I can work out where's best to start first.'

'Son, if you're here to waste my time, you'd best pack your bags now.'

'I'll show you what I've done so far, but I'm worried I'm starting in the wrong place. All I know is the cab. I've done firing – well, once – and Tom showed me up to the incline.' He knew he was gabbling senselessly.

'It's time you took a break and a cup of tea.'

Josiah walked off and Dafydd followed him to a small tin hut. Josiah re-emerged with two steaming mugs.

'See, what I'm worried about here is old Tom being a bit soft since he lost his first born,' Josiah said. 'He obviously thinks well of you, otherwise he'd not ask you to come over from Welsh Wales. But you're a bit on the old side for an apprentice. My experience is them as has worked a bit don't change. A labourer is a labourer, in my book. But I'm not one for making judgments: just prove yourself and we'll see how we stand.'

'Josiah,' Dafydd replied quickly. 'I don't know I'll make you believe me, but I've always done what I can. I proved I can turn my hand to anything and once I set my heart on it, I'll get it done.'

'Actions speak the loudest son. Best you work on the motion or you'll have a pretty beast only fit for a museum.'

'What'll be done with her after?'

'She's on the scrap line, son. It's what we do with all things that are found to be useless.'

'Oh! Look at you, aren't you a state,' exclaimed Mrs Tom when they got home. 'What on earth will you do for clothing? Your jacket's torn and your trousers black with oil. Come in now. Kitty! Set up the bath tub out back, he can have a scrub.'

'Shall I help him?' came the soft reply from the girl, although to look at her, there was no interest either way.

'Less of your sauce, young lady,' Tom said sharply.

'We can give him John's old boiler suit,' his wife continued.

Tom was silent for a moment, and then nodded. 'Aye, you're right there, woman.'

Dafydd noted Tom's silence for the rest of the night, and had an idea who John might have been. He didn't see Kitty again, though he was uncomfortably aware she was not far away as he sat in the tub. The oil and grease were not easily shifted, but at least his spirited attempt to clean up quickly warmed him up. As he settled down to bed, he caught a glimpse of a shadow hovering by the door. A fleeting glimpse at that, quickly away, as if fearing to be discovered.

Tom was back to his normal self by morning, when they made for the Castle Works once more.

Dafydd chose his moment and, with some trepidation asked, 'John was your son?'

He feared for a moment he'd created another day-long silence but presently, Tom took a deep breath and replied. 'Well, yes. Fine lad too. Would have made a good engineman. Would have been around your age now. He caught a chill, tried to ride it out and wouldn't take to his bed, our John. No medicine neither. Never trusted doctors. It went to

145

pneumonia and... well, he's gone now. I expect people's talked of it to you already.'

'They have, I think they're thinking... '

'...That I'm getting you to live the life of my son? No, I'll put it to you this way. My son was a good lad, all primed and ready for the engineman's trade. Leaving so early in life was a waste. Then I goes to Wales and I sees you there. I talk to you and I see you at work. Fate's not been kind to you and I'm thinking there's a mind there what could be put to better use than shovels and the like. I could not help my son, but I could help you with a future. You stick here a while and learn what you can. Listen hard to Josiah, he has a lot to give you.'

Josiah still wasn't much for talking, though. Dafydd worked hard on the rusting engine, feeling Josiah's judgemental eye even when he couldn't see Josiah.

'It's what good enginemen have to do. You have to know your engine inside out.' But he wasn't going to tell Dafydd anything useful.

The days at work went by much the same. Back at the house, things were becoming stranger. A few nights in, Dafydd was woken up by a noise downstairs and decided to check. There was a faint glow in the fireplace and from that he could see a shape of someone sitting in the chair nearby.

'Are you all right?' Dafydd asked.

There was a snort in response and a young girl's voice came back in reply.

'Just keeping warm. Only chance I get to sit in a proper chair by the fire.'

'Kitty.'

'Not that I begrudge you my bed. God knows the money comes in handy for us all.'

'You should sleep.'

'What? In my bed? With you?' Her voice was mocking, making Dafydd's back shiver.

'I'm taken,' he tried.

'What? Some girl back in the hills? You'll be away a long time. Do you think she'll wait?'

'Go to your bed, woman,' Dafydd muttered.

He could see the gleam of her teeth in the firelight. She looked like a fox.

'I'll do that,' she said, then stood and curtseyed.

She was quickly up the stairs. He raked the fire and crept back to his room, trying to avoid the steps that creaked the most. He climbed into his bed – and nearly fell out again in shock as Kitty grabbed his waist. She curled her leg over him. She had shed her nightshirt.

'Get out!' he hissed.

'You told me to go to my bed,' she giggled.

'I'll throw you out.'

'And I'll cry out and where would we be then? It won't look so good for you, will it? And you just taken our hospitality.'

She snuggled her head to Dafydd's chest.

'Besides, it's warm and cosy like this, is it not?'

'All right, be out of my bed by morning and don't prod me.'

He could sense the curve of her smiling lips, as her fingers caressed him.

'But you never know, mountain man. You may enjoy the night yet.'

Her fingers moved lower and lower, then her head followed. He watched the sheet moving and felt the gentle touch of her lips. He was caught between fear and animal excitement. It certainly wasn't something they had prepared him for in chapel. He doubted if the minister knew of it, because Dafydd was sure he had never read of it in the Bible. He put his hand in his mouth to silence himself. Afterwards, he lay there with his arm on her shoulders, wondering how he could feel warm and relaxed whilst dirty and impure.

He tried to think of Gwen, waiting. He tried to picture her, but he feared he would see Kitty looking back. In the morning, Kitty had gone. The next night though, she was back and very soon he was once again a sinner in the eyes of God. Gwen appeared in his dreams, always wearing black. She drifted sadly over the smoking ruins of the ropewalk.

At work, his lot got no better. He cleared a mountain of muck and rust. Inch by inch he greased, scraped and then oiled the grey metal to protect it. He'd worked out a lot of how things connected from the cab. He'd looked at the tubes inside the cylindrical boiler. The exhaust system that threw out the combination of smoke and steam. He'd gone into the firebox to chip the clinker off the brick arch inside. He'd been right over the beast, but no-one was coming to tell him what to do.

Was Josiah happy to leave him as ignorant as the day he had begun?

He appeared from time to time, to ask what Dafydd had done. He would then just shrug his shoulders and point to something else that needed fixing.

'You'll never be on the plate unless you know your stuff. And you'll not get close to that until I'm happy with you.'

Dafydd was on his own by day, worrying. By night, he was not alone. He welcomed the comfort of a warm body beside him but he felt a traitor and a fool, far away from home. Worse that it had been chance that had got him to this point, but now he was a sinner. Kitty acted as if he didn't exist by day, then was all over him when the house was asleep. And always the mocking smile.

This went on for months, until Tom decided it was time to give Dafydd a lesson.

'You'll fire with me for a day, Dav. Both Josiah and my regular are needed elsewhere. Besides, Josiah says you're coming on slowly; let's try and speed it up.'

Dafydd was happy, but wary. He lit the fire and started tidying around the cab. Coaling up was something he knew, at least, and he would make a nice beehive shape of the coal as soon as he could. When the engine was ready, they moved to the coaling stage and he loaded a few buckets of coal into the bunker. He looked out to the chimney and the smoke was clear.

'There's too much air going in the firebox, David,' Tom shouted. 'Flatten the fire a bit. Too many holes. You've put in enough there for a trip and a half. You going back to Wales with her or something?'

They moved on to the water column and Dafydd struggled to open the water tank. The crane was next and he didn't know where to start. To his relief, Tom jumped down and swung the crane over. Dafydd fixed it in place as the water gushed out. He was careful to note what Tom had done. He'd be wiser if he got the chance again. They did some shunting in the yard, Tom tapping the water gauge to remind him, before he fed more to the boiler.

'Keep concentrating, David,' he said. 'Smoke's a bit black now and all. Open the firebox door a bit to let some air in.'

Dafydd carried on as best he could, keeping an eye on what Tom did. They broke for a meal and Tom took him to a shed where a few men were drinking tea and eating their sandwiches. Dafydd sat at the back, wishing he was one of them, with their easy banter. They talked of events of the day and debated politics, just like the miners of Frongoch. All they needed to do next was form a choir.

They returned to the engine and Tom sat on the steps to finish his pipe. He gave one of his fatherly smiles.

'I don't know what is going on here, David. You learn fast. Everything I showed you, you've picked up damn quick. Thing is, you should have been learning all that. What you been doing, son?'

Dafydd sighed, he was never keen to tell tales, but he'd had enough bullies in his life. He led Tom to the back of the yard where his rusting hulk stood. Tom looked it over, shook his head, and smacked the water tank with his hand.

'There's a bit of elbow grease been put into this, son.'

He climbed into the cab and fiddled around with a few levers before hopping back out.

'You're working with me the rest of the week, David,' was all he said.

It was the happiest week Dafydd had had in Stafford. Kitty let him be also. It was enough to persuade him there was a God after all. However, the week passed and he was back with Josiah once more. When he saw Josiah hammering a frame into place. Dafydd approached him in trepidation, hoping Tom had had words and the future would be brighter.

'What do I do today?'

Josiah gave him a look that said everything. 'You're working on that engine until I say so.'

Dafydd sighed.

Josiah scowled, and pointed the hammer head threateningly at Dafydd. 'You used to leaving jobs half done then? You're learning a valuable lesson here. You're working on that engine until I say and you'll not leave her until she's steaming.'

'You know she'll not steam again, Josiah.'

'So you're the expert now? And don't give me any lip or I'll sling you out the gates before you can say Yucky da.'

'Tubes are broken, brick arch is cracked, baffle plate is burnt out and the water tanks are as thin as paper in parts.'

Josiah stared a while in silence, his face turning rosier with anger. 'How do you know that?'

'I've been firing the last week in the yard.'

'Who said you could?'

'Tom did.'

His lip curled. 'Dirty Welsh monkey boy! You got given a job that wasn't yours to take and as sure as hell is warm, I'll have you out of it and gone before I'm finished with you.'

He swung his hammer restlessly and spat.

Dafydd found himself more angry than frightened. 'You point that thing at me again and I will ram it down your throat.'

Josiah grinned. 'Try and take it from me then, fool.'

They stood glaring at each other for a while before Dafydd realised someone was calling. Tom's fireman came rushing. 'There's been a change. Tom's taking on David from now and I'm your new boy.'

'Says who?'

'Tom – he's cleared it with the gaffer.'

Muttering a curse, Josiah walked past Dafydd. He made sure their shoulders banged as he passed. The fireman gave Dafydd a wink and a grin, and then patted his shoulder before he ran off to follow.

CHAPTER THIRTEEN

Sudden Endings, New Beginnings (1900)

I<small>T WAS LIKE</small> a door opening to a new world for him – the one Dafydd had expected months ago, the one with a future that included happiness, maybe even Gwen. He was back in the cab, with Tom directing him, but this time there was more to do; shovelling coal, checking water, checking the steam pressure, coupling, uncoupling. It was hard work and Dafydd loved every minute of it.

Dafydd realised now how much there was going on at Castle Works. Whilst those in the works built and repaired, Tom and Dafydd moved the engines in and out the sheds, supplied coal and materials from the yard and tested the new engines. That was Dafydd's favourite job, being the one to take the plate as the newborn took its first fiery breaths and rolled forth. It was always a special moment.

He was getting to know people. He was no longer alone at tea breaks, and new confidence brought a new strength.

The next time Kitty slipped into his bed, Dafydd stayed still and kept his eyes shut, tired of all the games. She grew impatient and Dafydd held her shoulders to stop her.

'What's up with you?' she whispered angrily.

'I don't want it, least not from you. I don't love you, Kitty. This is all wrong.'

'Never stopped you before,' she grumbled, but Dafydd held her away, feeling her body go stiff with annoyance.

'Listen, I don't love you either, Welsh boy. This is only play.'

'It's wrong and I'll not keep doing it.'

'Boy taken your fancy?' she sneered.

'No, I love another. Should have saved myself for her, and I will from now.'

'How noble! Who do you think you are, Lord La-di-da?'

Dafydd turned away. There was no point replying. She snuggled up to his back and her voice lowered as she stroked his arm.

'Come on now, lover boy.'

Dafydd pushed back, causing her to fall off the bed. A low curse came from the floor and in the gloom he could see her stand up and rub her behind.

'You'll pay for that.'

'It's over, Kitty. I should never have let it happen.'

'I'm going to tell my tad what you done. He'll throw you out and you'll lose your job and all.'

'And what will happen to you? What will you be telling him anyway? That I forced you to come into my room every night?'

There was a silence. Dafydd could sense something else.

'You've done this before, haven't you? What happened? Did you get rid of him? Do you think you'll be believed a second time? Strange it would happen again, isn't it?'

She muttered another curse and Dafydd was left with no doubt.

'I love another, Kitty. Always have. Go now, there's nothing for you here.'

The slap came out of the dark, making Dafydd's jaw creak. Then she was gone and Dafydd was left seeing stars, but feeling that it was a fitting end to this nightmare.

A few days on, Mrs Tom was bustling around at breakfast when she stopped and gave him a hug.

'What was that for?'

'I'm pleased for you, dove. You've come around. You've come out your shell. Tom says you're doing well and all. You're more content, son, I can see it.'

'I'm learning so much, Mrs Tom, I can't help but be happy.'

She beamed back. 'Good lad. Kitty, bring us some milk. Kitty! What's got into the girl? She's gone more mardy, if that's possible. Kitty!'

Kitty thrust a letter into his hand. 'Here, this come for you.' Dafydd looked at the creased envelope and had a panic that his slow reading in English would show him up. 'It's from your girl, I think,' Kitty said, moodily. 'There's perfume on it. Well, I smell lavender at any rate.'

There were two small flowers pressed inside the letter. The words slowly came into focus and Dafydd realised he hadn't seen Welsh for so long he'd almost forgotten what it looked like. It was not a long letter, but it didn't need to be.

Dear Dafydd,
I hope this finds you well and you're learning a lot. I hope one day you will be working on the Aber trains perhaps? They do say there's a new line going up to Devils Bridge that needs building. Anyway, I hope so. I'm thinking of you.

I think of you every time I see the sun set from Pen Dinas. I know you had to leave and I hope you find what you seek. If you do come back, please remember me.
Love, Gwen

Dafydd read it again and breathed the lavender. He looked up to see Kitty glaring at him from the kitchen. He ignored her and read it again.

'Lavender is for luck in Wales,' was all he could think of to say.

'You deserve it, dove,' Mrs Tom said, patting his shoulder. 'You deserve it.'

From that moment on, the *hiraeth* burnt brightly in Dafydd's heart more than ever before. He loved his job, he learned more every day, but his heart was back by the harbour, with the girl from Turkey Town.

Tom was always by his side, encouraging him. Dafydd began to guess how the future would be and a few months on, when they were in the yard waiting for trucks to be unloaded, Tom told Dafydd what the young man already knew. 'I'd love to keep you here son, honest I would, but your heart's not here no more.'

'Has Josiah been bad-mouthing me again? I'm doing the best I can!'

'Nothing like that. I put paid to all that nonsense, but there's a few things have happened.'

Then he looked Dafydd straight in the eyes, and his words sent a shiver down his back.

'Kitty's with child.'

Dafydd turned to shovel coal in the firebox. A slam of the door and a tap of the gauges later, he knew he must face Tom.

'I haven't, I mean, I never...'

'I know, son. It'll be Josiah's boy be taking her down the aisle. He's the father.'

Dafydd stared.

'Well, more than likely it's him, but no matter: he's the one as will take her. Thing is, we need the room, when they're wed they'll need more space what with a baby to bring up and all.'

'But if it's not his...?'

Dafydd stopped himself quickly and Tom gave a strange smile.

'I'd not worry, Dafydd. He'll have her and she tells me it's his. Look, I know you're a bit soft on her, but I'll not let you do it.'

'What?'

'I'm sorry son, I'm a fair man and you're a good lad, but you're not English and I'll have an Englishman for a son. And a grandson too. Besides, your heart's elsewhere, allus has been.'

'Right.' Dafydd felt the pain of rejection. Up to then, Tom had been fair, kind, fatherly even. It was a bitter pill for Dafydd that in the end he was being judged by his place of birth. Even though he would never have wanted to be Kitty's husband, the rejection made him feel alone again. His mind began to race and think of a way to go home. Was he ready? Did he have enough skills to find a good job? Tom's words broke through his thoughts.

'There is something else. Go in that shed and have a look at *Treze de Maio*.'

The name was familiar, but Dafydd's mind was still spinning over Kitty. He stumbled over to the shed and looked in.

The engine was half covered in tarpaulin, but Dafydd would know the little girl anywhere. He moved the tarpaulin as best he could and rubbed dirt from the name, so he could see the gold letters: *Talybont*.

Dafydd grinned and let out a whoop. The tank was dirty and rusting in parts, but he let out a whoop and kissed it before rushing out again.

'The old girl has come home and no bugger has bothered to claim her,' Dafydd said, as he caught up with Tom, who was grinning as he leant out of his cab.

'You all right son? Looks as if you saw a ghost.'

'What's going on, Tom?'

'The Plynlimon line shut. It never made money, they tell me. Bagnalls were still owed, so they had her back. She's to be regauged and sold to a contractors from Devon called Pethick's. They'll want us to test her when they're done. You in?'

Dafydd nodded like a fool.

'There's one more thing. Pethick's are building a new line, so that's what she'll be doing. They're short of a fireman and asked if an apprentice is ready and willing to go and work for them. Interested?'

Dafydd didn't know what to think, He was still wondering where he'd be living when Kitty got married.

'They're building a line to Devils Bridge from Aberystwyth.'

Dafydd's jaw dropped and Tom roared with laughter.

'I'll put in a word if you like and they can take you on. It'll get you back to where you belong.'

'Am I ready?' Dafydd asked.

'You're ready for this, David, trust me.'

'But how do you know so much about it?'

Tom tapped his nose with a grin. 'That would be telling. Let's just say, old man Pethick come asking in my earshot and all the other boys are too comfortable by half in Stafford.

Now if it were in Crewe, they'd be screaming to go, but a shunting job in Wales? Short contract, year at most, well...'

'A year?'

'Well, yes. They're only building the line after all. Still, it's a chance to be called 'a passed fireman', and there's a few lines over that way as would take a youngster like you. Might give you time to sort out that woman of yours.'

'Gwen?'

'You don't really belong here, Dav. You should be at home in Wales with your woman and family. It's your tad that should be sitting down of an evening to have this talk with you, not me.'

'I don't know if my tad is still in the valley. The mine was on hard times.'

'Well, now's a good time to find out. Don't worry, Dav, we'll see you right.'

There was something of the situation Dafydd didn't like – a vague note of guilt and shame. He had done nothing to stop Kitty all those times. He worried that it had all been down to his lack of will. Perhaps a move now was his chance of redemption. He had dreamt for so long of going back to Aber as more than a common labourer. But would it be poisoned if he did it for the wrong reasons? He sought Kitty out when nobody was looking.

'You're with child,' he said.

'My goodness, you catch on quickly,' she replied.

'Is it mine?' Dafydd asked.

'What if it was?' She said with a sneer.

'Then I'd stay and marry you,' he replied. 'For it would be my fault for getting you into trouble.'

'But you don't love me. You've said it enough times.'

'Nor you me, but that is not important. The child is. If it's mine, I'll do what's right.'

'Bit late for that, don't you think?' She giggled. 'Anyway, Tad wouldn't have it, you not being English. He'd have you with open arms if you were, but he'll never see a foreigner as one of the family.'

'I would find a way – or we could move.'

'What? To your barbarian home? Not a chance.'

Dafydd bit his lip and she placed her hand on his arm.

'It's not yours, I know. Well past that, I was. Always careful with you, but I'm not past a bit of fun if you've changed your mind.'

'Are you certain?'

'David, I wouldn't have a baby by you. I made sure of that.'

Dafydd had no idea how she would do that. He had an inkling it was bravado, designed to belittle him. However, it made him feel a release. He had an awareness of the timings of such things and it had been nearly half a year since he had finally shed himself of Kitty's furtive pleasures.

Dafydd worked hard for weeks to prepare the little engine. As soon as she was regauged, he cleaned off all the muck that had been allowed to stick on her. He had her firebox free from the clinker that crippled many an engine. There was a new drive in him to make *Talybont* look her best. She had become the symbol of his planned progress in life.

He looked upon her new cab, with a roof covering the back, and vowed she would never be hidden in canvas again. Even if the cab back was wooden, it made her look fine. Finally, he polished the levers in the cab and looked out through the spyglass windows at the front. In his mind, he was racing to the Hafan quarry incline, all hell to play with smoke and steam and the coach banging against the engine, as it tried to keep up.

Finally, the day arrived when he could open up the doors of the shed and prepare for the engine to be turned out. The engine had a new name, *Rheidol*, now painted in white on the cab side. For a brief moment, he wondered if they'd notice if he changed it to *Gwen*. Then he hitched a ride on the cab, as the engine was pulled out to the water tower.

It took a few minutes until the cascade of water from within the tanks told Dafydd they were full and he could swing the crane away. *Rheidol* shone back, gleaming wet as it was pushed to the coaling stage. A few bucketfuls were gathered and Dafydd put some chunks on the top of the tanks for good measure. He started the fire as he'd been taught. It took a while to grow it; it always did with coal, but soon it was glowing away. He built up the fire and watched the smoke colour to make sure it was clear. The water pressure gauge stayed put for ages. Then it quivered with a flicker of greeting and slowly began its journey around the dial.

There was a welcome hiss of steam. Dafydd smiled and grabbed the oilcan to walk the engine and top up the moving joints, ready for the first run. Well-greased as she was, *Rheidol* still screeched as she moved across the yard. Satisfied at last, Dafydd raced back to the cab – and found Josiah waiting.

They had not spoken since the day of confrontation, and Dafydd wondered what to expect now. Josiah tapped the gauges and gave him a blank look, which Dafydd took as the signal to jump on board. As soon as his foot was on the plate, Josiah had the regulator up and *Rheidol* began to move.

Dafydd was proud of the little engine as it responded and inched forward. He didn't want the moment spoilt by Josiah. He tried not to show it, but he was full of trepidation as he stood on the steps and saw the engine into the yard. Josiah ran *Rheidol* up and down a few times before he spoke.

'Needs some oil on the coupling rods.'

Glad to be released from the cab, Dafydd moved down the engine with the oilcan. He quickly squirted a few times onto the metal rods on either side, then Josiah pointed to a ground frame and Dafydd went to change the points. *Rheidol* sailed past, Dafydd followed on foot, keeping his distance. He coupled up the trucks and neatly jumped away when Josiah sounded the whistle and made off again.

Josiah finally brought the engine to a stand after a few runs. He took out a pocket book and started making notes, tapping the gauges, opening the firebox, all without a word. Dafydd stood there wondering how this was going to end. Josiah wasn't going to even look at him unless it was absolutely necessary. He wondered how they had achieved so much with so little communication. Josiah jumped from the cab and lit his pipe. He walked around *Rheidol* and checked the outside, before opening the smoke box door at the front. Dafydd went to sit on the cab floor and watch the fire.

Time slowed down. The man was taking ages, what was it with him? Dafydd thought the fire was looking a bit off, so he put a few shovels of coal into the back. Then Josiah climbed back on and tapped the gauges again.

'Water pressure's good,' he rumbled, out of nowhere. He stooped to gaze in the firebox. 'Good fire going, but no need to stack it all in the front. This little one rocks about so much, it'll all get shook up too quickly. Little and often is the key.'

Dafydd listened to his words, but made no reply. 'You'll be all right if you keep your nose clean. You're good enough now for shunting, and you'll be able to talk your gibberish to the locals there. So, do you want to fight now?'

'What?'

'You and me, we don't get on. Do you want to fight me for it?'

'I've had enough reasons to fight in the past, but this isn't one of them.'

'Why not? You took the apprenticeship I thought my son was due so I tried to bury you in a corner and let you rot. That's worth something, isn't it?'

'Not any more.'

'I mean, father's got to look after son, right? Or do you even know who your father is?'

'My father let me leave and made sure I was safe.'

'Why's that, mountain man?'

'I thought I'd killed a man.'

'Oh yes? Big tough man are you?' Josiah pushed Dafydd in the chest. 'Want to have a go at killing me?'

There was an almost pleading look in Josiah's eyes. Dafydd was embarrassed by a desire to laugh. A cough became a chuckle. Josiah scowled. Dafydd gave up and laughed aloud. After all the things that had happened, this felt like nonsense. Playground stuff. Dafydd could have fought, but it seemed soft – and now he couldn't fight for laughing.

'You're mad,' Josiah grunted. Then he gave a puzzled smile and before long he was laughing too. He shook his head, and then reached for his knapsack.

'You ever ate a clanger?'

He unwrapped a small parcel, with two savoury-smelling pastries inside. Dafydd took one, noting it was still warm. He bit into the middle. His mouth was filled with the taste of meat and veg, but mixed with a sweet fruity taste. He coughed in surprise.

'It's two courses, son. Meat and veg on one side, jam in other. Easy way to carry a meal. The wife's a Bedford girl and it's what they do down there.'

Dafydd started on the meat end, and it became less confusing for his palate.

'It's old Tom who's to blame,' Josiah said. 'He paired us together, after he'd got you in before my son. I expect he thought I'd get on with it, but it was hard. He's got me son in now though.'

'I'm sorry, Josiah, I didn't know. Least it's sorted now.'

'I don't hate you, son. A man's got to look after his own, but that's gone now. I'll go and get a couple of brews and then you can tell me how you nearly killed someone.'

It was the nearest Dafydd would get to an apology, but now he understood the proud man a bit more. It was strange to be talking with Josiah about his past, as if they were old friends, but it served to release the tension between them.

'It's a hard time you've had, son,' Josiah said at the end. 'But maybe it's moved you to a better place. Look at it. A labourer at the mine, a labourer at the ropewalk and a labourer on the tramway. Now you have a good trade. You'll move up the links and you'll be on moving engines. Then? Who knows? A driver?'

'A driver! Every time something good happens, I go round the corner and there's a block on the next step. If not, I wouldn't be here – I'd be settled.'

'With your girl? Well, that's as maybe. You'll never know what would have happened if you'd stayed. I do know you learn quick and you think quick. You'll get on.'

'I never thought I'd hear you say anything like that, Josiah.'

Josiah sipped his brew and shrugged. 'In truth son, my boy is a good lad, but he's a plodder. Not half as sharp as you. He's fine for the yards here, as he's no ambition. Just as long as he earns enough for himself and that infernal Kitty girl. You're damn lucky she didn't get her hooks into you, that one.'

Dafydd coughed nervously. 'I'm in a spin now. There's you,

you're all right now, and Tom who looked after me here like a son, and then treats me like a lesser man.'

'Tom is a fine man and he thinks well of you. He'll drink with you and defend you to the last. But in his mind, folk should stay with their own. He'd love to see you married, but to a good fine Welsh girl. That's how he is. I daresay there's some in Wales would think the same of an Englishman.'

'I understand, Josiah. I'm grateful for that.'

Dafydd listened to the little engine, gently hissing by his side. She'd been through the mill and come back. Now she sported a full cab and looked every part the lady. He had to smile.

'I tell you what, though. I'm fond of this old girl here. She's been bashed about and not used well. She's been left to rot in my homeland and then plucked back out and fitted up. Now she's better than ever and ready to start afresh. I like her, for she reminds me of how things were and how things can be changed. She's still ready to stand up and come out fighting. She's doing what I should be doing.'

'No, she's doing what you *are* doing. She's a fighter, Bagnalls never produce owt less. And there's a few years in her yet. Go back to your girl and show her how much you've changed.'

Dafydd laughed, but felt a tingle down his back as he remembered Gwen's beautiful smile. In his mind, he was all but there at the station, bag in hand and one foot in the railway carriage, ready for the new beginning.

But would she still be waiting for him?

CHAPTER FOURTEEN

Reunion (1901)

*R*HEIDOL'S CAB, WITH its new matchwood back, was a welcome shelter from the heavy rain that hammered all around. He was happy that his driver had told him to build up a large fire. No more getting soaked gathering spare coal from the top of the engine's tanks, not since he had been allowed to stack coal on the lip of the cab back and inside. Instead, he could stand by and watch the poor trackmen toil in the torrent, thanking God his luck had changed.

One thing stung him, though: Gwen was nowhere to be found. Dafydd was back lodging with Mrs Owen in Trefechan, as was his driver. Gwen had left with no message there, and no word of where she had gone. If Mrs Owen did not know, Gwen might as well have gone to the moon. All the hopes raised by her letter had come to nothing.

Although his heart was heavy, he wanted to learn his trade and get a good job on one of the railways in the area. He had signed up for the line's construction; he could only hope it would help find him a home in the future. Now he stood in the cab, looking out at the streams of rainwater running past the track, it all felt so far from the future he had planned. He had been wet through getting to work and the warmth of the cab was complemented by the smell of damp clothes.

His driver was not helping his mood, so Dafydd just tried

to keep himself busy. The silence between them reminded him of awkward days with Josiah, and made Dafydd feel the absence of Gwen more. He now had too much time to dwell on it.

'They're too bloody slow!'

'Huh?' An unexpected comment from his driver, Smithson, caught Dafydd off guard.

'Track should be built halfway up the valley by now. They're far too slow.'

Smithson was right about the track, but Dafydd didn't mind. He wanted the job to last as long as it could, so he could stay in Aberystwyth. 'We had to wait for the bridge over the Rheidol to be built first,' he said. 'We're over past Capel Bangor now and then it'll be quick, you'll see.'

Silence again.

'Still, they say they're slower again up top,' Dafydd added.

Smithson growled. 'It's all right for you Welshies, jabbering away in your monkey language. I could do with being back in Plymouth.'

'It's not that bad. Don't you speak Cornish, anyway?' Dafydd knew he was being provocative, but it was a quick way of getting back for the monkey jibe. By rights he would have felled the man if he didn't want the job so much.

Smithson looked fit to burst, so Dafydd grabbed the oilcan and jumped out to check the axles. When he came back, the man had calmed down a bit.

'You got a girl in town, haven't you?'

'No.' Dafydd flushed underneath the layers of grime.

'Family?'

'Somewhere in the hills. I haven't seen them in years.'

He nodded slowly. 'Town's as much a stranger to you as me.'

'Tell me about it.' Then Dafydd stopped, for he didn't

want to see Smithson's black mood return. 'I'd better start paying more attention to chapel. It's the best way of finding who you need to ask permission from to speak to the town girls.'

'Chapel,' Smithson said, in a tone that ended the conversation.

It had made Dafydd think, though. What would keep him here now, once he was trained up? What would he do when the railway was done?

Dafydd was sent into town later on for supplies. He noticed a train had arrived at the Cambrian Railways station and he hurried to watch the bustle of people. He took great pains to keep out of the way, lest the porters chase him off at the behest of some rich passenger.

There was the usual mix of folk. Gentry trying to pretend they weren't too close to people. Children being fussed by nannies. Farm folk, old and young, on their way to market, a cheek full of baccy or a pipe in hand.

One woman in particular caught his eye. Her dark hair was pinned up under a hat. She moved with purpose towards the greengrocer that was set up by the entrance. Dafydd watched her as she checked the vegetables. She had a slim figure and was full of purpose. He liked the way she moved. Then realisation hit him like a flash of lightning and he was at her side.

'Fine cabbages on the shelves, madam.' Dafydd said.

She smiled tightly, but said nothing.

'Don't I know you?' Dafydd tried.

She frowned, and Dafydd grinned. He remembered her look just so, when she was chasing a wasp from the kitchen. Not one to kill God's creatures, even when one didn't want to leave.

'I know it's been a while, Sioned *bach*, but you could at least say hello.'

She finally saw through the railway grime. Her mouth formed a circle. She whispered his name with a sob of amazement in her voice. She dropped her bag and flung herself into his arms. A wave of relief swept through Dafydd and he clung to her, his only link to his past, until he remembered his dirty state and stood back, checking to see he hadn't put grease on her clothing.

'I'm so sorry, Mr Jones,' she said to the greengrocer. 'This is my brother – I haven't seen him in years.'

He had missed this so much – so different from the longing for Gwen, this unquestioned warmth of family. As a single tear fell down his cheek, he promised himself he'd go to chapel and give thanks.

'You must come and meet my husband, Donato,' said Sioned, as he helped her with her bags.

'Donato?'

'Yes, he's one of the Italian miners who worked down Frongoch mine. We've just rented a café in town. We started with sweets and all, but we found everyone just loves coffee these days. It's hard work, but better than the mine and its problems.'

She stopped and gave him a warm smile. There was sadness in her eyes, though.

'You been away so long, you wouldn't know half of it. Are you busy?'

Dafydd nodded. 'I got to go, Sioned. I said I'd only be five minutes.'

'Come quick, I'll show you where we live. Come straight after work and I'll have food ready and a warm bath out back.'

'I don't want to cause trouble.'

'Nonsense, Daf. You've been gone so long, I'm not letting you go again so easy. Besides… well, that's for telling later.'

He wanted to go right then, but there was an afternoon of work to get through first.

The day ended and Dafydd rushed to the small café in the centre of town. He remembered to look for the little notch in the line of houses, where the street briefly lost its straightness. Behind the door, the café was dark and closed. Shapes of chairs turned upside-down on tables could be seen through the frosted glass of the door. A sign would have made the place look proud, but for now there were just the simple white words on the front window:

Donato's Café
Coffees from around the world
Italian food

He could see movement inside and opened the door. A man in shirtsleeves and waistcoat was polishing a table carefully. He turned to look and Dafydd saw a slight man with dark hair, olive skin and a pencil-thin moustache, not Welsh-looking in the slightest, Dafydd decided. There was a quiet strength in the way Donato carried himself. Dafydd started to stammer a greeting, but the Italian was already over, grabbing his hand with a smile.

'Signor Daveed. You look like your father.'

His voice was low, almost a murmur, yet so calm.

'Thank you,' was all Dafydd could manage.

'Come in, go through. Sioned is cooking. She is so happy. I will join soon.'

Dafydd found his sister in the kitchen.

'There's a hot tub out back. You go there now. I'll wash

169

your clothes if you want, when I've done with this. Go on.'

Dafydd sat in the tin tub, feeling his joints come back to life. Soon he had settled into a doze, only woken by his sister's approach with a bucket of hot water.

'Here, I'll scrub your back, then take those towels and I'll be washing your clothes. We'll dry them by the fire and then you can sit and have food with us, all right?'

After a good soak, Dafydd sat by the fire, wrapped in towels, waiting for the fire to dry his clothes. Donato came back in.

'My boy sleeps now.'

'You put the baby to sleep?'

'Sure – we are only two parents and always work. Whoever can, must do.'

'Just the two of you at the café?'

'No, signore. We have a Harri, of course.'

Dafydd looked around the small living room, noting it was fairly clear and tidy. A picture stood in its frame above the fireplace, the faded brown photograph of a family, now heavily creased. Next to it was a small wooden bird, perched and ready to fly away. Only a lack of colouring stopped it from being real in Dafydd's mind.

'Is that a robin?' Dafydd asked.

'Yes,' Sioned's voice came from the kitchen. She came in to pick up the bird.

'Donato's first present to me. He couldn't make a love spoon.'

'Didn't need to,' Dafydd muttered, running his hand over the smooth carving. He raised an eyebrow at a scrubbing noise from outside.

'Clothes washing themselves, are they?'

Sioned laughed and shouted to the scullery. 'Harri, dry your hands and come in, girl.'

The girl came reluctantly, wiping her hands on her apron, looking ready to run back outside at the drop of a pin. When Dafydd cried with delight, she started in shock. Then a quick whimper and she was tearfully in his arms. His little sister, Angharad, one he had not known long before he had left. Now a girl not far off becoming a woman.

'All my girls!' Dafydd laughed. 'So where's Mam and Tad?'

'Perhaps we eat and talk,' Donato said and Dafydd sat in his towel, while Sioned found a blanket to put on his shoulders. She went off to bring the food and Donato filled plates for all.

'I have talk with the fishermen and we barter,' Donato said, as Dafydd looked at his plate.

They laughed a bit, and began to relax together.

'We used to live down that way, when we came here,' Sioned said.

'I was in Trefechan, still am.' Dafydd replied.

'We were in Rheidol Terrace.'

Dafydd winced: something wasn't being said. 'I heard them houses were grim. Must have been hard for you and Harri.'

'Harri wasn't there.'

'Look, what's been going on?'

'We don't know where Mam and Tad are,' Sioned said as gently as she could. 'Least we think we know, but we're not sure. Donato, *cariad*, Tell him what happened after he left.'

'Signor Daveed, perhaps easier I explain from the start. Your mine, Frongoch, was sold in 1899, to Belgian smelters. They think to control the market by owning from the ground to the ingot.'

'You should see what they done, Daf,' Sioned said. 'Huge new mill at the Wemyss end and a tramway running across Frongoch to get to it.'

'And water,' Angharad chipped in quietly. 'They use it to

make their electrics. Lights underground, they do say.'

Donato smiled sadly. 'They come here with big plans to make a big mine, but the old miners, they gone. Old mines gone long ago, so men leave. They take us men from Bergamo. We think we can go to England and send money back to feed our family. We come to Frongoch.'

'Seventy of them in a wooden shed,' said Sioned exchanging grim looks with her husband. 'But they made it a happy place.'

'Sì, we take the old chapel of the Cornish. We make a church and we sing. Then we find – the company, they cheat us. We pay for barracks, we pay for travel also. This not said before. We have to work extra, we who stayed. The Welsh, they not understand why and much trouble.'

'More like some caused trouble.' Sioned snapped.

'No!' Donato said firmly. 'The men, they welcome us. Your father – a good man. We have big party when we arrive, hundreds come.' He smiled to his wife. 'Is where we meet.'

'The Frongoch men were upset for the Italians working Saturday afternoons and Miners' Day.' Angharad said, eager to talk now. 'They were scared the company would make them do it and all. Dan Hughes told me,' she added to her sister's frown.

'You were young then, Harri.'

'Young, but not stupid.'

'You've grown up fast,' Dafydd said.

'Well, there was more trouble after that and we even had policemen staying on the mine.'

'What kind of trouble?'

'Strikes.'

'What? There's never been strikes at Frongoch!'

'Well, I seen at least four, Daf,' Sioned said. 'All for silly things. They pay the trammers to build a new dam then dock their pay when they go back underground. There was a rockfall one time and they suspended the Welsh miners working there but let the Italians carry on.'

'And there was a boy who was sacked for riding a tram without lights, but his butty was let off and him on the same tram!' Angharad broke in with excitement.

'All right,' Sioned said, her hand up to calm Harri. 'Then it got worse. Explosions started happening at night. At Cwmnewydion House, where the mine manager was living. Then the lander of the big wheel. Then by our house – someone didn't like me with Donato.'

It was all madness. It would never have happened in the land Dafydd had known. What made it worse was the quiet way that his sister told the tale.

'Who done it?'

'They don't know. Tad reckoned Dai Cochyn knew and when he found out, old Cochyn went and had a quiet word with them, like.'

'They found dynamite in my barracks,' Donato said softly.

Sioned snorted. 'Right, as if it's the only time someone's hung onto it. How do you think the locals fish? Light a stick, throw it in the lake and...' She blew out her cheeks. 'No-one ever bothered too much to count the sticks of dynamite. You just shoved what you didn't want in an open box by the shaft at end of shift. Anyone could use their stock – or take someone else's.'

'Your father, he say "enough", Daveed. He know the mine was poison now. He got us married and send us up here. Before it all died.'

'He sent you and all?' Dafydd asked Harri.

'Yes, I went to Aunt Myfanwy's in the hills. They were going to follow, Tad had had enough of the mine. Even David Treveglos had left and gone south to the coal.'

'Who's left?' Dafydd asked.

'The mine is closed,' Donato replied, standing to stretch his legs.

'Then what happened to Mam and Tad?'

'We don't know for sure,' Sioned said. 'We think they may be in Talybont. We just have no time to go, for the café takes all our time. We built it up from nothing, you know. Donato makes friends quickly and there's some good people in this town. They lent him money with no extra to pay. We just try and pay them back as quick as we can now. Coffee is fashionable, so we do all right, but we have to keep the place open as much as we can to do it.'

'Can't you send Harri? Just for the day?'

The room went very quiet.

'They say Talybont is a rough place and Harri's not good for going on her own at present.'

'Well, can't you get Idris and Myfanwy at the farm to…'

Dafydd wasn't allowed to finish. Harri got up and walked out. Sioned rushed to follow.

'What's happening?' Dafydd's voice was on the edge of panic.

Donato gave a grim smile.

'Harri, she run away from the farm. She have problem with a person. A man like her and she go before it get too bad.'

'Who was this man?'

'Signor Daveed, he not touch her. I think she leave before she find that she love. This a time ago and she not woman enough. There have been many changes, I think. The land is not how you remember. The mine, she change for ever now. Your family, they move. They have no reason to stay.'

'What of the house?'

Donato just shrugged.

'I take Sioned here, we find a place, Rheidol Terrace.' He caught the look and smiled. 'Perhaps it make me work hard. It not a good place, not a well place. I make friends, there are good people in this town. They help me buy what I need, soon we pay them back.'

The women came back into the room. Although they said nothing, Dafydd could see both had been crying. They sat down to eat – in silence, until Dafydd worked out something to break the unease. '*Duw*! It's enough to send me back to chapel, the way this has turned out. I should offer a prayer.'

'Well, you can come with us Sunday down the Catholic church,' said Sioned.

Dafydd frowned and Sioned gave him a gentle smile.

'What? I married in a Catholic church, where else would we go?'

Dafydd held up his hand. 'Don't read into things, girl. I've seen so many changes... Well, nothing surprises me no more.'

There was laughter and Sioned patted his arm. 'Well, you're here now and you've found your family.'

Dafydd had been on his own for so long he had forgotten the warmth of belonging. His voice wobbled as he spoke. 'And you got me and all. And I'll stand with you if anyone comes wanting trouble.' He coughed away the emotion. 'Right, what I think is, we write a letter. I don't know when I got time to get to Talybont, to be honest. Work is busy, they are behind with things but I'm sure I can find someone who can take it, and I know some in the village who could get it to Mam and Tad.'

'I can't write letters,' said Sioned sadly.

'And I can't think of the words, but together we can do it.'

'I can get some paper. Won't be proper, mind,' said Harri with excitement. 'And we got a pen.'

Her face flushed and she ran off. Sioned smiled and mouthed one word: *Diolch*. Harri soon returned and sat close to Dafydd, like an eager puppy, waiting for a stick.

'What about you then?' She asked, with a hint of mischief in the tone. 'You walking out with someone?'

Dafydd smiled back. 'None of your business, little mouse. Besides, I only just got back here.'

Her smile grew cheekily. 'But you haven't left some love behind or found some Aber girl at chapel yet?'

Dafydd shook his head and groped for a suitably cocky reply. Where to start, how to explain? Running from home, being found by Gwen; working on the Hafan and finding Gwen once more; Kitty's unwanted advances, Gwen's passionate promise; it all rushed through his mind. Always, it left one beacon of light. She'd saved him, she'd given him hope and there was now a huge gap in his life.

'She said she'd wait...' Dafydd whispered, then tears fell. Then he was sobbing into the warmth of Sioned's shoulder, as all the years of pain, frustration and loneliness flushed out of him. 'She promised, she did. She said she'd wait.'

At length, Dafydd settled down to tell them the whole story. He felt ashamed at his lack of fight. He felt bad about the times he could have come back to the family, but didn't. Yet all the time he spoke, little Harri sat on the floor next to him, holding his hand. Her touch was warm and Dafydd took strength from it. Her eyes, large with sympathy, did not judge him.

'I'm a fool, you know,' he said at last. 'I should have stayed and tried to find work here. I could have and all, I'm sure.'

'You can't change everything that's been,' Sioned replied after a silence that felt like hours. 'All you can ever do is take what's happened and let it make you stronger. '

'You can't just forgive like that. I done wrong!'

'Yes, I can, for you've been through the wars and come back. You're still here, fighting. You're still a good person.'

Dafydd stared into his tea, sensing Harri's eyes on him, waiting for him to accept his redemption. Sioned put her arm gently around his shoulders.

'Besides, I've had my brother delivered back to me, who I thought was forever lost. It's a moment I've prayed years for. I can forgive who I like.'

Dafydd squeezed Harri's shoulder, bathing in the warm smile he got in return.

'Since when did you get so wise, then?'

'Since I ran away with the man I love, and had to build my life up from nothing,' Sioned smiled.

'For the man you love,' Donato murmured, eyes glowing.

'So what now?' Dafydd asked, trying to smile away the pain.

'We find your Gwen,' said Harri with another squeeze of his hand.

'How can we do that?'

'I will ask, Signore Daveed. I have people who know me in the town. They will tell me, for sure.'

'But I don't want people to know...'

'Ah, I will be discreet. The girl, where she is, an old friend needs to speak, perhaps? Nothing more.'

'How will they know?'

'Oh, you silly boy,' Sioned chided, just like her mam. 'The daughter of Joshua, ropemaker of Trefechan. He who died after the fire that ruined his place. Tragic. She worked in a baker's, where the harbour folk went. Someone will know something. You can't move in this town without someone knowing something.'

'And then what?'

'Well, that's up to you, lovely boy, ent it? It's your story, only you can write it. First we have a letter to write. We need to use the back of a bill, but that's more the better. They'll know where to come. Then you get it to Talybont and we'll see if we can't have a really special time in town. As one family, like old times.'

Dafydd left late, his clothes cleaner and dry, ever conscious of the significant rustle of the letter in his pocket. His body wore less grime than it had for a while and a warm, warm feeling of love stayed in his heart. There was hope for the future now, that it would be all made right.

CHAPTER FIFTEEN

News

A FEW WEEKS on, little *Rheidol* was wriggling its way up the valley, pushing a line of trucks laden with material for the gangs to complete the track-laying. The railway had developed, so the gang working towards Aberystwyth from the Devils Bridge barracks was now close to joining their track with the gang who had started from Aberystwyth. As he watched the world go by from the footplate, Dafydd remained fond of *Rheidol*, although she grumbled a lot with heavy loads and was very contrary at speed.

However, he was concerned. It was 1902, and the company had been building for four years, but the railway was still incomplete. He was trying to avoid conversation with his moody companion, having already been scoffed at for asking why they weren't pulling the trucks instead of pushing them.

'Because we're going to the track-laying gangs and they don't like walking past the engine to get their rails,' Smithson had said, in his normal grumpy manner.

'Well, they'll walk past the guard's van.'

'We'll take him off when we get close to the top. Then run us to the end of the track. Honestly, you'd think you've never worked on a railway!'

The tart words were the only exchange between them as

they wobbled along towards Capel Bangor. Dafydd looked out of the wooden back of the cab and admired the long straight. The rails at Glanyrafon ran directly towards the town, as if they were going straight to the foot of Pen Dinas, which rose up, green and majestic. The stone cannon-like tribute to the Duke of Wellington stood like a beacon on top, waiting to lead him home, or so Dafydd dreamed.

With a sigh, he looked to the engine, as they rolled on higher into the trees.

They made good time, though Dafydd was forever checking the grate to make sure the fire was still there. The shaking of the little engine was now so bad that Smithson clung to the cab, holding onto the regulator as if it was a lifeline.

When they began to climb after Capel Bangor, *Rheidol* slowed. Gone were the long straights and plains around Lovesgrove in the mature valley. Now the woodland began to meet the railway. The track hugged the valley side and Dafydd watched the lines of new fencing. He needed to keep his wits about him, for there were many old paths that crossed the railway and the locals had not got used to the idea of railway line safety.

'Nantyronen,' Dafydd called out as they passed the clearing for the next halt. It stood out like a short plateau at the foot of the steep green valley side above. Smithson pulled the whistle chain. A farmer stopped his cart sharply at the sound. He glared in outrage at the train and Smithson's shouted response won him no friends.

Dafydd looked back and saw the railway had gone a half circle on its journey. The steep part of the climb had begun.

The next stop was the tiny station of Aberffrwd. Like all the others on the valley side, it had no platform, only a tin shack for a shelter and, important for the engine, a water tower. *Rheidol* was very thirsty. Dafydd quickly filled her as

Smithson went round with the oilcan for some quick top-ups. Dafydd knew the man still wasn't happy, from the way he returned to light his pipe.

'See you've given up the tidy beehive in the firebox,' he grunted.

'There's no point. I'm losing it all down the grate; the old girl's shaking up so much.'

'She'd not be so bad if they'd done the track proper.'

'You think?'

'Son, I've been doing this a while now.'

'I know,' Dafydd said. 'Not arguing, but…'

The Rheidol being a wide engine that had been made to fit on a narrower line had something to do with it, but Dafydd let the thought go unsaid. Smithson would not listen, he would always be one who must be right at all times.

They started off from the station, crossing a road track as it dipped down towards the river. The railway wound through a series of cuttings.

'You know they call that the Stag,' Dafydd called out pointing at a patch of grey in the woodland opposite. 'The mine was good for lead and they would bring the ore out and tip the waste down the valley. It closed, then they reopened to work the zinc. They made a tramway under the spoil and started tipping again. Only this time it's bigger. And nothing grows on lead spoil, so you're left with the upper heap as a head and the rest forming a body and two legs below. The shafts at the very top, where they tipped the ore out were straight down to make a line like antlers – just like a stag.'

Smithson stared straight ahead. Dafydd sighed. The man had no interest in his land.

The valley got steeper as they passed the Rheidol's small lead mines. Dafydd wondered how they had managed to stay open. When he had worked at Frongoch, the market was already hard and prices low. As they rounded a sharp curve, he caught sight of a man on one of the spoil heaps. He wore a jacket as grey as the rock he was tipping out of a tram. Once, Dafydd had so wanted to be like that man. Now he was happy to be anywhere but at a mine.

The track ran on a narrow ledge that the gangs had gouged into the side of the rock. Dafydd was proud to see how far they had progressed, especially when he looked at the steep drop to the river below. *Rheidol*'s wheels began to squeal in complaint as they edged around a tight curve, with check rails keeping the wheels in place. The bend was such that Dafydd could wave to the guard without leaving the cab. The trucks screamed as they were pushed ever upwards.

Then they reached their stop, a small station on the mountainside. The nearest housing was deep in the valley below. Ahead, the line continued, notched into the craggy rock face. The valley was now deep and steep-sided. The view made Dafydd gasp. He jumped off the footplate to check the wagons. At least two of them were riding rough. He needed to lengthen the coupling.

'Dafydd Thomas!' A voice sounded out of the blue. 'What the 'ell you doing 'ere, then?'

A ganger was striding towards him, pick in hand. A brown, toothy grin inside a tangled black beard – Dafydd knew at once who it was, for all that the man had changed in the two years since they'd worked together.

'Huw! What the 'ell are *you* doing here?' Dafydd said, before he was locked in a hug and had his back slapped until he wheezed.

'What happened to the Elan dams?' Dafydd managed to say.

'Gone, done. They needed men here to finish the job, so I came back. Had to really – Cardi boy and all that.'

'John and Jim?'

'Gone back to England. Leastways that's the mind they had when I left. Jim was talking of South America, but I thought that was the ale talking.'

'Good to see you, *bach*. You're looking big and strong these days.' Dafydd said, buoyed by the sight of his friend, after the tension of working with the tetchy Smithson.

'And you're looking smart, like you always was. You the driver now?'

Dafydd hid a grin, as he spied Smithson's expression. 'No, fireman just now. Only for the building contract.'

'Aren't we all? You got that girl yet? All right, you can tell me later, I'm lodging in the town as it is. Got time to share a tea with me, Daf?'

Smithson shrugged, and so Dafydd followed his friend to a brazier with his tin cup.

'Well,' said Huw, 'we were hoping for a lift up the valley, like. On the trucks. Do you think he will mind?'

Dafydd looked at Smithson, who was slowly following. 'Not if you find another cup and I talk sweet to him.'

They sat and chatted in the tool hut. The brazier outside was busy brewing for other arrivals. Dafydd thought Huw tougher and perhaps a bit rougher at the edges. A good man to have with you, but a bad enemy. Dafydd was glad he had managed to befriend him when he was younger. Huw's gang drifted over, as did the guard, Evans.

'It was tough in the Elan,' Huw was saying. 'You had to have your wits about you. The English boys looked after me and in the end I learned to do it for myself.'

'I heard it was lawless down there,' Smithson said, and some of the track gang laughed.

'You always needed to watch your back,' said Huw. 'There was drinking, disease, whores – and building those ruddy dams. Coming back here is peaceful by comparison; though Devils Bridge has got the reputation. Old Lincolnshire Jim done that a while back. Had a few and fell off the edge up top on his way home, silly bugger.'

'Silly *dead* bugger,' said another, to more laughter.

'Your tracks should be tighter,' Evans blurted out, and the group went quiet. 'Well, it's not a smooth run up the valley,' he added.

'*Rheidol*'s all over the place,' agreed Smithson. 'I never had one so flighty. Poor boy here can't fire the engine for the coal dropping through the grate.'

'And very welcome it is too. We need the coal for our brazier,' Huw said, to roars of laughter.

Dafydd noted how Huw had lightened the mood. His gang was kept relaxed, in spite of the train crew's complaints.

'Don't you boys care about your work?' Smithson persisted. 'You've not enough sleepers, for starters.'

Dafydd began looking for a weapon to defend his driver with. He caught Huw's eye. His friend shrugged and raised his hands, as others began to mutter.

'We do what we're told to do,' said Huw. 'We get told to miss every other sleeper and that's what we do. We're not stupid; sleepers are like anchors, they stop the track moving along with you. I know that, gaffer knows that, surveyor knows that, and all. But if them Pethicks say do it for less, we do what we're told.' He looked at Dafydd and winked. 'Am I right, Lucky Jim?'

'You're not wrong, Pendle John,' Dafydd replied and they smiled at everyone else's ignorance to their joke.

'Sleepers are bad, ballast is poor and lumpy as shit and the railway's been had over the rails,' said a ganger. 'Rail's half as heavy as it should be, brittle as anything. They'll need us to fix this line for years afterwards.'

'So you see, Mr Driver,' Huw said. 'We know how bad it is and if we're given the tools, we're more than happy to oblige. But we're not, so all I say is this. Watch your road.'

Smithson got up and sighed. 'Thank you for the drink, lads.' He walked off.

'He's all right really,' Dafydd said. 'Just wants to be home in Plymouth.'

'Well, he's the wiser now. Listen, if you feel a rough ride, just tell us where and we'll sort the road out. Though some of the old boys are saying it'll never be passed like this. Tell you what, I even suggested we all went to Talybont and lifted the track from there!'

Dafydd sat up. 'You still go up Talybont? I think my family moved over by there and I got to get a message to them. Know any way I can do that?'

'Give it to me, Daf. I'll get it to them and no mistake.'

Dafydd handed him the letter that had been burning a hole in his pocket. It would soon be on its way. He could almost taste his Mam's bread in his mouth.

'You're right on the track, Huw. This old girl was never this bad on the tramway.'

'That's *Talybont*? Well I never, seems things always to come back to you, you lucky bugger. We're hoping to stay on as the track gang after this is open, just like on the P & H. Could put in a word for you?'

'Thanks,' said Dafydd, 'but not for the track, mind. I think I've had my fill of that. Anything but the track! I'll share a drink with you at some time, Huw. We'll be the best-behaved navvies in town!'

Huw laughed once more. 'We will at that. Look after yourself and we'll talk again.'

Dafydd got back in the cab, and found Smithson waiting to speak to him. 'I don't mean to be hard on your friend,' he said, 'I think he was right. Look at the track! It's as bad as he said. The rails are brittle, sleepers green with moss, and ballast like a sprinkle of pebbles on a sandy beach. Are they trying to get things done on the cheap?

'Well, not much I can do. Just hope I'm gone before a rail bows out or snaps and sends a train down the valley.'

A few weeks later, the line was connected. With navvies, the event could have led to either a fight or a drinking party. Dafydd decided the good folk of the valley would probably have preferred the former. They locked up their daughters, dreading the temptations of the working man.

The line further up was steepest. The rock face was close to the trains on some curves, slowing them right down. The navvies were right about the way the line had been built. Work pushed on regardless, directors complaining about delays and contractors about costs.

'They're blaming this old girl now,' Smithson told Dafydd, slowing the engine as they rode up the valley in the morning sun. 'She don't pull enough wagons, they say. Well, that's as maybe, but they chose her. Their fault, their problem.'

'This is Rhiwfron station,' said Dafydd, 'Why are we stopping here, and not at Devils Bridge?'

'There's a gang here – your friend is with them. He's flagging us down. The damn track's bending, what with the ballast being too thin to pack the sleepers tight.'

Dafydd ran over to find Huw. 'Dafydd! I found them!'

'What?'

'Your parents! I found them over in Talybont. Your tad works in a mine in the hills. Your mam is in one of them woollen mills. I got your letter passed to her.'

The relief was overwhelming, Even the normally taciturn

Smithson clapped Dafydd on the back. Dafydd's mind raced. Could he get over there on a Sunday? Everyone was so worried about delays to the line building, could he be asked to work instead? Even on a Sunday?

'Another thing,' said Huw. 'The boy I met who told me said your uncle Idris – remember him? He came to the tramway that time – anyway, he was keen to see you.'

Dafydd wasn't so sure he wanted to meet Idris – and to find out who had been worrying his sister Harri.

Dafydd's hopes of a visit weren't easy to realise. His sister must needs go to church on a Sunday. That weekend, he waited outside the Catholic Church while they had a few words with friends, then walked back to the café. It was getting late by then. When they arrived, someone had smeared mud on the café door.

'Now who done that?' Dafydd growled.

'Wait! Words, it is,' Harri exclaimed. 'It says *iawn.*'

Then they all saw it.

Popeth yn iawn, Mam a Thad
(All is well, Mam and Tad.)

Sioned disappeared, and returned quickly with a smile on her face. 'The neighbours say they saw them. Reckon they went to the beach.'

'Let's go!' Harri shouted.

'Wait!' Dafydd shouted back. 'We'll lose them in the Sunday crowds. Someone must stay in case they come here.'

'I will do so,' said Donato.

'Right,' said Dafydd. 'Sioned, go to the pier and back, Harri, towards the cliffs. I'll go on the beach and we'll come back to meet by the bandstand.'

The day was hot and sunny and the promenade crowded. People were making the most of the weather. A tramway stretched across the strand, for moving rock from Craig Lais to build a new promenade around the college and castle. Strollers were bunched up in the remaining space. Dafydd jinked and dodged, trying to catch a glimpse of his mam's long curly black hair or his tad's bushy grey moustache in the throng.

Everyone looked the same to Dafydd. All men wore caps and moustaches. All women were in dark clothes and bonnets. He moved onto the beach and started scanning the groups on the gritty sand, and those baring their ankles to the ravages of the cold sea.

He headed for the pier, but soon realised his parents would not be there. They would not have climbed over the groynes on the beach, and probably wouldn't be queuing for pleasure boats. He made for the cliffs. His mam and tad were not to be found. Sioned and Harri had similar tales to tell when they met.

'What now?' Sioned asked.

Dafydd looked up. Midday sun warmed his face. '*Iesu Grist*! What if they went straight back to the station? We're probably too late for the train, Sioned.'

They tore off down the road. Their parents were not there, nor were they on the last train of the day that followed. Downhearted, Dafydd followed his sisters back to the café.

'We'll go next Sunday,' said Dafydd into the despondent silence.

Dafydd was keeping his counsel as *Rheidol* went up the valley. Although the line was complete, there was still plenty to do as they slipped and bucked to the top. They ran engine first, which allowed Dafydd a good view of the upper section. The engine lurched around the sharp bends in the cuttings, as if she wanted to kiss the rock.

The last stretch was a mass of twists and turns, some of which gave Dafydd a frightening view straight down the valley side. Green layers of grass and trees fell away beneath him, grey and brown in places with heaps of mine waste. Rhiwfron now had an aerial ropeway set up to a hopper on a siding.

'Could we sell tourists rides in the buckets down to Cwm Rheidol mine?' he asked Smithson.

No reply. Smithson was in another mood. Pethicks were being nagged over delays in finishing the line and Smithson had said he felt he was the scapegoat – they were still blaming *Rheidol*'s pulling power.

The rocky ledge became a horseshoe bend that cut through an old mine then straightened up and bore them past the tree line and into a long cutting, then past the navvy barracks above and the mill below. Curving again, they lurched towards the final cutting, bursting through the gap to the station. Dafydd had been up a few times in that week alone. The cutting was the point *Rheidol* would start to nod like a pigeon. Today, he was watching the sheer rock sides go past when *Rheidol* gave a sudden jolt that made him hit his head. Smithson shouted out and made a grab for him, but he collapsed to the floor. White spots appeared in front of his eyes as he sat up. His legs buckled when he tried to stand.

'Come on, we'll sit you down and see to that head.'

To Dafydd, the driver's voice sounded far away. He put his hand to his face and stared at the blood on his fingers.

'Your friend is here. Hey!' Smithson shouted, and Huw's voice joined the echoes around him.

'What on earth were you doing, Dafydd? Kissing your damned engine or something?'

'Well, she gave me a smack back.'

'The wound's not deep; head cuts bleed forever.'

'Best we clean it and have you lying down for a while.'

'Can you cope without him?'

'Yes,' Smithson replied. 'For my poor girl's been hurt bad this time.'

'Did he just speak nice of my *Rheidol*?' Dafydd asked Huw.

'Yes, he must have had a blow to the head and all. I'm going to have you rest in the station, and stay away from work tomorrow.'

'What you saying? I'll be all right after a sit down and a mug of tea. I'll not be docked wages for this.'

'You won't. We've heard talk that the company will be giving you another engine. One of the new ones, stronger. Pulls more than four trucks, they say.'

'How do you know this?'

'Because everyone talks in front of navvies, like we're not there. That new engine won't be here for a few days and your one's in need of repair. Couldn't be better. It gives you a day off and me time to get you up to Talybont to your family.'

'We had a message, they're all right,' Dafydd said, feeling very sleepy.

'Fine. We can have tea with them and tell your sisters all about it.'

There was something in his voice that Dafydd couldn't place, but he was losing focus again, and his head hurt. He wanted to sleep. Next thing he knew, Huw was rousing him.

'Dafydd, it's the end of the day and you need to get home.'

'*Rheidol*? Is she all right?'

Huw snorted. 'If you could be as mindful of your women as you are of that pile of junk, you'd be a very happy man for life. Can you get up? Slowly now, or the blood'll rush from your head.'

'How do you get to learning all this doctoring, Huw?'

'I learnt a lot at Elan, I can tell you. More than enough. Now, your engine's back on the rails.' Seeing Dafydd's expression, he explained. 'The track flexed and she fell off it. You slept through the resetting…'

'Your bloody bad work again,' Dafydd grumbled, rubbing his head. He felt really woolly.

'Yes, you're right, but until we get them to stop penny-pinching and blaming everyone else, we're stuck with our bloody bad work.'

Huw helped Dafydd walk to the engine, which was hissing away with steam in the evening light. Smithson was busy on the plate. He'd stocked up with coal and was using the shovel to good effect in the firebox. Dafydd felt weak at the thought of working back down the line and Smithson must have seen it.

'You're still looking pale, lad. I'll handle it all downhill, you just sit in the corner.'

'You can't do that and watch the road. You'll need to look out and tend the fire – little and often, remember. Huw's handled a shovel before. He used to work with me on the Plynlimon and Hafan, didn't he?'

Huw's face was a picture and Dafydd shrugged.

'I'll keep an eye on him.'

'Well, if you say so.' Smithson didn't seem to really believe Dafydd, but went along with it.

Huw looped a rope around Dafydd's waist.

'You'll be sitting out of harm's way. I'm not having you falling off when no-one's looking. There'll be no-one to find you if you do, as all my buddies will be in drinking dens that make the Black Lion look like a gentleman's club.'

The engine set off and they ambled down to Aberystwyth. Smithson took it easy and Dafydd weakly waved his hands when he wanted coal in, or the door shut or open. He squinted up to watch the pressure and water gauges. His head felt leaden as he rested it on the cab side.

When they arrived, Smithson lowered *Rheidol*'s fire and promised to check her over the following morning. It seemed from talk around them that they were indeed going to borrow one of the new engines, so there was no working until it arrived.

'That's Pethicks' excuse, until they find another,' Smithson snapped with contempt.

'Don't take it so personal,' Dafydd told him, sending Smithson off into another fit of cursing.

'Course it's personal. It's a comment on my performance. Besides, you grow to like the old girl. She's rough and ready, but still keeps coming back for more. I'll not need you tomorrow, Dafydd. If we're waiting for the new engine, you can rest your head over the weekend. I'll not tell and they can pay you for it.'

'He's playing the father now,' said Huw as they left the yard. 'Make the most of it.'

Dafydd staggered back to the café, where Sioned got out a needle and thread and set about closing the head wound.

'What's Huw been using to clean this? An oily rag? Don't they know about gangrene? Honestly, you men are just plain hopeless!'

Dafydd stayed over at the café, as Sioned said she wanted to keep an eye on him. The morning after, she had him roused and ready for the early Sunday train out of Aberystwyth.

Huw met him at the station and they were soon sitting in the carriage. Huw held his pipe in hand, staring out of the window. Just like old times, as he was keen to point out.

'We've come a long way, you and I,' he said as the train clattered its way to Llanfihangel. 'I'm certainly not the scared young buck I was. But you are one of the few people I trust, Dafydd *bach*. I hope you feel the same way?'

'Yes, we're friends now and always have been. Apart from the first time we met, of course.'

Huw chuckled and sighed, puffing his pipe for a while before looking Dafydd in the eye. 'In that case, I have something to say and you have to trust me as to why I kept it from you.'

They got off the train at Talybont, and Huw led Dafydd not to a house, but to a graveyard.

CHAPTER SIXTEEN

Rescue

DAFYDD SAT ON the grass next to the new grave. Hunched up, hugging his knees for warmth, he gazed out at a beautiful view. The hill dropped sharply to marshland below. Dafydd looked down on the distant brown morass. Far off, the village of Borth huddled on a strand of shingle between the marsh and the sparkling blue sea. To the north lay the Dyfi estuary and the brooding hills of Meirionydd. The land of his ancestors lay beyond, under a cloudless sky promising warmth to come.

'The gravestone will be provided in the week,' Huw said quietly. 'Not too large, but not too small neither. Organised by one of the men.'

'It's beautiful,' Dafydd muttered.

'Why a church cemetery?' Huw asked.

'They were married in church.'

'Oh, I suppose,' Huw mumbled. Then he went on, 'Their lodgings was all paid up. The man at the mine saw to it. I think they all chipped in. We can talk to him on the way to Idris's farm.'

'There's a few things I want to say to Idris.'

'There's a few he wants to say back, I'm sure. Right fond of your tad, that one.'

Dafydd grunted. 'Well, there's nothing to keep me in

Talybont, then. We may as well start up to the tramway now.'

'All right, I'll be up top when you're ready.'

Huw walked back up the hill as Dafydd put his hand on the grave and closed his eyes. The soil felt warm, and he couldn't stop his tears.

'Mam, if I could find one as bright and alive as you, I'd be in heaven down here. I wish we'd been faster, I wish...' There it was. All he could do was promise, 'I'll do my best. I'll look after the girls. Sioned's already found a fine boy, but you'll know that already. I'll keep them safe, I'll find... If Gwen's the one, I'll find her and you'll be happy, 'cos I'll do you proud, Mam. Sleep easy, for I'm not running away no more.'

Dafydd wiped his eyes and moved back up to the road. Huw suggested they took in the Black on the way for a spirit to dull the pain. Dafydd was tempted, but shook his head.

'So why didn't you tell me before?' he asked Huw, who puffed away at his pipe.

'About your mam? I didn't know until it was too late. Then what was the point in telling you something you couldn't fix?'

'Well, at least this is something I can.'

They walked up the valley in silence. The sight of his mother's grave made him sad for all the time he'd been away. He thought of her black curly hair, her laugh like bells and her smile so loving and warm. He wiped his eyes as they reached the tramway. 'Look how good this track is against that on the Rheidol,' said Huw. 'I've a mind to take it all up and move it over to Devils Bridge.'

Dafydd said nothing. He was busy wondering why he'd so rarely talked to his father.

'Look at that!' Huw exclaimed as they came into sight of a

new building. 'Bwlch Glas mine has got bigger. They've only gone and built a lead mine over our old line.'

'Bit too late now,' Dafydd said quietly, looking at the buildings of corrugated iron, standing out of the valley side.

'Why did they bother building a tramway here?' Huw asked. 'Where were the passengers ever going to come from?'

'An Englishman came gambling. He looked at the mines and the quarry and dreamt of the dams of Elan to be built, the promenade in town and all. He thought if he got the contract to supply stone, it would be the new Klondike. The one them newspapers go on about all the time.'

'Don't know much about newspapers,' Huw replied. 'But the mines are dying in most places. Come too late, all them ideas. We'll be up Idris' farm soon enough. It's not far once we're up the incline.'

'I owe you a lot, Huw.'

'You owe me nothing at all, Dafydd *bach*. Just wish I could have brought better news. You showed me once how to be more than a man with a shovel. I may still be a labourer, but I've done more and I know I can do more again. I've learnt a hell of a lot these last few years. Most of it good, some not so. I learnt how to stay out of trouble and what to do if you can't. But I also learnt about friends and you've been a good one to me, Dafydd. Hey, remember the time you ran off my cousin down by the river in Aber? Tell you what, if I saw him today, I'd knock him halfway across the Rheidol.'

Huw talked all the way to the mine and past, Dafydd giving occasional replies. Huw was stronger in mind and body than the boy Dafydd remembered. He was growing to be a useful ally. As they approached the end of the valley, Dafydd saw the large semi-circular silhouette of the old mine waterwheel which signified the bottom of the incline. It filled him with conviction. Now was the time to start giving back to his father, at least for his mother's sake.

The two struggled up the incline and past the quarry until the waterwheels of a little mine came into view on the hillside. Bryn-yr-Afr, the hill of goats.

The sight of the wheels brought back Dafydd's memories of his family working in Frongoch. His mood became worse as they made for the mine office. After a few words with the manager, Huw and Dafydd elected to split up. Huw went off to fetch Idris from his farm, whilst Dafydd made for the mine barracks in a small valley behind the spoil heaps.

His guide was a miner from Taliesin village, slightly built but wiry with it, like many miners Dafydd remembered. The gap in his front teeth was so large that they called him Twm-y-Twll. Dafydd started off thinking Twm was annoying with his ready laugh, but soon he was glad of the man's good humour. His father had gained a valuable friend who had shown much concern and compassion.

'Your father's not been over here that long, but I tell you what, he knows his stuff.' Twm said, as they walked from the mine. 'Come up with some ideas, he has. Some of the boys didn't like it, but that's always the way. Some can't change and are scared of it.'

'How is he?'

Twm stopped and scratched his head below his cap. 'I'll be honest, Dafydd. He's weak. When your Mam died, he couldn't face living in the village. Just packed and left. I tried to get him set up as the housekeeper in the barracks, so at least he would have work and the boys would chip in for him for food and the like.'

Dafydd looked blankly back at that, so Twm continued.

'Well, up here it's a long way to go back home every night

to Talybont and Taliesin – after a long day of digging and what have you. Many stay in the barracks through the week and go back Saturday afternoon, coming up again Monday morning, like. Sometimes them that can't work well no more, they get paid a bit by the boys to keep the place tidy and cook the food and the like. Them that's got nowhere to go back to.'

He coughed.

'I mean, your tad was a good miner, don't get me wrong. But he was getting on and seeing as he wasn't wanting to go near Talybont no more, I thought he'd be happier at the barracks. Problem was, he got the fever. I think it's what saw your mam off, to be honest.'

'Is he dying?'

'I'm no doctor, *bach*, but I'd say if we don't get him from the barracks, we'll be burying him next to your mother soon enough. I try and care for him when I can, but I got family in Taliesin and I'm working.'

'I understand and I'm grateful and all.'

'He's my butty, what else would I do? He's been more than all right to me, I just want to give him something back. But you got to take him away where there's those that can care for him or he's dead, I'm thinking.'

'My uncle's coming with a cart.'

'The farmer? Good one, he is.'

Dafydd bit back a reply, remembering Harri's look when he had first met her. She was like a frightened rabbit every time the name of the farm was brought up.

'Better road to Ponterwyd,' Twm said. 'Maybe you should take him that way.'

'But I need him in Aberystwyth.'

'Shame the tramway's not running no more,' said Twm and the clouds cleared in front of Dafydd's face.

'You are a bloody genius!' he shouted. Twm looked on bemused at the outburst.

'Don't know about that. If I was a bloody genius, I wouldn't be digging rock in these hills.'

The barracks was warm inside, the embers of a fire still giving a glow to the room. The air was stale, or perhaps Dafydd had lived too long in places where clothes were scrubbed clean. They walked through a grey cloud of smoke to the end bed, closest to the fire.

The beds were big enough for two people. Dafydd remembered his father saying that's how things were in these places. Two to a bed and with regular shifts, the ones returning would wake up those in the bed and take their place under the dirty sheets. Twm pulled some chairs up to the bed and Dafydd finally looked at his father.

The man lay without moving and fear gripped Dafydd. Were they already too late? His tad seemed to have shrunk, and was greyer than Dafydd remembered. The fever laid a speckled sweat on his brow. Dafydd sought, and found, a slight rise and fall of the chest – and a faint whistling which, in Dafydd's troubled mind, sounded like last breaths.

'*Iesu Grist*!' he muttered.

His tad's eyes opened at the sound of his voice. They stared at each other, Dafydd thinking of all the things he'd never said and done.

His father croaked a word. It sounded like "Tad".

'He's delirious,' said Twm. 'Been like this for a day or so.'

'Tad?' His father's eyes narrowed.

'Mam always said I looked like his father, my tad-cu.' Dafydd said.

'You're not my father.'

Dafydd smiled in relief. 'No, I'm your son. Come back to take you away from this bloody mine and back to the girls.'

His father sighed. 'About bloody time,' he whispered and then was lost once more to his dreams.

Huw turned up with Idris and the cart soon after. Dafydd's back stiffened at the thought of meeting the man he felt was responsible for Harri's flight. Part of him still couldn't believe this kind, strong father was capable of it, but if it came to a fight that day, Dafydd was more than ready.

'Go stay with Tad,' Dafydd said to Huw, as Idris jumped off his cart. 'I need to have a word with my uncle.'

'Dafydd!' Idris cried, clapping his shoulder. 'It's good to see you. Let's get your tad loaded up and back to the farm.'

'I'd rather not,' Dafydd said.

'We got to get him somewhere,' Huw said. 'Whilst we work out how to get him back to Aber.'

Dafydd looked at the three men standing around him, waiting for what he would do next. He wasn't even sure himself what that would be. 'I want to talk about Harri,' Dafydd said finally.

'So do I, Dafydd,' Idris replied. 'But we need to sort Owain out. We can talk on the cart now.'

Grudgingly, Dafydd agreed and they loaded his father up, wrapping him in blankets. Dafydd shook Twm by the hand as they prepared to leave. 'Twm, you are nothing short of a hero in my book for what you done for Tad.'

'He's a good man,' said Twm. 'And well, he was all right to me. Most around here see me as a bit of a joke.'

'If I get to hear any more of that, there'll be trouble,' Dafydd growled and got a toothy smile in response.

'That's what your tad said! Go easy now.'

Dafydd loaded his father up then sat with Idris as he drove

the cart. He seemed pleasant enough, but Dafydd couldn't help feeling wary.

'We'll take him back to the farm. It will be better for him away from that stuffy place. Fresh air and fresh food.'

'It's the doctor he's needing,' Dafydd said, with a sharp note in his voice.

'So what do you suggest?'

'Stop the cart!'

'Careful, Daf,' Huw cautioned. Idris pulled back the reins and looked quizzically at Dafydd.

'I want to know about Harri,' Dafydd said.

'Harri was like a daughter to me,' said Idris with a pained look. 'She came to us and just fell in love with the place, and we loved her for it.'

'So why did she run?'

He sighed. 'It's all my fault.'

Dafydd tensed, ready to hit him there and then.

'I should have seen what was happening. I was blind to it.'

'I think you better step down.'

He nodded. 'I deserve a beating, for I was quite blind.'

'Do you know what you done?'

'Yes, I've been quite foolish.'

'You've ruined her!'

'Yes, if I could have stopped him. Said something – I don't know...'

'You... what?'

'Hywel, my brother.'

Dafydd had to stop and catch his breath.

'Dafydd,' Huw's voice was urgent. 'Your father is sick, everything else can wait.'

'Yes...' Dafydd felt really faint as he got back on the cart. He didn't speak again until they reached the farm. His father was put straight in bed and Dafydd went outside with Idris to help put the cart away.

'I'm sorry, Idris. I'm sorry for what I thought.'

'I can see how it looked,' Idris said with a sad smile. 'My brother was a quiet one, bit stuck in his ways. He never really mixed, and Harri was kind to him. She made him a friend. Shy boy he was, though, and he took it to heart. Then I suppose he started thinking of doing things that chapel girls don't.'

'Where is he now?'

'Long gone. Harri ran and he knew he'd done wrong. He took off without a word also.'

'Is he chasing her?'

'I have heard he was seen over Llanidloes way, so no.'

'How do you know?'

Idris sighed and tapped his chest. 'In there. I saw his face when he knew what he'd done.'

'Can you look for him?'

'Dafydd, I have a farm that don't run itself and I'm already a man down for it. You tell me Harri is safe and I'm so happy, I could cry. I'm guilty as hell already, but if he's gone, where to? Cardiff? If I'm away, who's going to bring in the harvest and feed the family? This farm needs work, a lot of it, just to keep going.'

He looked around his farm as if talking of an errant well-loved child. 'This is a harsh land here. I'm sorry if that's not what you want to hear. I keep asking the questions – I have friends who go to markets and they ask. I don't think Hywel would come back close to here for the shame.'

'All right, Idris. I'm sorry too. It's your family scratching over what's left. I need you now though, to get Tad back to town.'

'I'll take him to Aber.'

'No, Devil's Bridge. I'll get him on our train.'

'Are you sure they won't be giving you the sack at the end of the journey?' Huw asked.

'No, I'm not, but that doesn't matter.' Dafydd snapped. 'My whole life I've spent running from problems, but that's stopping now. My mam's in the ground and my tad is close to following her. I can't help her, but by God, I'll help him and if they want to turn me out for it, I'll walk from their bloody job with my head held high.'

There was a long pause and then Huw nodded. 'You'll need some help.'

'This is my look-out.'

'You'll need help,' Huw repeated firmly.

Dafydd was surprised Huw and he had got back to Aberystwyth for the morning after. Idris had driven them back to the Hafan quarry, which had helped, By the time they arrived in Llanfihangel, they had lost any hope of catching the last Sunday train. They had been lucky, a travelling trader allowed them a lift on his cart. Dafydd had managed little, if any, sleep with his mind racing with the plan to get Tad back to Aber. He was roused early, as always, by a judgmental Mrs Owen, and went off to fire the engine. He still wondered how much to tell Smithson and the guard, Evans.

Smithson was in no mood for talking, so Dafydd left him to it. He just made sure his tin mug was full of hot tea to keep him awake as he shovelled. Dafydd considered leaving his driver half asleep, but they had seen too many broken rails, and there was a new engine to take out today. He therefore made an extra mug for Smithson, received with a curt nod.

Rheidol was under a canvas, in need of a new axle, so he could admire first-hand one of the railway company's new tank engines. It seemed a stocky beast to Dafydd. The water tanks dwarfed the boiler. He missed *Rheidol*, but the new one was a powerful workhorse and he was soon dreaming of what she'd be like with a rake of coaches.

He delayed his appeal to Smithson until they were ready to leave. 'I've got to bring my father back on the train today,' he shouted, above the din of rising steam.

Smithson shook his head. 'No passengers, we're not a bloody service.'

Dafydd knew Smithson would not be budging, and his heart was in his mouth all the way up the valley, because Dafydd was not budging either.

He realised he'd been over-coaling the engine at one point, as if burying his nerves in hard work. The engine attacked the hill bravely, and Dafydd could see she did not need much coaxing in comparison to his little *Rheidol*. Even so, he hung on to his loyalty for her.

The trucks were loaded up with rubble and made their way back down the valley. Dafydd couldn't help noticing how smooth the journey was. Even so, it seemed an age as they unloaded the spoil. Would they get the empties back up to Devils Bridge to meet Idris? A few more trainloads were filled and taken up the line, the nerves in Dafydd's stomach seeming to knot tighter with each one. Finally, the last train of the day reached Devil's Bridge, bursting through the cutting into the station yard. Dafydd could see Idris on his cart in the trees, on the road below the station yard.

Smithson brought the train into the loop and Dafydd took the oilcan round the engine as the trucks were loaded. He spilt a lot. He could feel Smithson's eyes on his back the whole time. He wished the day could start again and he could ask his favour differently. They were ready to leave when Huw ambled up, pickaxe in hand.

'Get by the guard's van. We're going to have to be quick.'

Dafydd rushed after him. 'What's going on?'

'You'll see.'

There came a shout from the yard, then a few raised voices. Dafydd saw a lot of dust and a few fists flying.

'Bloody gangs fighting,' shouted Smithson, jumping down from the cab. The guard stood in the doorway of his van watching. Dafydd, feeling guilty as hell, realised the man would have to be told.

'What you up to, Dafydd?'

'My father's ill. He might be dying. I want to get him down the valley to Aber, so my sisters can nurse him. Please don't tell, I'll put him in a truck and cover him so Smithson don't see.'

The guard looked Dafydd long and hard and then shook his head. 'Get him into my van. He'll be safer there.'

Dafydd didn't need to be asked twice. He waved Idris into the yard. Dafydd's father lay in the back, wrapped in a blanket like a shroud. Huw and Dafydd bundled him in the guard's van while Idris looked on.

'Good luck, Dafydd. Send word if you can.'

Then the cart was away down the road and someone gave a shrill whistle. Like magic, the fight stopped, leaving the foremen standing with their mouths open trying to fathom what had taken place. As diversions went, Dafydd thought, that was probably one of the slickest.

The guard chuckled. 'You can see their gaffer still trying to work out who started it. Now, I'll keep an eye on the old boy; just make sure Smithson gives us a smooth ride.'

They set off back down to Aberystwyth, the gangers travelling in the empty trucks, the new engine rattling along happily as ever, and Dafydd gazing anxiously back down to the van.

Then with a shudder, they came to a stop. A wheel had derailed. Thankfully it was the front wheels of the engine – the pony, bouncing along the sleepers – not the brake van or a truck. Small derailments had become such regular occurrences by now that Smithson was waiting for it to happen and was quick to slam on the brakes. The guard did the same in the van, and nodded an "okay" to Dafydd as he jumped down from the cab, ready to knock the rail back into shape. They backed up slowly, and Dafydd used a hefty sleeper to help lever the wheels back onto the rails as the gangers used a couple of crowbars.

'Useless,' Smithson grumbled. 'You know the gangs want the rails to break so they can throw away the rubbish that's been laid and put in new.'

He unwound the brake and raised the regulator. The engine began to shudder.

'Evans's still got his brakes on, what's he playing at?' Smithson was out of the cab and marching down the track to the guard's van. Dafydd jumped down and ran after him, but what to say when he caught up?

'He's all right now, he just waved,' he tried desperately.

Smithson brushed him aside. 'No, I've had enough today. I'm going to give him a piece of my mind.' He climbed into the van and saw Dafydd's tad. 'What the…? You're up for it now, Evans.'

'No,' Dafydd shouted. 'It's my fault. My father is very ill and he needs me. He's had a bad fever, it killed my Mam and it's left him weak as a kitten. I've got to do this. I was too late to save my mam, but I'll carry him down to town on my back if I have to.'

Smithson stared at Dafydd as his young fireman wiped the tears from his face. 'You're lucky I like you, son,' he said at last. 'All right, tie him to the bench, stop him rolling about the van and let's get going. Hope you're in voice, Dafydd, for you're to tell me everything on the way home. I don't like people working behind my back. How the hell did you expect to get away with this?'

'I don't know, I just had to. I'm sorry.'

'You should trust me more.'

Dafydd told the whole story as they worked the train back to Aber, how he'd lost touch with his parents, how hard it had been to find them when at last he'd returned to Aber. Smithson listened, with his hand on the regulator, to the tale of Dafydd's life punctuated by their shouts to and fro, acknowledging the clear crossings.

The railway took a long curve, hugging the riverside before popping under the lines south, past the small shed and into the station at Aberystwyth. Dafydd caught sight of Donato on the street pushing a hand cart. Smithson brought the train to stop at a point where Donato could access the guard's van. Dafydd's father was loaded on and the Italian wheeled him away before anyone else noticed. Smithson took the engine back to the shed and then reached out to stop Dafydd, who was furiously raking the fire in the engine.

'Look, I know I'm a whinging old bastard at times, but it doesn't mean I don't have feelings. You know I miss my wife and kids in Plymouth. It was a good thing you did there, even if we could all have been sacked for it. We're nearly done here as it is. I been told they're looking for loco crew for this line now. I been asked and said "no", but I thought of you.'

His smile was warm. 'It's as a passed cleaner. You'd be cleaning, preparing engines. Some shunting and filling in when other firemen are absent. You're driver material, Dafydd boy, and I thought you'd be better moving on to another job away from here. From what you've told me now,

I think you should stay. Take the job, heal your tad, find your girl and bide your time. There's talk of extending this line to Aberaeron and if that's the truth, they'll need folk and you'll be there waiting to bite their hand off when they come asking for drivers.'

CHAPTER SEVENTEEN

She Is
More Than That

DAFYDD KNEW HIS future would be one of oil-soaked rags and cleaning engines, but it was enough to be back with his family. Gwen had never left his heart but he had little time to dream.

He was not required for loco duty when the inspectors came to finally pass the line for opening. They had left with hard faces and harsher words. In the cab of the new loco, debate raged, as they moved to restart the works trains.

'Them inspectors left no doubt about what they thought,' Dafydd said. 'The ballast is rough and loose. The rails are brittle in places. The sleepers are rotten; all that them gangers said. How Pethicks expected to get away with it, I have no idea.'

Smithson replied with a heavy hint of sarcasm. 'Well, we loyal workers did our best to try and hide things, but the little engine's pony truck slipping off the rails on the inspector's train was a bit much to hide. He was quite amused by it, though. Nice that something made him happy.'

'So you're here for a while longer.' Dafydd said.

'Yes,' he replied. 'The wife and kids will have to wait a bit.'

At the end of the day, Dafydd called at Donato's. His father was still poorly. The situation seemed hopeless and Dafydd blamed himself.

He ate with Sioned's family and afterwards his sister and Donato sat in front of the fire with him in their parlour. The coffee was good – it always was when Donato made it.

'Looking back, they would have been hard pressed to prove I *could* have killed the boy, with the others there to defend him,' Dafydd said, staring into his coffee. 'I should have stayed to clear my name. I would have done my growing up, had a clearer head – been there for Mam and Tad.'

'But you *weren't* grown up and you *didn't* know that,' Sioned soothed, 'and it's not as if you went bad – you were sent away and gained a trade. Where was loading carts for a living at Frongoch ever going to get you?'

'But what good has it done? I'm back just cleaning engines.'

'You wouldn't have got to know Gwen,' Sioned said, looking up from her needlework. The fire seemed to crackle in agreement.

Dafydd's mouth tightened. 'Well, then I would have been saved the pain.'

Sioned sighed; there was no winning in this mood.

'Tad's getting better, I hope. He wakes a while and then he's drifting off back to sleep.'

'It's been days, and it feels like forever, Sioni.'

'I know, but every time he wakes there is hope, Daf.'

Then Harri's voice cried out from the hallway. 'Help me!'

Dafydd was through the door in a flash and found her on the stairway holding their father. He was sprawled face down on the steps, panting with exertion. Dafydd could see he was not fully conscious, which worried him even more.

'He keeps trying to come downstairs,' Harri said. 'Help me get him back to bed.'

'I'm all right, leave me be,' Owain whispered, as they carried him back to lie down. He was asleep before his head touched the pillows and Harri gave a groan of relief and a wan smile.

'Has this happened before, Harri?' Dafydd asked.

'Many times.'

'Why you never told me? Look, you'll have to stop holding him back and start helping him down the stairs.'

'What do I do then?'

'Have a chair ready for him to sit on at the bottom.'

Dafydd called in the next day and was astonished. His father was now sitting in the back garden, a blanket around his shoulders, sipping a mug of tea. He looked pale and his cough was harsh, but he was alive and that was enough for Dafydd's heart to leap with pleasure.

Owain grasped Dafydd's hand in greeting.

Dafydd wanted to hug the old man, tell him how sorry he was for leaving without ever saying goodbye to him, but feared an emotional display might blow his father over.

'You've got a moustache now,' his father said softly.

'Yes,' Dafydd sought for more to say. 'It's what everyone does round here.'

Owain grunted. Dafydd sat on a nearby windowsill. He'd brought tobacco, just in case, and began to roll a cigarette for his father. 'How you feeling, Tad?'

'I'm all right, son, just not quite ready for a shift down Frongoch yet.'

'How was it there?'

He shook his head. 'Them bloody Belgians, they ruined it for all of us. Had us fighting with the poor Italian miners. You like Donato?'

Dafydd nodded, and Owain continued.

'Well, would you fight him? They were all like him in my book and they were done down by everyone. Your mam and me, we moved out. Lots of people were going by then. Even the Treveglos family had gone south to the coalfields. Mam wouldn't go with them, not when she knew you were so close.'

'I'm sorry about Mam,' Dafydd said softly.

'Yes.' Owain's eyes glistened with tears. They sat in awkward silence for a time, before the old man finally spoke. 'We went up Idris's farm after we left Trisant village.'

'Idris?'

'Yes, he looked after us. Always has; too bloody generous by half, I expect. We helped him bring in the harvest. Then he found me work and us a place to stay.'

'He helped bring you from Bryn-yr-Afr to here. I brought you back on the new Rheidol railway.'

'What railway?'

'The one from Devils Bridge. I've been helping them build it. I fire the engine.'

Dafydd decided now wasn't the time to tell him how he would be falling back to cleaning and preparation soon enough. He told him of the past, and how he had gone from digging embankments in Talybont to the Bagnall works in Stafford. He missed out the bits he was not so proud of; they were for him to carry.

'I need to do something, Dafydd,' Owain groaned. 'They're working all hours as it is in the café, without having to support me.'

'Well, I'm chipping in as well now, Tad, and you need to get better. That's all you need to do for now.'

Owain grunted and the air seemed to buzz with his frustration.

'You got a woman yet?'

His father noticed his expression and nodded understanding.

'I... there is one, Tad,' tried Dafydd, 'but I don't know. I don't know where she is for starters. She said she'd wait, but since I came back I can't even find her.'

Owain tapped his chest. 'Follow your heart, son. If it's there, it's worth fighting for. I did, and it's the best thing I ever done in my life. Even if it hurts like hell now, don't have regrets. Go wherever, do whatever. At least you know then that you tried your best.'

That was Dafydd's dilemma – now he had found his family, he had no desire to go off looking for Gwen. True, he regretted not telling her how he felt, he regretted not taking her with him. Most of all, he regretted letting her go...

The door at the end of the back yard opened and a man stepped through. Dafydd recognised him as the town street cleaner. Bald and tanned like leather, he was a regular around the area, but Dafydd had never spoken to him.

'Look who's here, Dafydd. Don't you recognise your Uncle Gwilym? He moved to town four years back.'

Dafydd's heart sank. Gwilym was his mother's twin brother. Dafydd had never had much to do with him, and he wanted even less now as he looked into the man's eyes, so much his mother's eyes.

Much as they wanted him to stay, Dafydd made his excuses and left. He knew Tad was in good hands, for although Uncle Gwil may have appeared to be a joker back around the mine all those years ago, he was family. Dafydd made his way back to Mrs Owen's in Trefechan to do some thinking.

'So we're finally up to standard, then?' Evans the guard asked Dafydd. Aberystwyth station was so open that the weather would roll through the platform unchecked. Only the warmth from the engine protected them from a sharp autumn coastal breeze as they stood waiting.

Dafydd smiled. 'Well, having been laughed at by the inspectors, they had to loosen the purse strings and do it right, didn't they? Sturdier rails, sleepers of good wood and wider cuttings. Can't complain really.'

Evans rolled his eyes in mock despair. 'That why the directors have got excited?' He pointed his thumb at the carriages behind him. 'This special's for the invited few. We take the men to Devils Bridge, then go back up again with their wives and children. A picnic is to be laid on at the top station for the young and fair. And rich.'

Dafydd laughed. 'In November too. You are right, they *have* got excited. We get to take the train with one of the new engines. I don't know why their own railway crews are not involved... not that I'm complaining,' he added with a wink.

'Perhaps they think you know the line better, and won't send the train crashing down the valley,' Evans said with a quick dig of his elbow.

'I think Smithson wanted me here as a sort of farewell. I should be grateful, cos it's shining the brasses on an engine from now on.'

'Here they come now,' Evans said. '*Duw*, some of these men are either related to crabs or so full of drink they can't see a straight line, let alone walk on one!' he grumbled.

'Mustn't get above our station now,' Dafydd said, jumping down from the cab to join them.

'We'll behave better than our betters, that's for sure,' Evans replied. 'I'd say the ministers will have their hides come Sunday chapel, 'cept there's a few of those holy gentlemen in this party as it is.'

'Come on,' Dafydd said. 'They want a picture by the train. It's our chance to be famous.'

'Some of the buggers can't stand up properly,' Smithson said from the cab. 'Let's prop them up against the front of the engine, Daf.'

Heavy-set men lumbered up, many with red cheeks from too many similar occasions in the past. Others were stood around, swaying in the wind like grass. Dafydd hoped they would look all right in a still picture. One was sick straight after the photograph.

'Glad I'm not cleaning the carriages,' Smithson said.

Dafydd wondered if that would be his problem in future.

'See that one?' Evans said, 'He's a type. Thinks he's a Lord, does John Rowlands.'

The slim, neat man stood looking around with an air of disdain.

'God help his wife,' Smithson chuckled.

As merry as they were, Dafydd didn't know how the passengers had managed to get in the coaches, but the train finally got away and the journey out felt smooth. Perhaps the passengers might keep their stomach contents after all, he thought. They passed *Rheidol* in the shed and Dafydd wished it was her rolling under his feet. The new engine was so much stronger, keeping Dafydd busy with its coal needs as it raced up the valley, but he and *Rheidol* had been through so much together.

By the time they reached Devils Bridge the guests had decided they needed to give each other speeches. Huw came over to Dafydd, shaking his head.

'What you doing here, Huw *bach*?' Dafydd asked.

'Goodness knows,' he said. 'What do they expect us to do? Run a new siding or serve some high tea? Just like Hafan bloody tramway all over again.'

'You are supposed to listen respectfully and learn,' Smithson said with a wink. 'These are proper speeches. Big speeches, ones that set you wishing you hadn't sinned so much to deserve them.'

'You wait until the second train arrives,' Dafydd warned Huw, and he laughed. Eventually, Dafydd and Smithson took the train down the valley with their cargo of respectable drunks.

'Least they are singing hymns,' Dafydd shouted over to Smithson in the cab.

'Wives and children on the next one,' he replied. 'Fewer drunks and no bloody speeches!'

The valley dripped with autumn's moisture, the trees now bare of leaves. Dafydd found this weather difficult. He was warmed by the engine, but as soon as he looked out, his face froze in the cold wind. The line ran down to the riverside and finally around the tennis courts to the station. A big crowd waited there, with much cheering and flag waving. The wives and children of the guests, along with many townsfolk who had come down to see what the fuss was all about. Without thinking, Dafydd looked out for pretty girls.

One lady took his eye immediately. Slim and elegant, dressed in a white dress with puffed sleeves and a parasol, she stood apart from the rest. Her parasol shielded her from the fine rain that now fell. Dafydd liked the way her face lit up when she smiled. For a fleeting second their eyes met. It was Gwen.

Dafydd ducked back into the cab in a panic. That smile had been for another. Try as he might to concentrate on the engine's needs, he could not stop himself looking at her again as the train moved past.

'Arrogant cuss, that Rowlands,' Smithson was saying. 'Thinks he is so grand he can parade his mistress about. Come on, Dafydd, she's not for the likes of you. Uncouple us and we'll run the engine round to the front.'

Shocked speechless, Dafydd jumped down to uncouple the engine. He tried desperately not to look at the platform. Gwen was Rowlands' mistress?

'You there! Come and give the ladies a hand!' It was Rowlands, shouting at Dafydd. With a snort of frustration, Dafydd carried on working, praying the man would pick on someone else. 'Do you hear me?'

Dafydd could not reply for fear of screaming at the man.

'Mr Rowlands, I would send Dafydd down to assist,' Smithson's voice came from the cab, where he stood wiping his hands on a greasy rag. 'But railway work is a dirty business and we wouldn't want to spoil the ladies' fine dresses.'

As if to prove the point, he opened up his hands to show his dirty palms.

Rowlands turned and walked away without a word. Dafydd scrambled to the ground frame and set the points for the engine to run around. He caught a glimpse of Rowlands helping Gwen into a carriage and growled.

He coupled the engine back onto the carriages and dived back into the cab.

'Look out for Rowlands, he's a new director,' said Smithson. 'Thinks he knows a lot more than he actually does.'

'Arrogant dog!' was Dafydd's best reply. 'I'd like to wipe that smile off his face.'

'Don't let him get to you. Looks as if he's got back on. He's on heat, for sure.'

In his mind, Dafydd laughed at fate. Laughed and cried

and screamed at it. His guts cramped at the thought of taking Rowlands and Gwen on their merry journey... being the instrument that helped deliver them to their happy day together.

He wanted to close his eyes and make everyone go away. Or at least get off the engine and walk back to Donato's café, to weep on Sioned's shoulder. His throat was sore with tension.

Smithson tapped the glass of the gauges. When Evans blew the guard's whistle, there was an answering blast from the engine and he lifted the regulator. The engine responded with a blast of steam. Dafydd checked the firebox, receiving a blast of hot air that matched his temper, and kicked the door shut.

'Hey! Watch what you are doing!' Smithson shouted amid hisses and blasts of steam. Dafydd glared back.

'What's got into you, son? Ever since you saw Rowlands you've been ...' He tailed off and sounded the whistle. A bystander stepped away from the track.

'Keep alert on your side, Dafydd,' snapped the driver.

They stopped talking, bar the essentials. Dafydd leant out to watch the driver's blind side. Beyond confirming when the crossings were clear, their silence continued up to the water stop at Aberffrwd. Dafydd's thoughts boiled, dark and despairing.

He prepared the engine for water. Smithson swung the arm over from the water tower and Dafydd fed the canvas tube into the tank of the engine. Smithson pulled on the counterweight, hanging by a chain, and soon there was water gushing out of the feed. Dafydd raced to put it into the tank.

His breeches were soaked from the splashes. His stomach raged; even his face ached. Many heads popped out of the carriages to see what was happening. Dafydd could hear a few calls of 'What's going on?' Some were obviously drunk. He ignored them, knowing his answer would be too sharp. Some of the male passengers wandered off to relieve themselves, others stood outside to smoke. The tank was finally filled and the engine was ready to move.

'What should we be doing now?' a man shouted.

'Getting on board, if you don't want to be left behind,' Dafydd snapped.

There were a few noises made about that, and some mocking laughter. Dafydd bit his tongue.

'Come on, Dafydd,' Smithson gently steered him to the cab. Once there, he patted Dafydd on the shoulder. 'It's her, isn't it, your girl as was? She's on board. I realised as we were driving.'

Dafydd didn't reply, and Smithson sighed. 'All right, son, I know it hurts. Just stay away from folk and the day will go faster.'

The approach to the top station was normally a joy. The railway clung to the side on a narrow ledge. Far down below, the river wound its way like a blue ribbon past the lead mines. Some travellers cried for fear of falling. On the sharper curves, where check rails had been added to help keep the engine on the tracks, the screeching of metal as the train climbed the hill added to the drama. It was truly a lovely sight – on other days. Today, Dafydd's heart had returned to the mood of a lonely boy, a new arrival in town, who'd lost his girl. He could not lean out of the cab without pondering the best place to jump.

A hand gripped his shoulder, calm and firm, holding him back from an evil deed. At last, the train dived through that large cutting into the station, with its neat buildings of corrugated iron. The roofs were decorated with bunting ready for the party.

The track gangs had obviously finished off the drink from the first train. They raised a great cheer when the train arrived and received one back from the carriages. The station was as busy as an anthill. Dafydd saw Rowlands help Gwen down from the carriage and he turned away to shut out the scene. He helped uncouple the engine and Smithson moved her forward ready to run her round when there were fewer people milling about admiring the engine and trying to get run over. Dafydd leant back behind the engine and took a deep breath.

'Come and join us in the station office, Dafydd. It's quieter.'

Dafydd followed him into the narrow corrugated-iron booking office. The world was shut out there, save three small square windows. The wooden walls felt to Dafydd like shelter from a storm. Smithson handed him a mug of tea.

'I wish I could fix this for you, son,' he said. 'I'd let you sit on your own somewhere, but it doesn't help. It would just eat at you inside. You're best with folk and a good cup of tea.'

Huw came in and Dafydd saw immediately that he already knew the story. Dafydd wanted sympathy, yet he didn't. He wanted to pretend it wasn't happening.

'They are all at the Hafod Arms tea rooms,' Huw said. 'Some might make it to the falls, but the way some have been going at it, you may see a few of them floating past you at Capel Bangor.'

'Well, it's not often you get a free meal,' Dafydd said. His voice sounded cold and strange in his own ears. 'I need some air,' he added. Outside once more, he walked off past the train towards the cutting. For so long Dafydd had held the dream of a happy end to his journey. He had found a trade, he had found his family, he had even found his love again – but she was not for him.

He ambled along the track until he noticed the sound of cascading water from a local mill, and birdsong, sweet and bright. It spoke of freedom and happiness – for others. For himself, the old urge to run far away and start anew was upon him. But this time, he had to fight it. He had vowed to be there for his father and to protect him. He knew that all he could do was rejoin the play and wait for his own part in it to come alive again.

The track curved away past the navvy barracks. Dafydd followed it, idly looking for stray lumps of coal in the track bed. Ahead was another large cutting, an old quarry broken through by the line. Dafydd walked close to the jagged side until he found a place where he could sit out of sight and see the railway curving off around a horseshoe bend. Tears clouded his sight. His shoulders shuddered for a while, then it was all locked back inside, where no amount of forcing could bring it back out.

He jumped at the call of an engine whistle; Smithson had moved the engine without him. With a deep sigh, he headed back to the water tower set into the hillside close by the station cutting. Still away from the merry crowd, Dafydd got on with topping up the tanks.

'Coal her up here and then check the lubrication,' said Smithson. 'I think we could do with a spot of oiling in parts and...' he smiled sadly. 'It keeps you away from the train. We'll couple up just before we're ready to go.'

Dafydd moved to couple up the train, pretending he could not see Gwen and Rowlands getting back on board. He hurried round to the other side of the engine.

The journey back was a bad dream. Looking out of the

cab to check for danger, trying not to focus on the carriage interiors. He was soothed by the sound of the engine as it ran down the valley into town. This had been the first real chance he had had on the new locomotive and deep down he knew it had performed beautifully. He knew he would have enjoyed the experience had his past not flown at him so unexpectedly.

They reached Aberystwyth to find the station a bustle of people shouting, singing and laughing. A few passengers approached to thank the crew. Dafydd grabbed his oilcan and turned his back. If only they would all just go and leave him alone. He thought of the old Trefechan lime kilns. There would be no people there on a November evening. It would be a place to think, to remember, to grieve.

'They don't wear much on such a cold day.'

It was Gwen's voice.

Rowlands was haughty in his reply. 'Well, they work in such heat, my dear. There is no need for it.'

'But not outside,' Gwen replied. 'Here, give me your scarf.'

Dafydd was being played, and he had nowhere to hide.

'Here, take this. It will keep you warm. Please.'

He turned to look at them both. Gwen reached out with the scarf, her eyes pleading. Rowlands stood as if aloof from the woman on his arm. The scene was beneath him, the offer so trivial.

Dafydd looked at the scarf. Not to take it would appear churlish. He took hold of it without meeting her eyes, but managed a nod of thanks. He turned back to his work and when he next dared look, realised she had not recognised him.

They put the engine away and as Dafydd finally closed the shed doors, the working day was over. He saw Donato

222

hurrying towards him, running as best he could, yet trying to keep his composure.

'Daf, Daf. I have found her!' His words spilled out in excitement, breathing heavily with the effort. 'I found her, the Gwen. She is in the town. She is a housekeeper at one of the big houses on the Llanbadarn Road. I have the address.'

Dafydd said nothing.

'Daveed. Your woman. You can find her. I say she is a housekeeper.'

'No, my friend,' Dafydd's smile almost cracked his stony face. 'No, she is much more than that.'

CHAPTER EIGHTEEN

The Broken Promise (1903)

OWAIN HAD CREATED a haven of peace in the garden at the back of the cafe. Whatever grass had been there had been dug up and tilled for vegetables. Dafydd knew his father would never have a problem with hard work. He had used string and long branches of driftwood to support the runner beans and peas. His tomatoes were reaching out and up, and his cucumbers showed promise of a decent harvest to come.

He had been given a small table with two chairs, tucked away in a corner of the yard. It was in a shady place that suited his lifetime underground. Even now, very bright days brought pain to his eyes. He sat at his table, drinking his coffee, and smiled when Dafydd came through the yard door. Dafydd thought that loss was etched on his father's face, permanently now. A cough and spit, however, the legacy of years of lead and zinc, were all that broke his otherwise tranquil greeting to his son.

Dafydd looked around appreciatively. 'There'll be vegetables aplenty in no time,' he said. 'I like the way you've made a greenhouse from bits.'

'It's better now I've sorted out the slugs,' Owain smiled. 'I found an injured hedgehog in the road. Must have been hit by a cartwheel or something. He's here now, healed and feasting on the slugs and snails.'

Dafydd smiled back, thinking how his father's face would always be pale, etched with lines of dirt. A cat jumped over the wall and padded over to Owain, tail up in greeting. 'I find cats tend to show you where they want to be stroked, don't you, Morgan cat?' said Owain.

'I wish I had your peace,' Dafydd said

Owain shrugged. 'Everything has its time, son. You've got to carry on as best you can and not be a burden,' he nodded at his vegetables. He was not fit to work in the café, but at least in the garden he could create something in his own way to help pay back.

'You are right. This will be a tidy crop when it all comes to bear,' Owain said with a laugh. 'Yes, that's where you need patience. Although when the days get really bright, I'm more likely to be sleeping in the chair. Not used to all that sun. Never seen it regular since I was a boy, only the time I broke my leg.'

'And your father-in-law came to bully you to leave the house,' Dafydd smiled. He had heard the tale a few times from his mam. 'You were saved by Uncle Gwilym, who roused the neighbours all the way along the road to Frongoch. Must have been tough, him going against his own family.'

'Well – aye, it was, but he was saving his own sister, who meant more to him than his drunken brothers. Why don't you get on with him?'

'I just don't like the way he doesn't seem to care.'

'He does, *bach*, he just hides it. Been through a lot, that one, and he saved me and your mam many a time. Stubborn, he is and all. Just like your mother.'

Dafydd had to laugh. 'Well, there you have it. I think it's because he's too much like Mam.' The laughter stopped. 'I miss her. I can't forgive myself for not getting to you sooner.'

'What would you have done? She was ill, she was going to die anyway.'

'Yes, but if I'd just done some things different...'

'Son, you have your life and it's not that of an English squire. You can't just drop everything and come running.'

'I never got to say goodbye.'

'Neither did I, Dafydd *bach*. I was living at the barracks during the workdays, and her with a bit of warmth on her brow when I left for it on the Monday morning. She was dead before the end of the week. There's always regrets in life, but then there's always something worth living for and all, if you look.'

There was a silence between them for a while and then Dafydd whispered, 'I just wished it could have been different, that's all.'

'Me too, Dafydd. Me too.'

The cat jumped onto the table and demanded more fuss, a useful distraction to them both.

'So what of your woman, Dafydd?'

'She's not my woman, Tad. Never was. Donato and my sisters are talking too much about me.'

'They don't say much, son. They're just worried for you.'

'I'm fine. I do my job, I go home to rest. It's all I need.'

'Cutting yourself off from everyone isn't a happy place to be. I know it hurts, I've tried that kind of idea and I nearly killed myself for my trouble. If it wasn't for old Twm-y-Twll, I'd be up in heaven with her and she would have had my guts for garters for not trying.'

'All right for you to say.'

'Yes it is. I can't fix what happened in Talybont, much as I'd like to – but you can move ahead with your life.'

'What do you do then, to move ahead?'

His tone was harsh, he knew, but his father carried on as if he hadn't noticed.

'I walk, Dafydd. To the harbour. It's hard work these days, but I watch and learn. I talk to the fisher boys. It all helps.'

'Well, next time *Rheidol* steams down the harbour, I'll give you a lift. That's the one run I'm allowed to fire these days, once the cleaning is done. It's not that often, neither.'

'That will be good, though I never see you down there.'

'That's because there's never a load to carry down there. Half the time they go down there just to make sure we keep the running rights.'

'Why are you still here, boy? You're a trained fireman. Could find a job on another railway easy, man.'

'I don't want to leave Aber. There's you and Sioned and Harri… I want to make up for the time I wasn't there. You need me now and sure as hell Donato can't look after you all on his own.'

'No, but you've got to look after yourself. I'm not long for this world, and Harri will be courting soon enough. I don't want you left alone in a town where there is no hope for you.'

'Are you telling me to leave?'

'I'm asking you to think about it. As my father told me to, before.'

'And you stayed.'

'And I'm still asking you now.'

There was a pause.

'In the meantime, Tad, I'll be helping in the garden and sharing your walks when I can.'

'That would be good. Just don't forget yourself, your way forward.'

It gave Dafydd something to think about whilst he was preparing the engines. He found the new ones easier to clean, and soon felt he could take them apart and put them back together blindfold. All the while, there was little *Rheidol* close by, now all fixed and good for light duties like the early train. It was like having an old friend standing by. The railway was now taking fares and running regularly. As Huw had put it to Dafydd: 'Within two years,' he'd said, 'we'll have replaced all the crap that Pethicks' put down. Strong iron and good wood will be the order of the day.'

The plans for extending south to Aberaeron had gone quiet. Now, there was no talk of any expansion. Dafydd still had the odd firing duty, mostly shunting, and very occasionally the early morning mail train up the valley. But the railway never grew further. It was not flush with passengers except in the summer: it became popular with tourists taking advantage of the chance to see the world famous 'Swiss-like' beauty of the Devils Bridge falls in comfort. Freight was lower than expected as the mines began to close. What was worse, the railway men were coming together as a tight unit, one it was difficult to progress in.

Dafydd had found his path, but the world had changed. The path led nowhere. There was no way forward, or so it seemed.

When the evenings began to lighten, he took to walking up the slopes of Pen Dinas. He often sat up there, within view of his long-ago moment of passion with Gwen, and the ruined ropewalk below. In his oily breeches and jacket, he sat and wondered about what might have happened and where the future might lead. All the while, a grey mist swirled in his head, hiding all the answers.

One warm evening as he gazed out to sea, enjoying the sunset in an almost clear sky, a small band of cloud just on the horizon formed pinkish strands in the sky above and a golden bar of light below it. He shielded his eyes as the red disc of the sun broke from the cloud and slid below the horizon. He knew this kind of evening. The sea would become a lighter and lighter blue, almost a gentle green.

He saw a woman approaching. A working girl, from her clothing. She was far off, but every time he tried to recapture the scene over the harbour, she was there in the corner of his eye and getting closer. Dafydd was not on the main path, he had moved along into the farmer's fields to protect his solitude, and yet she was heading straight for him.

She was probably one of the brewery girls. Surely she'd not come up this far to scrounge the price of a quart? Why now? Dafydd ripped up a fistful of grass in his annoyance. He'd been ready to quietly absorb the last burst of warmth on his face for another day. And then he remembered the bakery, ages before, when he had walked through the door and the sun had lit up the face of the girl there. Of course she knew he would be here. The old magic that pulled her back to him had not been lost. But what had become of the vision of finery from the train trip to Devils Bridge? And when had she lost that beautiful welcoming smile?

She came to sit by his side and for a while there was a silence. Not a comfortable one.

'How did you know?' Dafydd asked at last, not daring to look at her. A weight had suddenly formed on his chest.

'I still have friends in Turkey Town,' she replied. 'As do you.'

Dafydd wanted to shout and scream.

'It's a beautiful night,' she said, waggling her toes out of her shoes. 'They say you're a regular up this place.'

Dafydd shrugged. 'Beats sleeping on the bridge.'

'You look healthy. Stronger.'

'Why did you come?' Dafydd sounded sharper than he'd meant to.

Gwen just shrugged. 'We needed to talk.'

Dafydd looked away. 'That was a long time ago.'

A dog's bark echoed from somewhere below. Gwen sighed and started picking at the grass.

'Where's your fancy dress,' he asked, and got a bitter laugh in reply.

'Fancy dress,' she spat. 'Or I could have carried a torch up here and a big sign saying *here I am*! At least this way I blend in.'

'You don't want to be seen with me then?'

'I have no problem with you and every problem with people who would wish to watch. I also have no desire to... scratch the wound.'

'What wound?'

'The one that makes you hate me.'

Dafydd's eyes were pools of tears. 'You said you would wait.'

The sea was such a rich blue now. A boat was on the horizon, not in time to make harbour, Dafydd judged. It would soon weigh anchor for the night, so close and yet so very far away. Just like he felt.

Dafydd turned and looked at Gwen. He couldn't touch her. He wanted to touch her and *cwtch* away the hurt, but he knew he could not. He took a deep breath. 'You said you would wait and I clung to that when I was away, longing to come back and have you by my side, I was. When I had given up hope, you wrote to me all I wanted to hear. It gave me the strength to keep trying, to keep hoping. Then I had the luck to be sent here with *Rheidol* to work.' Dafydd had to pause for breath as his hands fell to his sides. 'And found out you were lost to me.'

'I waited, Dafydd. A long time, but you have to understand. Here in Trefechan, I am a poor woman. An orphan. No family, no support. It came to the choice of going into service in a big house or throwing myself on the parish. So I chose a master, but he was kind. I was offered a situation. It gave me security, shelter and food. What was I to do?'

'Couldn't you have told me? I would have come running back for you. I'd have taken you anywhere.'

'You never wrote back.'

Dafydd stopped, all his anger and frustration boiled away. 'I couldn't. I didn't have the words.'

'Then how was I supposed to know you hadn't settled down in England with a wife and children? How was I to know you were still alive?'

His head sank in despair. He knew she was right.

'You told me to wait, but was I supposed to grow old waiting, in the hope that you might walk through the door?'

'I'm here now, though, aren't I? And I'm staying and all. I've got a job, it may grow. Why not now? We could...'

She smiled her sad smile. 'Perhaps once...' She was not trying to give him hope. 'Things have changed. We are not the same as when we were at the ropewalk.'

'Do you love him?'

She looked down, her smile fixed. 'I have to go.'

'Do you love me?'

She made to get up and Dafydd grabbed her wrist, felt her tense, and let go. 'Answer me. You owe me that much, Gwen.'

'I owe you nothing, Dafydd Thomas!' she flared. 'I found

you shelter when you were alone. I got Tad to take you in. I got him to find you work when he was on his deathbed. And I waited. *I waited!* I waited while the world collapsed around me. I waited until there was no money left to buy the bread, and the bailiffs came to throw me out. And you never wrote. And you never came.'

'I wanted to come,' Dafydd whispered. 'I had to learn, I needed to be able to earn money, to keep a family. What use would I have been without a trade? I would have been penniless with you.'

Gwen wiped the tears from her face. 'But you would have been *with* me. And what has your trade done for you now? Cleaning, oiling, shovelling coal.'

'You told me to go,' Dafydd sounded, even to himself, like a lost lamb.

She knelt by him, as he hugged the pain out of his body.

'I did, and I said I would wait. The world has twists and turns and I would have waited until death if I could. But when you starve, it makes you desperate. Mad for food, all the time – it is all you can think of. In the end, I swallowed my pride and went to Mrs Owen's door. She found me work as a scullery maid at the Rowlands'. I had food and a warm bed, even if I shared it with another maid. I recovered myself and Captain Rowlands took a shine to me. I had nowhere else to go.'

She brushed his hair so gently it made him gasp. 'You had to find a trade, to be someone. I saw that. I could have kept you here and you would have hated me for it in time. All those memories of our times at the harbour and the beach, they would have crumbled into dust. I let you find your path, but it did not come back to mine. It was not meant to be.'

'It could now,' Dafydd grabbed her hand and drew her to him. 'We could survive.'

She shook her head. 'I cannot go back now.'

Her words said the matter was closed. Her face, her actions did not. She showed no fight as Dafydd drew her close and kissed her gently on the lips. The kiss grew deeper. The urgency to touch and feel grew, and the air seemed thinner.

It was like a high tide crashing over them, like a breaking wave, a build-up of energy released in a flash across the shingle. Just as quickly it was gone and they sat panting side by side, their hands close but not touching. They may as well have been miles apart. He felt raw and wounded, hot with passion and anger, unsure where to look or what to do next.

'I love you,' was all he could say in his defence.

'I know,' she said. 'I'm sorry. I wish things were different now.'

'You don't love me,' Dafydd said sadly. She took his hand.

'I never said that, Dafydd Thomas. I can't tell you what you want to hear and see you waiting for a chance that things will change. They won't. I have let myself be trapped. If I strayed now there would be no happy ending. I cannot love.'

'But then you must feel something for him, or you are behaving like a...'

'Imagine what you will,' she cut in. 'How I feel about anyone is really only my business. Please do not judge me.'

The night breeze seemed to blow through Dafydd's bones. 'I have no desire to judge.'

'No. Well, I came here for a reason, Dafydd. I know you, I think I know you enough to ask you to leave this town.'

'What? I have a job here and a trade. I have worked hard enough to get that far.'

'And what has it got you? An oily rag and a coal-stained

shovel! What future have you here? You walked away from me to better yourself. Now you are stuck. You can stay and clean engines here, with you and I falling over each other at every turn, or take a job in a big town where you could become a driver.'

'I have reasons for staying.'

She snorted in frustration. 'Have you not listened to a word?'

'I have listened,' Dafydd snapped back. 'You have said all I needed to hear. I have family, my father. I was never around for them before, but I sure as hell need to be now.'

Gwen nodded slowly. 'Perhaps, but within your noble thoughts you must still leave time for yourself. My master has influence. There are opportunities. I could assist you.' She produced a letter. 'This is a reference from the Rheidol railway to the locomotive superintendent of the Cambrian Railways at Oswestry.'

'Oswestry? What would I be doing in England again?'

'Working at a good job and, I dearly hope, finding happiness. Goodbye, Dafydd.'

Dafydd watched her walk back across the fields towards Trefechan. He hoped to see some sign of regret, but there was nothing. Her shoulders were not sloped in defeat, her hands swung loosely by her sides. He watched her walk past the brewery, giving a passer-by a cheery wave. Her voice drifted over to his ears, or so he imagined. A happy tone. How much of a fool he had been all those years?

He sat for a while before scuffing down the hill. In the street, he was drawn by the lights of the many taverns of Trefechan. He made for The Beehive, a small inn by the railway bridge. In the darkening gloom of evening, the flickering lights from its small windows beckoned.

'So, you've come off your bloody mountain at last.'

234

The man hit the floor. The landlord had Dafydd bundled out of the door as the laughter died in the onlookers' throats. The door slammed and there was a moment of quiet. Then Dafydd stood up, dusted himself off and made for Donato's. His hand still throbbed from the punch he'd thrown.

Donato was sitting among the stacked chairs in the café, smoking a cigar. Dafydd gave him a weary smile and moved on into the kitchen, where Sioned and Harri were rushing around. Sioned was the first to notice his face.

'What's the matter, *bach*?'

'Nothing. Can I help you with the washing up?'

'Only if you wash yourself first, *cariad*. I'll not have engine grease on my plates.'

'You'll look funny then,' Harri giggled. 'All white, and clean hands like a gentleman.'

'A gentleman with an oily rag, aye. Look, leave me to sort this, you go and sit down and have a rest.'

The water was warm and soothing, though his face felt as if it would crack if he blinked. Dafydd rubbed his face with his hot, wet hands. It helped, though it did not heal.

He had the plates and cups gleaming when Sioned came back with a tea towel.

'Go up and see Tad. He's in his room,' she said. 'Leave me to stack those now.'

His father had been given a small box room. Owain was sitting on his bed, a walking stick hung over the end. The *Cambrian News* was spread open beside him and he held a small magnifying glass. He had always said they were big readers of newspapers at the mine, though Dafydd had never thought much of it before.

Owain greeted him warmly. His voice was always softer

now, so different to the tone of the man who used to be shouting to his butties underground all day. He folded his paper and bade Dafydd sit next to him.

'So, Dafydd. The girls are telling me you have a face like thunder – there's truth in the tale and no mistake.'

'My sisters have wagging tongues,' Dafydd grumbled.

'And caring hearts,' Owain replied, leaning back against his pillows.

Dafydd grunted, then ran a hand over the little dresser squeezed in opposite the bed. 'How have you got so many things in your room?'

'Well, Donato is resourceful and even I have made friends with people who no longer want things.'

'Is that the old clock from the house?'

'Idris rescued it. Another resourceful man – and one I never got to thank.'

Nor I, Dafydd thought. *Or say sorry*.

'I found Gwen, Tad. Or, she found me.'

And then the whole story came pouring out. All his hurt and anguish came to the fore. Owain sat back and squinted at the letter through his magnifying glass.

'You know what this is?'

'Letter of reference for Oswestry?'

'Well, no. That would have gone to the Cambrian Railways. This acknowledges your references and invites you for interview for the role of passed fireman.'

'Well, that's Captain Rowlands meddling.'

'I don't know what you really expect then. Didn't you know he has links to the Cambrian Railways board?'

'I can't do this, Tad.'

'Why not? You'd be back at the level you were and on the road to being a driver. There's more opportunity there and all. You could be working on the expresses.'

236

'I can't leave you again. Then there's the café – you know I chip in a bit.'

'Well, you can send money down from Oswestry. Don't their drivers come down this far?'

'Rarely.'

'Well, it's up to you to befriend the guards and get free rides. I heard tell it's normal practice on that line. You'll be coming down at your leisure then, not darting in and out when you have a minute. It's the best thing for you. Look, me and your mam, we knew the score. You had to go when fate dealt its hand. We knew you needed to find your way; best we could hope for at times was to know you were safe. Your mam knew that. There's no guilt to be had there.'

'So what are you saying, then?'

'Go and see them in Oswestry. It's only an interview and a medical. They haven't handed you your cap yet but it looks that they might.'

CHAPTER NINETEEN

A Ball of Wool

OSWESTRY WAS ONLY two and a half hours away on a fast train, but it may as well have been in France. The train steamed out of Aberystwyth late, the talk in the carriage suggesting this was quite a normal event. Dafydd watched Plascrug Avenue go by and gazed at the castellated tower of the farm next to it. There would be a climb out of Llanbadarn soon, then a run downhill into Bow Street before dropping down again to Llanfihangel. His thoughts were broken by the blast of a whistle from an engine in the shed. A parting farewell, returned by the driver of Dafydd's train.

He felt his spirits lift. He wanted to be back on the footplate. The Cambrian was a big company of opportunity. As the train passed the abandoned tramway track, he relived his time in Talybont. His eyes filled with sorrow as he thought of his mam.

The carriage jerked violently as they rounded a corner and he gazed on the brown and green wilderness of Cors Fochno. They were arriving in Borth, a collection of houses on a strip of shoreline behind a few large chapels. A huge hotel marked the change from fishing village to tourist haven. Where the tourists would come from, Dafydd did not know. He had heard that Borth had lovely sandy beaches. Perhaps that was enough? After running across the flat sandy land, they crossed a road and ran through a small halt called Ynyslas. The traces of an embankment ran off from it, going nowhere.

'You're looking at the old deviation.' Dafydd's head snapped round. The man sitting opposite him was nodding officiously. The buttons of his jacket had the Cambrian railways insignia. 'Forty-odd years back now,' he went on, 'they were looking at a bridge across the Dyfi, just like the one at Barmouth. Would have come out at Penhelig – you know, Aberdyfi way.' Dafydd shook his head. If the man noticed, it didn't discourage him. 'Problem was, they sent surveyors off to the estuary with measuring poles and the mud was so deep in the middle, they bloody lost them! So we're stuck with this roundabout way and an embankment crafted with love but going nowhere.'

He cackled, and Dafydd felt uncomfortable. He would rather be left with his thoughts, but the man wasn't stopping.

'So they came around the coast and cut off Derwenlas. My tad was a fisherman there. The river silting up had all but killed off the town for boats, anyway. The railway made damn sure it would die. I remember it as a boy, though – we used to get slate from Corris and lead from Dylife to ship out.'

The man wasn't going to shut up, no matter how hard Dafydd tried to ignore him. He nervously took out his pass and started turning it around in his hands. The man was quick to spot it.

'You're off to Oswestry, aren't you? They do all the interviewing at Oswestry. What are you going for?'

'Passed fireman,' Dafydd muttered.

'You've been referred by Aber shed?'

Dafydd sighed, and decided to open up. There didn't seem to be any option.

'No, I work on the Rheidol. Shedman mostly. Though I fired the contractor's engine when they built the line and I done some firing in Bagnall's.'

'That's more than a start. Well, this is your lucky day, *bach*. I know this line like the back of my hand. I drove for the old Newtown and Machynlleth and then the Cambrian. Then I got old and moved into station work. But I know this place and I know how to coax an engine over all the problems. You pay attention to me and I'll see you right. They'll be so impressed with your knowledge that they'll be begging you to be top link driver.'

Dafydd wondered how much of this was the truth, but then it was a long journey. He might as well listen.

'It's a good level run here up to Glandyfi,' the man continued, 'though the track bed is only floating on the marsh. It can move sometimes and we put down markers for the gangers to knock it back in check. One problem you really have, though, is Talerddig. You'll be sweating so much you'll be clean of coal dust. I'll explain... Samuel Jones is the name, by the way... Now, where was I...?'

He left the train at Newtown, but not before he'd talked Dafydd through firing to Oswestry and back, down the Kerry branch and along the narrow gauge to Llanfair Caereinion. Dafydd hoped he'd remember all the important bits, but most of all, he hoped Samuel was right.

The train crossed the border at a junction with the North Western railway and sped onward past quarries and the old canal. Before long, Oswestry was in sight. Dafydd had been there before, passing through on the way to Stafford. It was a mass of large brick railway buildings, now stained black with soot and grime. The railway works had loomed threateningly in the dark then. They hadn't changed. Dafydd was struck with how small he felt in the middle of this railway town.

There was a footbridge over the main track, which gave Dafydd a view over a goods depot behind the station. In front of him, line after line of rails ran side by side as far as the eye could see. He wondered how the drivers knew their way in this web of iron.

He got directions to the shed and stopped to admire the size of it. Six lanes, rows of black engines; some gleaming and bubbling steam, others dead and neglected. Dafydd took an immediate fancy to the big express engines and wondered how long it could be before he fired one.

He found the foreman's office and knocked on the door. There was no reply. He knocked again, and still no answer. He tried the door. It opened so easily he fell through the doorway, to find two men sitting either side of a desk. The foreman gave him a look.

'I'm so sorry,' Dafydd mumbled. 'I thought you said come in.'

'I didn't,' the foreman replied brusquely. 'Now go back outside and wait.'

Dafydd removed himself quickly and closed the door, feeling stupid. Was it a fatal mistake? He wondered when the next train back home was.

After about five minutes the door opened. The other man came out, indicating Dafydd should go in. Dafydd took off his cap and waited for the worst.

'So, how can I help?'

'I'm here for an interview, sir. Passed fireman.' Dafydd gave him the reference papers.

The man read through them slowly. 'Where you from?' he finally said.

'Aberystwyth.'

The man scoffed. 'Well, they don't have a football team.'

'Yes, they do!'

Dafydd wished he hadn't opened his mouth, but he noted his unexpected warm feeling about the town that had caused him so much pain, and a football team he'd never seen.

'But they're not any good.'

'We won the cup in 1900! Beat the Druids!'

The foreman was trying not to smile. 'Well, I've never had much truck with the Druids. You'd best be off, this says report to the General Office in the station.' He opened the door and shouted down to the shed.

'Jim, take this lad with you.' He looked back at Dafydd. 'You're lucky – station pilot is here at the moment. He'll give you a lift. When you get there, if you see a door closed, wait until someone answers or opens it for you. That's my advice.'

Dafydd nodded, flushed with shame.

In a matter of moments he was on the footplate of a tank engine, squeezed into a corner amongst blackened friendly faces, trying to avoid getting the grime and dust on his Sunday best. The engine moved out and, with a few track movements and a wait for a train to depart, Dafydd was deposited on the long platform.

The office area was spotless, tidy, and quiet as a library. Dafydd sat in a corner in the hall, gazing at the yellow stone walls. He spun his cap in his hand; spent a while looking for specks of soot on his clothes. He seemed to be there for hours and was dying to get up and pace the room. He didn't, in case he was being watched, and judged accordingly. He turned his attention to the patterns of grain in the wooden benches; every loop a year of growth, his teacher used to say.

The wooden floor reminded him of chapel. Sunday school

pupils sat on the floor, with hymn books and a Bible in front. He remembered standing up as the minister came in and called for a hymn. Dafydd would reach down for the book. Once he'd yelped then, as a huge splinter of wood planted itself in his thumbnail...

'Mr Brown!'

Dafydd jumped. A man stood at the door. Dafydd took in the suit, waistcoat, gold chain and small pebble-glasses. He looked around, but no "Mr Brown" appeared – and the man was looking specifically at him, so Dafydd braced himself for the interview.

'Take off your shirt,' the man said as he reached for a stethoscope on the table.

Dafydd had been prepared for being taken apart by far-reaching questions about boiler pressures, raising and drawing fires, emergency maintenance and the rules and regulations. What he had not prepared for was a cold steel disc being placed on his chest as a stuffy doctor, reeking of stale tobacco, listened to his breathing.

He measured Dafydd's height, weight and chest size. Then he hit his knees with a small hammer, then spent far too long for Dafydd's liking poking things on his tongue and shining things in his eyes. Next he picked up a huge woollen ball and tossed it to Dafydd.

'Pick out two red strands and then two green ones.'

Dafydd looked at the great ball, it was a mass of different colours. He couldn't see any red ones to hand, so he started levering some blue ones out of the way. Then he noticed the man's expression.

'There's no red ones that I can see,' Dafydd pointed out. 'I'm trying to dig under these blues.'

What if he was colour-blind? Dafydd had never thought of it before, but he couldn't see any red threads. He knew he had seen red things before, but in the panic, he wondered if he'd been mistaken.

The doctor stared at Dafydd for a long while.

'Correct, Mr Brown. Now, just show me where there is a green strand.'

Dafydd did so and the man promptly threw the ball into a waste bin and retreated behind his paperwork. The examination went on and by the end Dafydd was sure it had all been a waste of time.

'What was your father's occupation?'

'Lead miner.'

'What did he die of?'

'He's still alive,' Dafydd said, part surprised, part angry.

'Can he do simple carrying activities?'

'Of course.'

'What weights? How is his breathing?'

It was all beginning to get upsetting.

'I have to say you have a poor opinion of lead miners,' Dafydd snapped. 'I can assure you they are good strong men.'

There was a silence whilst the doctor continued to write.

'Did you ever work at the lead mine?'

'Yes, for a while.'

'Underground?'

'No, on the surface. A few years in the mill and a short while loading trucks.'

'I need to test your hearing.'

He did, as Dafydd started thinking of the cleaning work he was going back to. And Gwen, even though she had sent him away.

'Why did you not go underground?'

'My father couldn't find work for me.'

The man stopped and looked up. 'Miners work for

tribute. He could have taken you on any time he wanted.'

Dafydd remembered standing on the lip of the old mine shaft, staring its black shadow in the face.

'I think he didn't want that life for me.'

'Why?'

'Because he didn't want me to die of the dust.'

The conversation stopped and Dafydd let the doctor finish writing up his rejection letter. Finally he put the pen down and leant back in his chair.

'Your father did you a big favour. It's kept you fit and healthy. Healthy enough to fire an engine and that's only for those who are really fit.' Seeing Dafydd's look of surprise, he added: 'My father was a lead miner in Snailbeach. He didn't send me down a mine, he sent me to school, spent every penny he could afford to, until I got a scholarship and could pay my own way. Lead miners are a hardy breed, Mr Brown, but the work takes its toll on you. Had you stayed longer, you'd be less likely to be able to wield a shovel, and be deaf as a post. This is your paper, please wait outside for the interview.'

He stood up and held out his hand to Dafydd.

'Good luck, Mr Brown.'

Dafydd was not just surprised, but worried. How had the doctor managed to get his name wrong? He knew he would have to get it put right. After a long while back in the corridor, another door opened and he was led into a room where a man sat importantly behind a table.

'Sit down, Mr Brown.'

'Could I just mention, sir, about the name...?'

'Yes, what of it?' The man held up a sheet of paper. 'I have a letter of recommendation here from Captain Rowlands for Mr David Brown of Cemmaes Road near Machynlleth. Are you this man?'

A scheme of Gwen's? Dafydd had to think quickly. What had she done? There seemed no choice but to go with it, so he nodded.

'Fine. Now, Mr Brown, tell me a few of the difficulties that a fireman on the Cambrian Railways would encounter.'

'Well, there are a few banks to deal with,' Dafydd said, rejoicing in the conversation he had had on the train. 'Commins Coch, Borth, Whittington. But the worst by far is Talerddig. It's where a fireman needs to do his hardest coaling and where the driver needs to be in harmony with his engine...'

The ordeal over, Dafydd was back on the platform, watching the pilot. The fireman leant out as he went past.

'Did you get it?'

Dafydd grinned, and waved a sheaf of paper. 'Medical, contract and an address for digs.'

The man showed a white toothy grin, creasing his blackened face.

'Well, we'll see you around then.'

With a cheery wave, the engine was away.

Dafydd was looking to catch a late through-train that would only stop at the main stations. It would give him a chance for some long sleeps in the near-empty carriage. As soon as the guard had disappeared, he was lying on the seat, feet hanging off the edge, exhausted by the strain of the day.

'What do you make of it?' Dafydd asked Donato over a cup of coffee on his return. They sat in the closed café, lights dimmed, chairs stacked on tables. It was a time of day Dafydd had grown to enjoy. The strength of the coffee and Donato's wise company were luxuries that he cherished.

'I donno,' Donato replied. He knew most things that happened in town. He knew who to ask and people came to him eager with news as they drank his coffee. Even so, Gwen was the one person he could never find much out about. It was as if she were a ghost.

'Maybe she just want you to be 'appy.'

'But why the name change? And why Cemmaes Road? They were ready to put me on the branch to Dinas Mawddwy!'

'This is a problem?'

'Only that I know nobody there – they'd soon find me out.'

'She want to hide you, or she think you need a new life?'

'Why hide me, my friend? She's done a good job of avoiding me these years.'

Donato shrugged. 'Maybe you find out?'

'How?' Dafydd only got another shrug in reply. 'How is Tad?' he tried.

'Owain is fine, Daveed. Old, tired, short of breath sometime, but fine.' He gave a large cough himself then. 'Sometimes he not alone. You know this doctor? He was a-right, he was very right. You are lucky man, Daveed Brown.'

'But why me?'

Another shrug. 'I donno.'

'My friend, I have kept you too long.' Dafydd got up to leave. 'There are too many questions and only one who can answer. I will find her. I knew all along how I could do that. I was just too scared to do it.'

'Then keep a wise head and do what is good for you.'

'Yes, yes. But if I knew what to do, I wouldn't be a railwayman.'

'This job, it will bring you back here?'

Dafydd shook his head. 'Not for now. I have to work my way up the links. Shunting and station pilot link at first. If I get to the next link, local freight and passenger. If I get to go further, the long distance freights, then stopping passenger. If I ever make it to top link, I'll be on the expresses.'

'If God wills it, it will be.'

'Course, I'll get to know folk and get to travel for free, so I'll come visiting sometimes.'

'Good, Daveed. Your coffee cup will be always here for you, and my conversation.'

Mrs Owen was strong, proud, yet soft as anything to Dafydd.

'You've been good to me, all these years,' he told her. 'I go, I come back, but you are always there with a room for me and hot water for the tin tub.'

'You're like a son to me, young man,' she said, as she busied about the kitchen.

'Yes, and you've always protected me.'

She met his eye then. 'I done my best, Dafydd *bach*. Especially when that Joe was trying to get you blamed for the fire at the ropewalk.'

'And Gwen…'

There was no reply. He watched the knife clicking away as she chopped her vegetables.

'Mrs Owen, tell me how I can speak to her?'

'It's best I don't, Dafydd. She's made her own road and that's that.'

'I have to talk to her.'

There was no reply.

'Even if it means going up to the door of Captain Rowlands.'

'Dafydd, fate has not been kind. She was for you, but the times she was there, you were not. Now she's gone. You have to accept it.'

248

'Not before I talk to her. She has to tell me why she's done what she done. Why's she got me a job away?'

'She's still fond of you, *cariad*.'

'Yes. And why then do it in a different name and address?'

'A mix-up? They do say the railway's not clever with them things.'

'I don't think so. I want her to tell me. I want her to explain,' Dafydd went over and put his arm around the old woman. 'I want to say good-bye.'

She gave him a big hug and he felt the pain once more.

'I'll see what I can do.'

The River Rheidol looped gracefully through the flat of the valley, on its way down from Devils Bridge. Odd-shaped trees grew here and there on its banks, and where the river straightened up past Pwll Simon towards the hill of Penparcau. In the background, an engine was about to leave to take a train up the valley. He didn't need to see it, the noise was enough. It was *Rheidol*. Wretched though they looked, the trees offered protection and shelter – from the weather and from prying eyes. Gwen sat on the bough of one such tree, waiting for Dafydd. Llanbadarn church loomed beyond, suggesting a prayer for the deliverance.

'You're looking well,' said Gwen.

Dafydd had no reply.

She sighed and looked away. 'How did the interview go?'

'I got the job. All in all it was easy, thanks to you.'

'I didn't write the letter.'

'No, but you got it written, Gwen. Why was that?'

'I wanted you to be happy.'

'How do you know I wasn't happy in Aber? You've been avoiding me long enough.'

'Well, if your idea of enjoying life is sitting moping on Pen Dinas every night, fine.'

'All right. My landlady spies on me for you, but I still need to know why you done this?'

'I just want you to be happy,' she repeated. 'You can't have been, just cleaning engines.'

'Why change my name?'

'Mix-up, I'm sure.'

'No, I don't think so. I thought that at first, but then I think back to all the things you've done. You got me a job at the ropewalk when I was sleeping rough. And a place to sleep. When the fire happened, you got me away to Talybont, and now you're getting me on to a better job again. You're like my own angel, but you won't let me be close. Why?'

'I want you safe, that's all.' She wasn't meeting his eyes any more.

'Why?'

'Oh, you're so stupid sometimes!' she snapped. 'Do I have to spell it out for you?'

'Yes.'

'Because I love you,' she shouted. 'Because I always have from the day I found you being sick by the river. Once you'd cleaned up, mind you. You keep on bleating *why, why, why?* I don't know why, I just do. And I want you to be safe and happy and settled.'

'Why not with you?'

She sighed and bit her lip. 'Once you asked me to go with you and I curse the day I said no. Now I can't.'

'I can't dress you in fine clothes or give you gold to wear, but I can make you happy. Come with me.'

Tears were streaming from her eyes as she looked at her feet. 'I can't… You wouldn't have. Oh, you don't understand! I'm expecting. I've made a mess of it all, but he's such a powerful man and I don't want you hurt by him – or what I done. I couldn't stand the pain of you watching me with child, seeing me in town. Knowing what I'd become. If I went with you, he would track us. He would make sure you never worked again. He might even get you hurt. You don't know him, how cruel he can be. I sent you away with a new name, so he couldn't find you.' She stopped and sighed, her voice no more than a trembling whisper. 'You can find someone who will look after you, like I never can.'

'How does he not know who I am?'

'He got his secretary to write it and I inserted the name and took the letter while he wasn't watching. They all think it got lost and are trying to forget about it. Oswestry is big enough to hide you.'

'Oswestry is big enough to hide you too, if you come with me. You could be Mrs Brown soon enough and we could raise the child as our own. He would never know.'

Her eyes widened, her mouth trembled. Dafydd kissed it.

'You would do this? After all that's gone? I thought you'd hate me.'

'I *love* you, Gwen, I always have. I've always dreamt of us being together. Please come with me.'

'I thought you'd hate me.'

'I could never hate my angel. Only protect and cherish.'

She blinked away the tears. 'Yes,' she whispered. 'Yes. I will meet you at the station on the morning we leave.' She hugged Dafydd and cried and kissed his eyes. 'Dafydd Thomas, you're a fool. But then, so am I.'

CHAPTER TWENTY
Partings

H IS NOTICE PERIOD had been completed and now Dafydd had packed. There wasn't much. A few bits of clothing, his shaving tackle and a brush was all he had to show for his life. No trinkets, no riches.

'The only thing I would take with me is the old clock from the house,' Dafydd said.

'Take it,' Sioned replied, as they all sat round their table after a farewell meal. 'Tad won't mind.' Owain had gone up to bed.

'No, I'll leave it with him. It's got more memories for him than me.' Dafydd said with a sigh. 'So, it's a strange turn of fortune I'm having now.'

'I think it's wonderful,' said Harri.

'Yes, well,' Sioned muttered and looked hard at her tea.

'You don't approve, then?' Dafydd asked.

'It's not for me to say,' came the reply.

'Sioned,' Donato said calmly. 'This is his time. We should be happy.'

'Oh, I am. Happy that you have a better job in a bigger town. More chance of bettering yourself than here. And you're not scared of moving away, you've done it before.'

'It's Gwen,' Dafydd replied. 'You don't think I should be doing this.'

'She's led you a merry dance all these years. And then just to turn around and fall into your arms. I don't believe it.'

'But she told me why, and I understand. She's had a bad time of it, all told.'

'Fall into shit and come up smelling of roses, that one,' Sioned replied. 'I just don't think you should be so forgiving.'

'He must,' Donato said firmly.

'Why?'

'It is his road to travel, he must see his journey through, not us.'

'I don't see...'

'Because he must!' Donato didn't shout, but his tone ended all discussion. Sioned got up, clattered the plates into a pile and strutted into the kitchen. The sound of banging cutlery faded as the door closed.

Donato sighed. 'I donno if this is good or no. But if you do not find out, you will regret. For all time, you will regret. For that reason, this must happen.'

'Thank you.'

There was nothing more to add.

'Will you write?' Harri asked eagerly as she took the remaining dishes. 'I would like to know what you are up to.'

Dafydd saw her blush then, and wondered where her mind had gone.

'Well, I suppose I could,' he said. 'And you write back, so I find out what you are up to as well.'

She was still looking shy. He didn't know what to think. He went into the kitchen, catching Sioned wiping her eyes before returning to scrub the dishes.

She tried to smile. 'I'm sorry, Dafydd,' she said. 'I'm not wishing you ill but I don't want you to go. She's not been good for you in the past, Gwen. I'm sorry I'm thinking that way, but there we are.'

'I know, Sioned. I'm sure it seems that way. But Gwen's really looked out for me over the years. She's found me work and homes when I've been on my knees. I can't turn away now she needs me.'

'As you will. Just be sure you have a place to go if things go wrong.' She touched his cheek. 'Go and see Tad before you go.'

'Won't he be asleep?'

'It's possible, but all the same.'

Dafydd went upstairs to Owain's tiny room. It was dark, and all Dafydd could hear was the ticking of the clock on the mantelpiece and Owain's heavy breathing. Dafydd closed the door softly, but then his father croaked out his name, following it by a familiar coughing fit. Dafydd brought the lamp in and Owain sat up slowly.

'Were you going without saying good-bye?'

'Never,' said Dafydd, 'just didn't want to wake you.'

'So, are you ready?' asked Owain.

'As ever I will be.'

'Is she coming with you?'

Dafydd nodded. 'She promised.'

Owain grunted.

'Do you think Mam would have liked Gwen, Tad?'

'I'm sure she would, son. She'd have been proud of you.'

'It doesn't seem right. I am forever leaving.'

'It has to be, son. This town's sapping your energy.'

'Oswestry is huge. The railway, that is. I never seen so many engines and other railway companies drive into there and all.'

'You'll do fine. Don't worry.'

'I hope so, Tad. I was talking to some of the men. There's

254

ways of getting tickets for free on these railways. I could get you up to see how we're getting on.'

'I'd like that. See you settled and all.'

Owain got up to wind the clock, fidgeting about.

'There's something else. How would you feel if I was walking with another woman?'

'Tad?'

'Nothing out of order, though that wouldn't stop tongues clecking. Just an old friend come back and I've kept her company on walks and such.'

'Tad, you're fine. Just be yourself.'

'All right, son. I just had to ask.' He stuck out his hand. 'Well, it's good-bye then, for now that is.'

'Good-bye, Tad. I wish it were different.'

'I know, Dafydd.'

Another woman in Owain's arms. A woman, who wasn't Mam? It was not wrong, and once again, Dafydd questioned his decision to leave.

Huw, now shaven, came and found him. Dafydd saw once again the youth of his face that had been hidden behind bushy whiskers when he was building the line, and thought how much his friend had mellowed over time.

'What happened, Huw?' Dafydd said. 'Have the deacons got hold of you?'

'Nothing so drastic,' he replied with a laugh. 'I just thought, well – now I have a job that will last a while, I should start tidying myself up, like.'

'Going well then?'

'Yes, I'd say. We spend our time fixing the rubbish that they had us put down in the first place. If I had a place to dry out all that rotten wood, I'd keep very warm this winter. May end up just dumping it down the closed mine halfway up.'

He was grinning, making it difficult to distinguish truth from stories. Then again, no-one was using the mine, Dafydd thought, and grinned.

'Are you ready then, Dafydd?'

'The number of times I've been asked that. Yes. No. What do you expect?'

'I expect you to do fine.'

'What if I don't?'

'Go to Crewe. It's just up the road and there's work to be had, I hear.'

'And Gwen?'

'You're really lucky, Daf. It's been a long time coming and you deserve it.'

'In truth, I don't know if I can go, now Tad's told me he's taken to walking out with another woman.'

'What? He's seeing more than one?'

'No, just the one. He lost my mam, remember. I don't know nothing about this. Don't even know who she is.'

'Mary Treveglos.'

'What? Uncle David's daughter? She's in England, surely. *Iesu*, she's not much older than me.'

'So what? I'm sure they are not looking to start a family.'

'But my sisters said nothing. Do you think they don't know?'

'I would be very surprised if Sioned didn't know. I knew. What's the matter?'

'It's not right. Mam's not long in the grave.'

'It's over a year, nearly two. Does it matter?'

'He hasn't got over it.'

'Sounds to me like you're the one who hasn't.'

Dafydd bit back a harsh reply. The silence extended.

'Look, Daf, Do you want him to be happy? Do you want him looked after? Sioned can't do that and all the café work and look after her son, can she? He hasn't forgotten your mam. I'm sure he thinks of her every day, but why make him be lonely?'

'I don't know, Huw.'

'All right, honest now: would she approve, your mam?'

Dafydd nodded. 'Yes, she was that generous. Do you know what the worst thing is? I had a thing for Mary Treveglos, when I was a boy.'

Huw boomed out with laughter. 'Coveting your father's woman? I'll have the deacons on you and no mistake. Be honest though, and I say this as a friend; how can you forgive your woman but not your father?'

There was a long silence, while Dafydd bit his lip. 'All right, Huw. You win.'

'Good. Now I've to ask your permission. I would very much like to walk out with your sister, Harri.'

'What?'

'I'm not like the other navvies, I changed to a track man now. I go to chapel. I've a tidy place to stay. The money's not brilliant, but it sees you right.'

'Why you asking me, you old *hwrgi*? You should be at the door of my sinful father.'

Huw actually blushed. 'I want you to be happy with it too. It's important to me. I'm learning reading and writing at Sunday school. I can do sums – had to with this track build. I'll not be a labourer all my life. I can do gang leader at least. I want to change, that's all. I want to be better, so I can talk to your sister with my head held high.'

'Huw, you are fine already. Go talk to my father, he's normally down the harbour on a day. Two things I will say. One is, don't put off tomorrow what you need to do today. The other is Harri. Be gentle with her. Don't rush. She had a scare before, if you remember.'

'I remember and thank you, Daf. And you – forget what has gone. This is a chance to take with both hands.'

'I'll forget the bad moments, but not the good people. They made me who I am. Take care, my friend.'

Dafydd went to the station with his heart in his mouth. Today his life would begin anew. He had the tickets ready. He sat in front of the ticket booth, waiting. The train he was to catch arrived, the station pilot bringing the coaches into the station. He watched the crew working hard and tried to follow what they did. Their banter made him dream of his own future.

He determined to learn every detail any way he could, so he could move up quickly through the links. The main engine was backing on the front and Dafydd itched to see its lines. He thought of the cab, the speed and the work involved to keep it fast. Then he thought about the future. A place to live, furniture, babies.

Gwen. His heart leapt. She was walking across the station forecourt. He marvelled at the way she seemed to glide. She was dressed smartly and carried a small bag. Not what you could call luggage. He stood up, clenched and unclenched his hands.

She smiled, a bit uncertain, and looked at the crowd. He wondered how she had left the house that morning, without wanting to show she was going. The dress would have to be her normal town wear. How could she have brought any luggage? Her nervous glances into the throng were for sure, her worry about her master – her lover – seeing her. He took her hand to reassure her. Her touch was cold and clammy. There was a faint tremble. Her eyes, her beautiful blue eyes, were wide, darting, to and fro. Dafydd ached to comfort her, but it was not a thing to do in public if you wanted to be invisible.

She shivered. 'I hate cold mornings.'

'Well, we'll be allowed on the train soon. Here, I'll get you a cup of tea.'

He went to the refreshment kiosk and returned with tea and a cake.

'The sugar will help.'

'You shouldn't have,' she said, taking a small bite. She moved seats, huddled in the shadows. 'The house in Oswestry?'

'It's all settled,' Dafydd said. 'The railway organised it for me. After you said you'd come with me a couple of weeks ago, I told them I was not alone, so they've got me a bigger place. I said we were married and they just filled in the paperwork.'

'England seems so far away,' she murmured, closing her eyes.

'Just over two hours from here and when I'm working for the railway, it'll be easy to get back. You just get known to the right people and keep your head down when the bosses walk around.'

'Where will you be going from there?'

'I don't know, *cariad*. I have a feeling, a great desire, to make it to driver. Even to the top expresses. I want to be working local, but I'm not afraid to move if it came to it. If that's all right with you, of course.'

She sipped her tea and stared at the crowd. 'How do your family feel?'

'They're happy for me, Gwen. They know how hard the journey's been and want me happy and settled down. Tad would have loved to have met you before we left, you know.'

'Why?'

'To thank you for all you done for me. The ropewalk, Mrs Owen... this. I think you'll like him.'

She didn't reply, just looked out at the people in the station.

'It seems such a long way back to when you found me on the bridge. We've come so far.'

'We are different people,' she said faintly.

It was early, and Dafydd was feeling a lack of sleep. He was not normally good for talking before a strong mug of Lipton's tea. Then there was the fear that Captain Rowlands would run in and stop them. Dafydd knew they'd be better once they were away on the train.

'We'd best get ready,' he said.

The tank engine suddenly blew its whistle and let off a large amount of steam in the covered part of the station. People jumped. A baby started to cry and a little boy put his hands over his ears in pain. Perhaps the driver hadn't had his Lipton's, Dafydd mused.

Tears streamed Gwen's face, and she bit her lip. He reached out to her but she shook her head. Finding a linen hankie from her sleeve, she dabbed her face and blew her nose.

'I must look terrible.'

'Don't worry, we'll get on the train and be away soon enough.'

She looked away and he knew then what had been staring him in the face. How he had missed the signs, he did not know. 'You're not coming, are you?'

She shook her head, that lovely fair head. She had stopped crying. Part of him wanted to shake her. The rest of him had fallen from the top of Craig Lais into the cold blue waters of the sea below. He sat down hard, then stood up again and paced up and down. He knew it was coming. He'd known – deep down in his heart, he'd known. He was still in shock though.

'I'm with child. I can't do this,' Gwen was saying. 'And the master said he will not cast me aside. Dafydd, I thought he would throw me on the streets, leave me to my own fate or force me to the workhouse.

'I would have had nowhere to live, no income and as the child grew, no chance of work. Do you know what they do in a workhouse? They house you apart. My baby would be taken from me and I would never see him again. I would never leave there, either. It's like prison. But the master has no children and he so desires to be a father. So he has said I will be looked after and my son will be raised as his own.'

'How do you know it's a son?'

She smiled her secret smile and, seemingly without thinking, patted her belly. 'He kicks, it's a sign, they do say.'

'What about us, Gwen? I would take care of you. I would work my heart out to provide for you. I would do anything.'

She shook her head sadly. 'It's not enough. Not any more. My baby is the most important thing in my life now. Nothing else matters. And what can a railwayman provide that a gentleman cannot, and more?'

'I would try.'

'But you are just a fireman, on the lowest rung at that. Where do you expect to go from there?'

'I'm going to drive, Gwen. I'll be on expresses in time.'

She stared at the crowd. The words were not there that would ever be enough.

'It is his son, it is his to choose. I knew you would do your best, but it is not the same.'

'A port in a storm, that's all I was. That's all I ever have been. Something to fall back on when the choices have all been exhausted.'

Gwen said nothing. There was no use in arguing, pleading or begging. Dafydd could tell it was decided.

'And you love him?' Dafydd asked.

Her lips tightened. 'I'm not going to compare him with you, if that's what you're wanting. It's not fair to start that.'

'Fair? When did fairness come into this? I have tried to be there for you, to work towards a decent living for us. I've never thought of anything but us being together. And you talk of fair?'

There was no reply, save a big intake of breath and a stiffening of her back. In all his life, Dafydd had never been in control of what happened with Gwen. It was always meeting when she wanted, going where she wanted. He had fallen deeply in love with the young girl, full of life and spirit. Now, he was faced with a woman even more used to carving her path to fulfil her needs.

Life had forced it on her, true, but he cursed himself for not realising it earlier. He had been a promised haven for her child when all seemed dark. Now the master had claimed his own. Dafydd was no longer needed.

'Were you ever going to come with me?' he asked.

She sighed. 'I know this is hard, but I must do what is right for the child. I hope you find happiness. I would love your blessing. I do understand though, if you feel you cannot give it.' She stood up to leave, straightening her skirts. Then she suddenly grabbed his arm and drew him forward, leaning to kiss him gently on the cheek.

'Were you ever going to come with me?'

'I…' she started, then thought better of it and turned to walk away.

As she moved into the crowd, Dafydd blurted out, 'God be with you!'

She did not stop, though he could swear her regular pace was checked for a moment. He watched her leave. There was nothing else to do.

He got on the train. Aberystwyth held nothing for him now – Oswestry was as good a place as any.

He'd wanted to have a look at the engine, but a small six-wheel coach had been placed at the front of the train. Probably one of the directors was travelling that day in his own personal carriage. The hostile looks Dafydd got from the crew as he approached confirmed his theory and warned him off.

He took his seat in third. It would be a long and painful journey, so he looked for a place he could settle down and try to sleep. The whistle sounded and the doors were closed in haste. There was a rush of steam and the coach jolted as the engine lurched forward. Other passengers settled into their own thoughts. Some read, some smoked. One woman was knitting. The train moved past the signal box, the signalman standing there jacketless, his shirt sleeves rolled up. He waved and shouted a last word to the crew before turning away.

Dafydd's gaze was drawn to the small green avenue of trees beyond the signal box, which led to Plascrug Castle. Seats were placed for convenience along the way by the paths. On one seat, he saw a woman sitting, dressed like Gwen. A rush of emotion caught him and he rushed to stand at the window, waving hard. One last goodbye, his heart screamed inside him. One last parting to allow him to move on, but it was futile. She did not look up.

Slowly, he returned to his seat and sat heavily, looking back. He had come so far, rebuilding his life from nothing. He had recovered his family and found a worthy trade, but all his dreams hadn't been realised. He had not won his Gwen.

As the crumbling tower of Plascrug Castle farmstead came into view, he began to roll back the images of the parting in his mind. It was Gwen who had managed to get him a job in

Oswestry, like she had at the ropemaker's all those years ago. She may not have given him love in the way he had craved, but she had shown him her love in kind. It was the only way fate would allow her. All he could do was repay it by making the most of the chance she had carved out for him. The train gathered pace, as he knew his life must. He moved across the aisle to watch the world come to him.

Glossary

ardderchog: excellent, splendid
bach: small, or an affectionate term a bit like 'love' in English
Beth sy'n bod?: What's the matter?
bradwr: traitor
butty: mate, friend
cariad: my love, my darling
cawl: soup, broth
crachach: posh people, the upper class
cwtch: cuddle, hug
diolch: thank you
Duw: God
ent: aren't, isn't, am not
hiraeth: homesickness, yearning
hisht: hush
hwrgi: whorehound
Iesu (Grist): Jesus (Christ)
mam: mum, mother
mam-gu: grandma, grandmother
tad: dad, father
tad-cu: grandad, grandfather
teisen lap: a kind of fruit cake
twll: gap, hole, opening
twll du: black hole
twpsyn: idiot
twp: stupid
tŷ bach: toilet

Also from Y Lolfa:

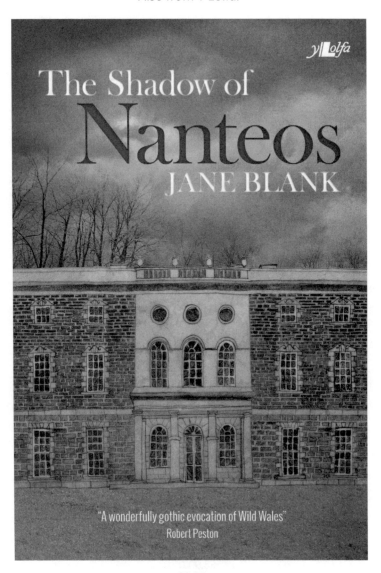

£8.99

ROB
GITTINS
HEAR THE ECHO

y Lolfa

CAFÉ · ICE-CREAM PARLOUR

CARINI'S

Two strong Welsh-Italian women...
separated by a lifetime, linked forever

£8.99 (pb)
£17.99 (hb)

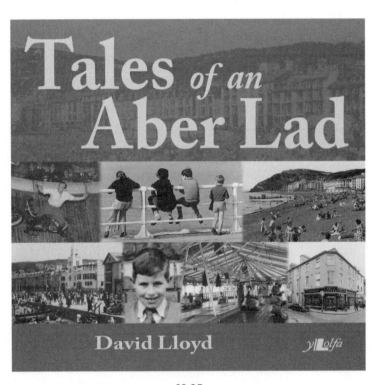

Tales *of an* Aber Lad

David Lloyd

y Lolfa

£9.95

By the Banks of the Rheidol is just one of a whole range of publications from Y Lolfa. For a full list of books currently in print, send now for your free copy of our new full-colour catalogue. Or simply surf into our website

www.ylolfa.com

for secure on-line ordering.

TALYBONT CEREDIGION CYMRU SY24 5HE
e-mail ylolfa@ylolfa.com
website www.ylolfa.com
phone (01970) 832 304
fax 832 782

Printed by Y Lolfa
Ask for a quote